Nor Forsake

A NOVEL BY JULIE PRESLEY

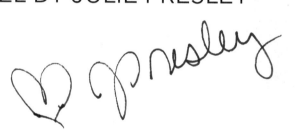

Printed in the United States of America

First Printing, 2016
ISBN 13: 978-0-9859291-2-1 (Paperback edition)
ISBN 13: 978-0-9859291-3-8 (e-Book edition)

Presley Publishing

Visit www.juliepresley.com for more information

Library of Congress Number: 2016908389

This is a work of fiction. Names, characters, businesses, places, events and incidents are either the products of the author's imagination or used in a fictitious manner with the exception of 21 Club, Zini's Pizza and Campisi's Restaurant, and all mentions of Central Park. Any resemblance to actual persons, living or dead, or actual events is purely coincidental.

For Anna,

Your support, encouragement, and bravery in the last year are what have inspired me to dare greatly and finally push this book out. You are an amazing book doula!

The ways in which this story mirrors parts of your own is incredible, as if time and space were transcended when I wrote Libby's story six years ago.

I love how the Lord has woven our stories together.

Thank you for your friendship and for being a consistent source of truth and love. I adore you.

"All I'll say is, good thing your agent is a girl!"

Prologue

JASON RANDALL SAT back in his chair, carelessly tossing a dismal excuse for a manuscript onto his desk. He stretched his arms behind his head and laced his fingers together, closing his eyes. For every best seller he'd launched into the market, there were a few hundred rejects lining his recycling bin, and that was even after his intern had screened them.

"I need a new intern," he sighed. "Amanda!" he shouted to his assistant.

"I know, Jas. New intern." The voice that came from the desk outside of his office was slightly sarcastic.

"I mean it this time."

"I know. You always do," she yelled back.

"But you never do anything!" Jason pointed out, leaning forward on his desk and pushing his fingers through his jet black hair.

"You made me promise not to, boss," Amanda appeared in the doorway with a fresh cup of coffee and a sweet smile, her dark hair perfectly cropped close to her jaw bone, bangs in a straight line across her forehead.

Jason sat forward, slapping his palms down on his desk. "Why did I do that again?"

"When you hired me, you warned me of your occasional temper

tantrums and that I was to ignore anything that sounded irrational and childish."

Jason stared at her through narrowed eyes. "I was half joking."

"I know, but you left it up to my discretion," she teased. She moved forward and sat the coffee cup on his desk and shrugged. "It's not Peter's fault. He's doing the best he can. He just needs to learn from you."

"There's something going on between you two, isn't there?"

Amanda's cheeks turned crimson and she quickly turned on her heel and left the room, shutting the door behind her.

Jason rolled his eyes and let them settle on the steaming mug. "Round two," he said bringing the mug to his lips while picking up another manuscript from his stack.

"All right, Stanley M Blackwell, let's see what you've got for me today." He flipped the manuscript open and began to skim through the proposal. Another synopsis that basically described every Sci-Fi show on TV right now. "Aliens, superpowers, blah blah blah." Jason threw his head back and groaned. "I do not get paid enough for this." He put the proposal down again and stood up, stretching his neck and taking another sip of coffee.

Ever since that *Twilight* spin-off had hit the top of the New York Times Best Sellers list, it seemed every amateur novelist in the world felt that they had the chops make it there as well. The very publishing houses that made it possible to keep the electricity on in his dimly lit office were ruining Jason's life. He needed to get out of the little brown box where he spent most of his time.

"I'm going to get some fresh air. Need anything?" Jason asked as he passed by Amanda's desk on the way to the elevator.

"Could you check the mailbox on your way back up?"

"Don't we have an intern for that?"

"He's busy making your life miserable," she said without missing a beat. She smiled up at him and took a loud bite of the apple on her desk.

"Oh, well, by all means, don't disturb him," Jason said sarcastically and pushed through the frosted door that read *Crane Literary Agents* backwards in front of him, catching a glimpse of his tired brown eyes in the reflection. Even his normally olive complexion seemed pale with exhaustion.

You really need a day off, old man, he thought to himself.

In the lobby, he checked the mailbox to see if there was something of interest to read–anything but more badly written prose. Five manila envelopes tumbled out along with a thinner white envelope with a handwritten address. He instantly recognized the cursive swoops on the letters and cocked his head to one side, his stomach tense. The return address read "Leanne Randall" in the same feminine writing.

"Oh, Lord," he sighed. "What are you doing to me now? I thought we'd put this behind us." He looked up at the ceiling, as if he could look straight into God's face, and cringed. "I haven't had enough sleep to deal with her today."

The verse about God moving in mysterious ways immediately came to mind, and his curiosity got the better of him. He shoved the rest of the envelopes back in the box and tucked the white one under his arm. The last time he'd received any mail from Leanne, the contents of the thick envelope had changed his life forever. That had been two years ago, and while the divorce had been mostly amicable, he never expected to receive an envelope like this from her again.

"This better be good," he sighed.

He stepped from the lobby onto the busy New York City sidewalk and quickly joined the masses heading in the direction of his favorite bakery, just half a block from his office.

Once settled into his usual seat by the window with an extra-large cinnamon roll, he ripped open the envelope, pulling out a magazine with a sticky note that read, "Thought you might be interested–L."

Jason swallowed a lump in his throat, remembering how his former wife used to pass her magazines on to him, dog-eared and marked in red pen, when a feature short story really got to her.

While it was rare that he actually pursued an author unsolicited, he knew his ex-wife had good taste in fiction. He peeled the sticky note off of the front of the page and rolled his eyes as he saw the huge red letters spanning the cover.

"*American Woman*. Thanks for that," he muttered under his breath. He pressed the yellow post-it note onto the envelope and then opened the magazine, folding it down the middle to hide the front page.

"'*Red Parks Ranch*,' by Elizabeth Abbott," he read. "All right, Leanne, let's see who you've discovered this time." He settled deeper into his chair, tuned out the chatter of the customers and noise of the cafe, and began to read.

Chapter 1

LEANING AGAINST THE wall of the elevator, Libby Abbott watched the numbers light up in consecutive order. She clutched the coat button directly under her breasts and squeezed her eyes tight as she tried to focus on breathing in and out. There was still time; she could still punch one of the buttons for a lower floor and take the stairs back down to the parking garage, and no one would ever know she'd been there.

Ignorance is bliss, right? she thought. "No," she hissed, trying to silence the voice that was pushing her towards self-preservation. She'd managed to get all the way to the office without turning her car around, and as the elevator continued to close in on the eleventh floor, Libby knew there was no going back. She needed answers. She needed to either put fear to rest, or be released to move on. The only way to do either of those things was to stay put until that bell chimed on the number eleven. She'd already prepared her heart for the worst. She just needed proof; she needed to see it with her own two eyes.

Never before had an elevator bell sounded so ominous; the sound rattled her thoughts as the doors opened to a deserted hallway. The only light at that hour of night came from the three silver wall sconces that lined the wall across from the elevators.

She'd walked the sleek, dark brown paneled hall hundreds of times. The steel accents had always made it seem like a cold and uninviting entrance, but now with the soft lights casting shadows around her, she found it appropriate. She didn't want to feel invited or welcomed into this situation. She took a deep breath, stepped out of the elevators, and turned left to the large mahogany door at the end of the hallway. The block letters seemed to shout at her.

BAKER, ELLIOT, and ABBOTT

Attorneys at Law

Libby pressed her hand over her last name on the plaque and took a deep breath, second-guessing herself for the last time as she moved her hand to the doorknob.

"You have a right to know, Libby," she whispered to herself. "You have a right to be happy." The only problem was that after walking through this door, she didn't know if she would ever be happy again.

She closed her eyes again, squared her shoulders and mustered up all the courage she'd had when she'd gotten in the car and driven herself all the way to her former place of work: her husband's office. As quietly as she could, she turned the doorknob and stepped in. The door made a soft swooshing sound as it closed behind her.

She blinked back tears as she took in her surroundings. This is where it had all started–her career, her first love, her marriage, two pregnancies, and it seemed that it would also be where it all ended. The career was over, the pregnancies had failed, and Libby was pretty sure that the marriage was about to meet the same fate.

The same brown paneling and steel accents from the hallway adorned the walls of the reception area. Although it was lit by just one lamp at this late hour, Libby still remembered all the details of this cold and male-dominated office. She eyed her old desk where the light came from. A vase of fresh flowers sat by the computer screen, the only evidence of a woman's touch. She wondered whom they were from, and then she shook her head at herself. She felt pretty sure that she already knew the answer.

A purse was sitting under the desk–evidence that Bria, the assistant that had taken Libby's place, was still in the office somewhere. The fact that Mark's car was still parked in the garage downstairs should have been enough to convict him, but Libby needed more proof than that. She took a steadying breath and continued to make her way down the hallway.

She trailed her fingers along the walls as she walked slowly, approaching the door with Mark's name on it with great hesitation but with an underlying determination that kept her feet moving one step at a time. She sucked in a breath as she reached the door and leaned her head softly against it.

You know how this goes, Libby, she reminded herself. Once upon a time she had been the girl behind the closed door, long after everyone else had left for the night. The only difference was that back then neither one of them had been married.

"Oh, God," she whispered quietly. "If You're still up there, please let me be wrong. Please let this be a client meeting, just like he's been telling me." Carefully she palmed the doorknob, turning it ever so slowly to avoid the click it would inevitably make if she moved too quickly. She pushed against the weighted door and stepped into the room.

Libby's stomach dropped to her toes; she immediately felt her legs grow weak. She grabbed on to the chair beside the doorway with one hand and continued to grip the handle with the other.

"Oh my god," Bria moaned from the edge of Mark's desk.

"Mmmm."

"No, Mark. Stop." Bria pushed him off of her and grabbed at the sides of her blouse to cover her bare breasts. Mark's head shot up and looked towards the door, his shirt unbuttoned, slacks held up only by the pressure of his legs against the side of the desk.

His face paled; he swore.

Libby heard a sob escape her throat and she turned to run out the door.

"Libs!" Mark called as the door shut behind her.

Libby's tears streamed freely as she raced through the office to the front door, her stomach in knots. She reached Bria's desk and paused abruptly, wanting to turn the whole thing on its side. Instead, she picked up the vase of flowers, took a few steps back and then threw it at the computer screen. The glass shattered all over the desk and Libby heard a sizzling sound behind her as she slammed her body through the door and into the hallway. She jammed her thumb on the down button and was relieved that the doors opened immediately. It was late enough that the building was deserted, except for a cheating husband, a slutty receptionist, a security guard, and a devoted wife.

Libby sank to the floor in the corner of the elevator and let the sobs shake her whole body.

Chapter 2

THE MORNING SUN assaulted Libby's eyes as it shone cheerily through the window. She groaned and tried to roll over on the bed, but the pain in her neck and stomach quickly reminded her that she wasn't actually *in* her bed. That explained why the sun was being so cruel and bright. There were no curtains or drapes to shield the light. The cold tile under her cheek was no more welcoming. Slowly, she pulled herself up and groggily took in her surroundings.

For a moment, panic seized her. She touched her hand between her legs and pulled it back quickly, expecting it to be covered in blood. She exhaled with relief. The last time she'd found herself in the bathroom like this, she'd lost her first baby. It took a minute for her breathing to regulate.

The scent of vomit assaulted her nostrils and she cringed as the events of the previous night came back to her.

"Oh, right," she sighed and reached forward to flush the toilet. She didn't remember driving herself home or even getting up the stairs to her bedroom.

The mix of emotions happening inside of her was overwhelming. Never before had she felt so betrayed and out of control. The last year of her marriage had been anything but happy, and now that her suspicions were confirmed, she was at a loss.

Libby pulled her knees to her chest and rested her forehead on them, rocking slightly. "What am I supposed to do now?" she cried.

She sniffed and wiped at her eyes. Overcome with exhaustion and the need for a soft mattress, Libby pulled herself to her feet and immediately had to lean against the wall for support while waiting for the room to stop spinning in front of her.

Stepping from the bathroom to the master bedroom, she took one look at their bed and grimaced. It was an eyesore; she'd always hated it. They'd fought about it until she'd finally given in.

"It's Tuscan!" he'd insisted when she'd balked at the picture he'd pulled up online for her. Oversized with pillars and scallops at each corner, it was so far from her style, she'd almost laughed.

"It's obnoxious, and it doesn't match any of our other furniture!" she'd argued.

"Then we'll get new furniture!"

In the end, Mark had purchased brand new furniture for their bedroom and Libby had just thrown up her hands in defeat.

Instead of being a place of peace and calm, the way Libby had once imagined it would be, their master bedroom looked more like a cigar bar with dark woods and leather accents. She'd tried to decorate accordingly but had decided instead to focus her efforts on the guest room, which Mark had given her free reign over.

Libby sighed sadly as she walked into her favorite room in the house. The ocean-blue walls and antiqued white furniture soothed her weariness as she pulled back the delicate lace bedspread and climbed in between soft sheets, stuffing her pillow under her head. She closed her eyes and conjured up her imaginary beach house, wishing more than ever that the place was real and that she could truly escape.

Over the next few hours, Libby replayed the last seven years of her life over and over in her head. Whirlwind office romance, marriage, rushed honeymoon, back to work, surprise pregnancy, ecstatic rejoicing, miscarriage, devastation. That was when Mark started taking business trips while Libby remained at the office, holding down the fort for the rest of the partners. When Mark had returned from the first trip, she thought she'd noticed something strange about the way he acted towards her. But after a few days, he seemed to shake whatever it was and life returned back to normal— as normal as it could anyway, while Libby tried to recover her heart from the devastating loss.

She'd been alone the first time, in the bathroom, just like this morning, and it had been the worst day of her life, until the second miscarriage.

The second miscarriage was followed by a longer business trip, and upon his return, everything changed. Under the guise of supporting her dream of being a writer, Mark had encouraged her to quit working at the firm, and began to distance himself from her even more. Her first doubts about his fidelity had begun to surface then, and out of self preservation she chose not to fight the distance between them. They'd never really recovered and had continued to grow further and further apart.

The first time Libby had met the new assistant with the huge chest and collagen filled lips, warning bells had rung so loudly in her head, she could hardly see straight. Mark had shrugged it off repeatedly and then finally told her to drop the subject for good.

What am I supposed to do now? Libby wondered. The uncertainty and fear became so overwhelming that Libby struggled to breathe deeply enough to fill her lungs. She squeezed her eyes tightly and clenched the sheets so hard her knuckles ached.

The phone rang, startling her. She sat up, thankful for a distraction, and reached for the cordless phone on the bedside table.

"Hello?"

"Libby? Are you okay?" Hearing her best friend's voice thick with concern made her chest tighten and she felt her eyes stinging with a surge of fresh tears. She tried to speak but the words caught in her throat and only a squeaking sound came out.

"Oh, honey," Elena said softly. "I'm on my way over. I'll see you in five minutes."

"Okay," Libby whispered and then let the phone slip out of her hands.

ELENA LET HERSELF in, started a pot of coffee, and then went upstairs to encourage Libby out of bed and into a fresh pair of clothes. She was surprised to find the master bed made, with no sign of Libby in the room. She glanced down the hallway and sighed. Of course, Libby was in the guest room.

She tapped gently on the door and it opened slightly. Libby shifted in the bed and stared blankly in Elena's direction. Dark streaks of mascara remained smudged on her cheeks, and her eyes were red-rimmed and bloodshot.

"Hey," Elena said softly, without too much emotion. She needed to get a gauge for where Libby was in her own emotions.

The broken woman looked up at the ceiling wordlessly, but Elena saw a tear slip down her cheek. Crossing the room quickly, Elena took a spot on the bed and sat on one knee. She grabbed her best friend's hand and squeezed it.

"I'm here," she whispered.

Libby nodded, still not saying anything, and blinked repeatedly, trying to clear her eyes.

They sat in silence for a long time, Elena at a loss for words, knowing her friend was too numb to speak.

"Are you hungry?" Elena asked, the silence becoming too much for her.

Libby shook her head.

"Well, you need to eat, even if you're not hungry. It's almost ten. Why don't I go make some food while you get dressed?"

Libby sighed deeply. "Okay," she whispered.

Elena smiled softly and stood up. "Take your time."

LIBBY EMERGED DOWNSTAIRS ten minutes later, having exchanged last night's clothes for a T-shirt and black yoga pants. She took the plate of scrambled eggs that Elena handed her and sat down on a stool at the island. She pushed the eggs around on the plate for a few minutes before Elena scolded her.

"Libby, I know you don't want to eat, but you need to. Just a few bites, okay?"

Libby sighed and shoved a forkful into her mouth. She stared thoughtfully at her friend. Elena was petite and thin with great hips and perfectly proportionate breasts, even if they were on the small side. Libby had always admired her best friend's outward appearance. Her pixie cut and dyed black hair framed her face, accentuating her ivory colored skin and big dark blue eyes. Libby was of average height and build, had the same blue eyes as Elena, but she'd never been happy with her curves, or lack thereof. She sat up straighter, pushing her chest out.

"Do you think I should get implants?" she asked.

Elena choked on a sip of coffee. "I'm sorry, *what?*"

Libby shrugged and speared another bite of egg. "It worked for Bria."

Elena cringed.

"They look amazing. I mean, it's no wonder Mark is cheating on me." She pressed her hands on her chest. "I can't compete with that."

"If all it took was a pair of fake double D's, Mark would've strayed a long time ago, honey."

"What then? Her vibrant personality?" Libby rolled her eyes.

Elena snorted. "Sure, yeah, that's definitely it."

Libby shook her head. "I just can't figure it out. I mean, I did everything right. I went along with everything he said, even when," she gave Elena a meaningful look, "it was the last thing I wanted to do."

"I know," Elena said softly. "You're beautiful, Libby, and I'd kill to have your rack. I don't know why you always complain about your B's. Hi, my name is Elena and I'm a double A, which is not the same thing as being a double D. Besides all that, you have been a fantastic wife to that jerk."

Libby rolled her eyes. "Maybe I should have put up more of a fight. Maybe I should have pushed back a little."

Elena shook her head. "I don't think that's the issue."

Libby set her fork down and looked up at her friend, eyes full of tears. "Then what did I do wrong?"

"Nothing," Elena whispered. "You are more than he deserved."

The doorbell rang then, startling them both. Libby wiped her eyes and pushed herself off the stool.

"That wouldn't be him, would it?" Elena mussed her hair with her fingers, her eyes darting from the direction of the door to Libby. Libby shook her head.

"He's not polite enough to use the doorbell."

Even though she doubted it was Mark, she approached the door cautiously and looked out the peephole before opening it. A man she didn't recognize stood on her doorstep in a blue button down shirt and grey slacks. She did a quick check in the mirror and cringed. At least she'd thought to wash her face, but her hair was a complete disaster. The bell rang again, and she quickly tucked a stray piece of blonde hair behind her ear and opened the door.

"Elizabeth Abbott?" the man asked.

"Yes?"

"You've been served, ma'am. Please sign here." He held out a delivery slip and handed her a large manila envelope.

Libby obliged him by signing his form and took the package. Confused, she shut the door behind her and walked back into the kitchen.

Served? Served what? she thought as she ripped open the package. Her jaw dropped as she read the words aloud. "Petition for the disillusion of marriage … *what?*" she cried out.

Elena hurried around the counter and peered over Libby's shoulder. "You're kidding me. How could he do that so fast?"

"He didn't. Look!" Libby pointed with a shaky finger to the date on the papers.

"February twenty-eighth?" Elena looked at Libby, confused.

"He filed a week ago!"

"And said nothing?"

Libby sank back onto the bar stool and dropped the papers on the counter. She felt as though her stomach had plummeted to her feet.

"That lying, cheating son-of-a—"

Libby interrupted her friend by standing up so quickly she knocked the barstool over with a loud clatter.

Elena jumped back from the island. "What are you doing?"

Libby shook her head furiously and stormed up the stairs with Elena on her heels. She blew through the door of her bedroom and threw the closet doors open.

"Libby?"

"Elena, you can help me, or you can watch, but you will not get in my way," Libby held up a warning finger, her eyes fierce with purpose.

Elena nodded, bit her lips together, and stepped back, watching as Libby pulled one designer suit after another out of the closet until her arms were full.

"Libby, what are you going to do?" Elena whispered.

"The only thing that makes sense to me right now." She struggled with the load in her arms and carefully made her way out of the room and down the stairs. Elena picked up a pair of slacks that had slipped off one of the hangers and followed Libby out into the front yard.

Dropping the pile of suits on the lawn, Libby began arranging them side-by-side on the lumpy grass.

"There's a brand new bottle of bleach on the dryer in the laundry room. Can you grab it for me?"

Elena's eyes grew wide. "Libby, those suits are worth thousands! Why don't you sell them instead? Or donate them? I mean, plenty of—"

"Elena, get the bleach," Libby ordered.

Elena nodded dumbly and disappeared into the house. She returned momentarily with a large blue-labeled bottle and handed it to Libby who took the bottle and opened the lid. She tossed it aside, unaware that one of her neighbors who had been watering her lawn was now watering the sidewalk and staring at Libby with a gaping mouth.

Libby stood away from the stream of the liquid and began dousing the suits. She smiled devilishly as she watched the bleach work its way through her husband's treasured business attire. She cursed them and Mark loudly as she dumped the last of the bleach on the suits.

Elena swallowed in concern. "Do you feel better now?"

Libby looked up; her eyes had taken on a slightly glazed look. "Almost." She dumped the empty bottle in the trashcan by the garage and then breezed past Elena and through the front door.

"What are you doing now?" Elena asked, hurrying to keep up.

"I need some new rags," Libby said, her jaw set and eyes locked on the stairs.

"New rags?" Elena had to take the stairs two at a time to keep up.

Libby walked over to the ornate dresser in her bedroom that she and Elena had made fun of for years and pulled out a pair of scissors. She opened and closed them quickly in the air, the evil grin spreading across her face again. "I think you'll want to help with this one. There's another pair in the bathroom." Libby tossed her head towards the bathroom and then walked back to the closet.

"Oh, hell yeah!" Elena grinned and hurried to find the extra pair of scissors.

An hour later, the last of Mark's shirts and ties were in a haphazard pile of scraps on the floor.

"There. Now I feel better."

"Really?" Elena asked, closing the scissors for the last time and laying them in her lap.

Libby lay her scissors down softly on the floor and took a deep breath. She looked Elena in the eyes and bit her lip. "No," she whispered, and tears spilled over her eyelids.

Chapter 3

JASON PICKED UP the *American Woman* magazine for the third time in two days and thumbed over to page sixty-four. Leanne had been right. The woman who had written that short story was incredibly talented. In fewer than ten thousand words, she'd captured emotional struggle, intense passion, and complex character traits that Jason had a hard time finding in most of the full-length manuscripts he received on a regular basis. But short stories weren't his market, and just because this Elizabeth Abbott could tell a good story didn't mean she could write a good novel. Still, there was something about her style and the grace with which she dealt with difficulty and loss. Jason couldn't shake the feeling that she was worth pursuing, despite the fact that he wasn't exactly in the market for a period romance novel at the moment.

Call her.

Jason stopped short. "Really?" He closed his eyes and prayed for God to speak again—if it had really been Him at all.

The feeling in his gut was undeniable and since he wasn't going to pass up a lead from God himself, Jason pulled up the contact numbers for *American Woman* magazine on his computer and dialed the extension for the editor.

"*American Woman*, Rachel Davis' office," a woman's voice answered.

"Hi there, my name is Jason Randall, I'm with Crane Literary Agents and I'd like to speak to Ms. Davis about an author that your magazine featured a few months ago."

"Certainly Mr. Randall. One moment please."

Jason picked up his pen and began tapping it on the desk in time to the hold music. "This is the worst hold music, ever," he grunted. "For crying out loud, why do we still have elevator music?" He shook his head. "Amanda! What kind of music do we have for our hold music?"

"Uh, I think it's like Kenny G or something?" she called back.

Jason groaned. "Can you find out how to change that? Seriously this time."

Amanda laughed. "I promise."

The music stopped abruptly and a nasally, high-pitched voice said, "Mr. Randall? This is Rachel Davis."

"Oh, hi, Ms. Davis. Please call me Jason."

"What can I do for you, Jason?"

"I'm looking for some information on an author that you featured a few months ago."

"Okay, let me just pull up my database. What issue?"

Jason flipped the magazine shut to find the issue number. "January of this year."

"Oh, you're looking for Libby!" Rachel's voice warmed.

"Elizabeth Abbott?"

"Yes, she goes by Libby otherwise. She's written for us a few times. Would you like me to send you her other submissions?"

"Yes! That would be fantastic! And her contact info as well?" Jason sat forward, surprised by the anticipation that stirred in him at the thought of reading something else of Elizabeth's.

"Absolutely! I'm sure she'll be thrilled to hear from you!"

"Thank you so much." Jason gave the woman his email address, said goodbye, and then immediately checked his email.

Amanda tapped on his door. "So, I did a web search on how to change the hold music and –"

"Shh! It's here!" Jason shooed Amanda out the door and quickly opened the attachments that Rachel Davis had sent him. Included in the files was a picture of Elizabeth Abbott.

"Whoa," Jason sighed and sat back in his chair. Dark blue alluring eyes stared out at him from under thick black lashes. It took a few seconds before he could look away from them and take in the rest of the portrait. Soft golden blonde hair curled in long layers around a heart shaped face with a smile that stopped his breath. "What are you doing to me, Lord?" he sighed.

LATER IN THE evening, while Elena had left to pick up supplies–hard liquor and pizza–Libby cranked the faucet in her shower as hot as it would go and stood underneath the stream, welcoming the distraction that the burning pain brought. Without bathing, she simply let the water run down her body, willing it to rinse away the stains that her life had been reduced to. She felt worthless, unlovable, and unimportant. Everything she'd set out to accomplish had failed. Here she was on the verge of thirty with nothing to show for it. As the steam began to fill the bathroom, it became hard to breathe, but she didn't care. She welcomed the struggle.

She kept her back to the shelf of Mark's things: his razor, body wash, the special loofah sponge he'd asked her to buy him for Christmas even though she'd teased him about it. Those weren't things that he would miss if she destroyed them, but she wasn't ready to do anything about them yet, either.

"Oh, God, how did this happen?" Libby sighed and leaned against the shower wall. "Where did I go wrong? Never mind, don't answer that." She didn't want to add any more failures to the growing list in her head.

As the hot water began to run lukewarm, Libby turned the shower off and stepped out. She pulled one of her oversized towels from the cupboard above the toilet and wrapped herself in it, burying her nose in the plush terry cloth and breathing in deeply of the fresh detergent scent. She went into the bedroom to find her robe and once again eyed the enormous bed that took up most of the room. She cursed her husband silently.

WHEN ELENA RETURNED, she found Libby upstairs, wrapped in a towel and hunched over a chainsaw.

"Whoa! Libby! What are you doing?"

"I'm trying to figure out how to start this thing! I thought we could use the bed for firewood! Do you have any idea how to work one of these?" Libby looked up, her hair hanging in damp strings around her face.

"Oh boy. Uh, Libby, you know I'm all for destruction of property and getting even and everything, but . . . don't you think you've done enough for today? I mean, seriously?" Elena cringed and took a step towards the chainsaw, seriously concerned about her best friend's well-being.

"But he loves this bed," Libby responded as if there were no question about her logic.

"Um, yeah. I don't think that's going to play out too well for you. Can I . . . can I have the chainsaw please?" Elena reached forward carefully and tried to pull the chainsaw towards her. "Whoa, that's heavier than I thought!"

"I know. I almost fell getting it up here." Libby sighed and sat down on the bed. "I don't even think it works at all."

"You don't even have a fireplace, either." Elena gave up on the chainsaw and sat beside her friend on the bed. "This is awful, one hundred percent. But, things are ugly enough, don't you think?"

"Honestly? I'm kind of surprised to hear you say that considering how vocal you once were about how much you didn't like him."

"I know. Trust me, I want to destroy him too. And we will, but not like this."

"We will? Promise?"

"Oh, honey," Elena said, giving Libby a serious look. "If it's the last thing I do."

"Okay," Libby gave a sad smile. "Did you get pizza?"

"And cinnamon sticks."

"Reggie doesn't mind you staying over tonight?"

"Nah, he's got a poker game or something else equally as boring going on anyway. He's staying at his place."

"Thanks for being here, El."

"Where else would I be?"

Libby smiled and after changing into some pajamas, followed Elena downstairs.

"YOU'VE REACHED THE Abbotts! We can't come to the phone right now, so leave your message after the beep!" A cheerful voice said.

"Hi, there, my name is Jason Randall. I'm from Crane Literary Agents and I was hoping to speak with Ms. Elizabeth Abbott. Please give me a call back at your earliest convenience." He left his phone number and then hung up, slightly disappointed that she hadn't answered and that the outgoing message had said, "Abbott's," which meant there was more than one of them. And that likely meant she was married. Or it could mean she was a lesbian. Or maybe she had kids. He could handle kids though, right?

"Whoa!" Jason sat up, jolted back into reality. "You're getting a little ahead of yourself, man."

"Everything okay in there, boss?" Amanda called from her desk.

Jason shook the thoughts from his head. "Yeah, I'm fine. I think I'm gonna head out early today, though." He began packing manuscripts into his shoulder bag and turned off his computer.

"No problem. Peter and I can close up," Amanda said as he passed her desk.

Jason stopped and spun around on his heel. "On second thought . . ." he gave her a disapproving look.

"Ew! Give me some credit, Jason!" Amanda giggled.

"You had better keep that under wraps, you know. Don't we have a policy on office romances? The boss might find out."

"You keep forgetting that you are the boss now."

"Oh, right. In that case, I'm leaving, and I'll be back in a week," Jason said with a grin. He winked at her and then left the office.

Sometimes he wished that his best friend and former business partner hadn't fallen in love and run away with an actress. When Kevin Crane had handed Jason the keys to the office and promised to file all the paperwork making him the sole owner of CLA, Jason had been too dumbfounded to speak.

"Bro, you'll thank me someday, I promise!" Kevin had vowed and then disappeared through the front door, never to return.

Six months had gone by and Jason had managed to keep the business on its feet, but even with dim-witted Peter's help, the work was piling up and he felt he was spending way too much time reading second-rate manuscripts when he should be shopping the good ones. It was either time to put a little more faith in Peter, hire another qualified agent, or admit defeat.

Jason sighed as he stepped off the subway and made his way up the stairs back onto the street level. He purposely blocked work from his mind, even though he'd brought a stack of it home with him. Jason had a meeting the next day with his friend and favorite publisher, Andrew Green, where he planned to pitch an author he hadn't even signed yet. He hoped he could reach Elizabeth Abbott before the meeting, but for now all he wanted to think about was the ice cold beer waiting for him in his fridge and the next episode of "CSI" in his Netflix queue.

Chapter 1

LIBBY DIDN'T CHECK her messages until the next morning after Elena left to go to work. They'd turned off all the ringers in the house and stayed up late, gorging on pizza and mojitos while binge-watching old TV shows on Netflix.

Mark's voice echoed through the kitchen, casting a chill about the room after she'd pressed play on the answering machine. Libby clenched her water bottle as he ranted about a phone call he'd received from the next-door neighbor about his suits on the front lawn. He ended with a firm, "Libs, we need to talk," which was followed by a loud click.

Libby took deep breaths in and out, trying to ignore the fact that he'd called her by her least favorite nickname on top of all the obvious issues she had with him currently. She deleted his message immediately. How quickly things change, she thought as she waited for the next message to play. A week ago she would have been relieved to hear his voice on her voicemail, to hear his key in the lock. She jotted a quick note to herself to have the locks changed on the house.

An unfamiliar voice started speaking. She couldn't conjure up a face to match the smooth rich tone of the speaker, but suddenly his words seemed to come to life. Wide-eyed, she replayed the message to make sure she'd heard right. Slowly she leaned forward and braced herself on the counter.

"Crane Literary Agents?" she breathed. Her mind raced with possibilities while her common sense told her not to jump to conclusions. She listened one more time and wrote down the number that Jason Randall had recited for her. Clutching the paper, she walked slowly and purposefully up the stairs to the room she used as an office and sat in the over-stuffed chair—her favorite writing place. She took a steadying moment and then picked up the phone from the table beside her and breathed in deeply.

Her fingers shook as she dialed the numbers uncertainly. Who was Jason Randall? Why was he calling her? How did he get her information, and what did he plan to do with it? These and dozens of other questions flew through her mind as the number tones played through the earpiece of the phone. She lifted it and held it gingerly to her ear while she waited for a ringing on the other end. All thoughts of her unfaithful husband, his voluptuous mistress, and the thousands of dollars of ruined clothes on the front lawn had been shoved as far back in her mind as they could be. Her heart pounded as the first ring vibrated against her ear.

"Crane Literary Agents, this is Amanda," a young voice answered.

"Uh, yes, um, this is Libby, I mean, Elizabeth Abbott," Libby stuttered.

"What can I do for you, Ms. Abbott?"

"Oh, sorry. I received a call from, uh . . . shoot, I've forgotten his name . . ."

"Jason Randall?" The voice asked sweetly.

"Yes! Yes, that's it. He asked me to return his call."

"Well, Mr. Randall is currently out of the office right now, but I will let him know that you called back, and I'm sure he'll be in touch soon."

"Oh, all right," Libby said, more than a little disappointed. "Do you happen to know why he was calling me?"

"Hmm, well, I would assume it would have to do with business since he gave you this number. Are you a writer?"

"Yes, well, sort of . . ." That answer made her feel stupid and she stood up, pacing the small room nervously. She wished with all of her heart she could have answered that question with a confident "Yes," but the past year had been so tumultuous, she'd been doing well just to write her grocery lists down. There was that short story that *American Woman* had run last month, but she certainly hadn't submitted it to anyone else.

"Then that has to be it. We are a literary agency and Mr. Randall is an agent, so I'm sure it has something to do with your writing. Let me just get your name and number again as well as the name of your manuscript and I'll pass along that you called."

"Um, my manuscript?" Libby's heart stuttered in her chest.

"Didn't you submit a manuscript?"

"Uh, no . . ." Libby felt her palms starting to sweat.

"Oh, well, then just give me your information and I'll make sure he gets the message."

Libby gave the information and then clicked the off button on the phone as she slumped back into the chair. She let out a long breath and looked sadly around the room. Then, because of the way her nerves had been tested beyond reason in the past twenty-four hours, she burst into tears.

ELENA WAITED FOR Samantha to grab her purse from the back room before flipping off the lights as they walked out of the flower store together.

"Are you sure she's okay?" Samantha shook her long brown hair over her shoulders as they stepped into the chilly evening.

Elena turned the key in the lock on the door and nodded. "It'll take time, but she'll survive this. She doesn't think she will, but I know her better than she knows herself."

"Well, when she's ready, maybe we can all go out to that new club downtown and let cute guys buy us drinks and then ignore them!" Samantha grinned.

Elena laughed. "I bet she'll be all over that. I'll keep you posted. You're going to open for me tomorrow, right? I've got to check out the venue for the Archer wedding this weekend."

Samantha saluted her. "Assistant manager at your service!" she grinned.

"I told you not to let that get to your head."

Samantha shrugged. "Give Libby a hug for me?"

Elena nodded and they said their goodbyes. Armed with more liquor and Ryan Reynolds' latest romantic comedy on Blu Ray, she drove back to Libby's house.

She eyed the mess on the front lawn with pride. Libby was sweet and thoughtful and didn't have a mean bone in her body – unless you crossed her or one of her friends. Then she could be like an angry mama bear, and Elena pitied whoever fell in the way of her best friend's warpath, present victim excluded. She would never give Mark the satisfaction of her pity. She stepped carefully around the suits and up the front walk to the door.

"Libby?" she called, trying the handle. It was locked. "Libby, it's me!" She tapped on the window. There was no answer, but Libby's car was still in the driveway. Elena walked around to the side entrance and tried that. It opened easily, and she walked through the laundry room in search of her friend.

"Libby? Where are you?" She heard a sniffle coming from the dining room, and turned in that direction. Her heart ached at the sight of her friend sitting at the long dark dining table with her head in her hands, long golden hair spilling over her shoulders and covering her face like a curtain. In front of her was a stack of papers and the manila envelope they'd been delivered in. The simple chandelier cast soft light around the only room in the house that hadn't been a source of argument between Libby and Mark. They'd simply left it as it was, white walls with a simple floral oil painting on one wall and bay windows on the other side.

Elena sighed and sank into the chair beside her friend.

"I can't bring myself to do it, El. I can't sign."

Elena reached forward and rested her hand on Libby's arm. "You don't have to. Not yet."

"But I want to. I want it over with."

"It's only been two days, you've got to give yourself some time to ease into the idea of this whole thing. To grieve."

Libby finally looked up, her expression like a tortured puppy: totally innocent, yet abused in the most hurtful way. Tears filled her eyes and began to spill down her cheeks. "I don't know what to do," she sobbed.

Elena scooted forward and vowed silently to murder Mark if ever given the opportunity. She put her arm around her friend, wishing that comforting words would begin to flow out of her mouth to heal the wounds Mark had inflicted.

Elena had never liked him. Ever. She'd raised questions about him only once before and had been shut down so harshly by Libby that she'd shut her mouth and simply put up with him for the better (or worst) part of the last eight years. She wished to God that she'd been wrong about him.

Libby sniffled and sat up, wiping the back of her hand across her nose. "One of the worst parts of it is just how stereotypical it all is. I know that sounds stupid, but he's just another lawyer screwing around on his wife, and I'm just another loyal wife, pretending it's not happening."

"Libby, you are the most genuine, beautiful, and honest person I know. He's the only stereotype in this situation. He can't handle how real you are. He needs fake Bria with her fake boobs and her fake smile."

"I know. But she's also stunning, and . . . she's me, with augmentation."

"What do you mean?"

"She's my replacement, El. Literally, in every sense of the word! It just makes me wonder if what we had was ever real or if I was just another conquest."

"He makes me sick." Elena sneered.

"Be thankful you didn't have to see what I saw."

"I'm sorry, Libby. I'm so sorry."

Libby let her arm hang loose again. "I dug my own grave, I suppose."

"Don't you dare say that. This is not your fault. Do you hear me? Mark is an ass and he doesn't deserve you. He's a complete ass."

"I just don't know what went wrong. I did everything right. I did everything he asked. Except one thing."

"Elizabeth Abbott," Elena warned.

"I couldn't give him a baby, El."

Elena sighed and sat back in her chair. "And you think he wants Bria to be the mother of his children? Please."

"I know, but we all saw it. After the second miscarriage, he totally changed."

"Well, that's not reason enough for him to screw around. You are more than amazing. You are way more stunning than Bria is. Nothing about her beauty is real. It's all fabricated. Paid for. You make gorgeous women look plain, and that's before you've even put your makeup on!" Elena exclaimed.

"Then it's not about looks, which is what I'm saying. It's about the baby. Or the lack thereof."

Elena rubbed her hand over her eyes. "If that's true, then he's even more of a jerk than I ever imagined. It's not your fault that you miscarried—"

"We don't actually know that, though."

"That's not what I mean. It's not like you wanted to lose the babies. It's not like you did it to hurt him."

"Of course not!"

"See? That's my point. You wanted those babies as much as he did. He was the one who refused to try fertility treatments; hell, he was the one who refused to go through any kind of testing! That doesn't give him any right to go bang the next chick who walks into his office!"

Libby turned her eyes to the ceiling and shook her head. "I know. It still doesn't explain what went wrong."

"Well, you may never know. You might just need to let go and move on."

"Let go," Libby said, as if trying the words on for size. "I think that's going to take time."

"Of course it is. No one is expecting anything of you right now."

Libby looked back at her friend and bit her lip.

"What? What is it?" Elena sat forward, the look on her friend's face concerning her.

"I got a call from a literary agency in New York today."

Elena's jaw dropped open. "Are you kidding me?" she squealed.

Libby shook her head. "I didn't actually talk to anyone but a secretary; the guy left a message and when I called back, he wasn't in. But, I asked the girl who answered if she knew what it was about, and she said that it had to be about my writing because he'd given me the office phone number."

"Libby! That's amazing!" Elena jumped up and threw her arms around Libby's neck.

"I don't know anything yet. She asked if I'd submitted a manuscript, and of course I didn't, so I'm trying not to freak out–"

"Um, it's totally necessary to freak out!" Elena pulled back and clasped her hands together. "Oh, my gosh, Libby!"

Libby smiled nervously. "Okay, I'm freaking out a little," she laughed.

"This calls for a celebration!"

Libby started to protest.

"Don't worry," Elena interrupted, holding up the movie. "I brought the party to you. Ryan Reynolds and margaritas!"

Libby sighed in relief and followed Elena into the kitchen.

"OH GEEZ, I'VE missed this! When was the last time we did this?" Libby laughed as the credits rolled on their movie.

"Last night?" Elena giggled.

"Well, I suppose we can do this as much as we want now," Libby smirked.

"Who needs men?" Elena lifted her glass.

"To not needing men!" Libby joined her in a toast.

"Amen. Or, uh . . . *no*-men!" They both burst into a fit of giggles.

After a minute, Libby sobered her gaze. "Thank you for coming, Elena. This really helped."

"Ah, you might not say that in the morning." She held up the empty tequila bottle.

Libby swore. "We didn't . . . did we?"

"Well, that's the first time I've heard *that* from a woman!" Elena laughed, "Oh geez." She clutched at her skull, "I've gotta remember that I'm not in high school anymore. Drunk isn't very attractive on 30 year-olds."

"Ha. You're on your own there."

"Yeah, yeah. Twenty-nine only lasts so long, my friend," Elena snorted.

"Well, until then, how about I just stay drunk?" Libby smiled as she pushed herself off the floor.

"I don't think that'll solve anything."

"But it'll be *fun!*" Libby swayed as she gulped the last of her margarita.

"Okay, enough of that. Where's your aspirin?"

Libby staggered over to the cabinet above the dishwasher and pulled down the bottle, dry swallowing three and giving Elena three of her own.

"Yeah, I'm gonna need water with mine."

"Fridge," Libby said as she hung over the counter. "Uuuuugh," she groaned.

"What was that you said about being forever drunk?" Elena smirked.

"Yeah, well, it was a nice thought."

"I'm gonna crash in the guest room, 'k?"

Libby nodded and pulled a water bottle out of the fridge. She went to make sure all the doors were locked and the alarm set and then bid Elena good night, not willing to acknowledge that she was going to be sleeping in her own room, in that awful bed, for the first time since her life had fallen apart.

She stood in the doorway, hesitating a minute before giving in to the exhaustion that was overwhelming her. She climbed onto the enormous bed and lay as close to the edge as she could without falling off.

LIBBY WOKE UP the next morning feeling as though she were experiencing an earthquake. Her whole body was shaking.

"Libby! He's here. Mark is here!" Elena's urgent tone of voice ripped through Libby's head like a siren.

She sat up straight, immediately regretting it as her hands flew to her head. She groaned at the pounding in her skull and the uneasy feeling she had in her stomach.

"I know, I know, but Libby, *Mark* is here."

"What?" Libby cried and started scrambling to get out of the bed, suddenly very aware of where she was.

"Calm down. Calm down. He's waiting for you downstairs. Just put on this robe. Here, let me just fix your hair a little bit . . . oh screw it, there's nothing I can do. You don't need to fix yourself up for him anyway."

Libby wasn't sure if Elena had meant that as a compliment or not, but she had bigger things to worry about just then. She pulled the robe tightly around her body, grimaced at her reflection in the mirror, and tried to square her shoulders and hold her head high.

She was about to step through the door when she froze with a thought and said, "Wait. I do *not* need to rush around here to go and see him when he decides I should. Screw him! I need some time to clear my head. I waited on him hand and foot for how long? And he made me look like an idiot. He can wait a few minutes while I shower and get ready." Mind made up, she strode purposefully to the bathroom and shut the door behind her.

ELENA STARED AFTER Libby, a little shocked at her friend's countenance. "And I'm, what, supposed to entertain him?" she cried, mortified. She heard the shower turn on and the lock click on the door, so with a sigh, she turned on her heel and worked to overcome the rage that had built up inside of her. Libby might frown upon a murder taking place in her home, even if it was the murder of her own lying, cheating husband.

Mark was sitting at the island in the kitchen, palms pressing down on it, his chin tucked into his neck. Elena eyed him warily before making her presence known. What could he be thinking? Obviously he'd be mad about the suits, but as for anything else, as far as Elena was concerned, Mark had forfeited his right to be upset about anything. She cleared her throat and stepped around the corner from the stairway into the kitchen.

"I can't believe you–oh, it's you, again." Mark stood abruptly.

"She's getting ready."

Mark let out a sigh and sat back down. "Did you stay here last night?"

Elena nodded.

"How is she?" His expression was serious, his eyes searching.

Elena narrowed her eyes at him and took a step forward. "I don't really think you have any right to ask that question, Mark. In fact, I don't think you have any right to step foot inside this house, and if it were me, I'd have you forcibly removed from the property."

"Elena, look–"

"No. You look, Mark. Look around at what you've just given up. Not just this amazing home, but the family that was building inside of it. The love and support of the most loyal, devoted, kind, caring, incredible woman that I know! I always knew you weren't good enough for her. I always knew you were capable of screwing this up somehow. But she trusted you." Elena got in Mark's face and pointed her finger at him. "So I kept my mouth shut and prayed that I was wrong." She shook her head. "You gambled your entire world, Mark Abbott, and you lost. You will never even realize how badly you lost."

His expression was unreadable. He looked away from her and stared at the fridge in front of him.

"Nothing to say for yourself?" She stepped back and put her hands on her hips.

"Not to you." He gave her a dark stare.

Elena clicked her tongue in disbelief. "You really have no clue do you? There is no one better than Elizabeth."

"Elena, can you give us some privacy please?" Libby's voice came from the doorway to the kitchen. Mark's head snapped towards her immediately.

With one last glare at Mark, Elena spun on her heel and left the kitchen, squeezing Libby's arm as she breezed past.

LIBBY HAD HEARD only the last few sentences. She had come down the stairs quietly and stood in the doorway, sensing the tension rising between her husband and her best friend. Her hair hung in a damp ponytail, her makeup had been applied quickly, but in her typical, soft style, and she'd thrown on jeans and an over-sized T-shirt that hung off of one shoulder.

Her breath had caught at the sight of him. His hair was perfectly combed forward, as always, slicked with product, but his deep-set eyes were tired with bags underneath them. Mark's dark suit was not unlike normal, but suddenly it seemed so out of place to Libby in the stark white kitchen with the stainless steel appliances. Suddenly he didn't seem to fit into the home that they'd made for themselves. She shifted uncomfortably.

"You've got some nerve coming here today," she said softly in a matter-of-fact tone.

"Libs—"

She held up a hand to stop him and laughed without humor. "Do not call me Libs," she sneered, her voice no longer soft but thick with irritation and warning.

"I just, I just wanted to talk . . ." he said, sounding a little nervous.

"Talk? What in the hell do you want to talk about Mark? What's left to say? You didn't tell me you'd filed for divorce. Well, I know that now. You didn't tell me you were screwing around behind my back. Well, guess what? I know that, too! I'm pretty sure there is nothing left to say." She walked over to the counter and pressed the button on the Keurig to make a cup of coffee.

"I didn't mean for—"

"You didn't mean for what? For me to find out?" she cried. "What *did* you mean for, Mark? Did you just want to divorce me quietly, behind my back? Did you think I wouldn't notice when you'd moved out all your things and we weren't *married* anymore?" She slammed the sugar bowl down on the counter, sending sugar granules all over the place, and turned to face him, her cheeks burning with anger.

"Libby, I'm sorry. I didn't know you were coming to the office, I didn't know that you were going to walk in, and I didn't know when the papers would be delivered—"

"Total b.s." she seethed. "None of that really matters now, does it?" She walked forward and stood directly opposite him on the other side of the island, arms folded tight across her chest. "Just what exactly did you expect to accomplish by coming here, Mark? You're not here to apologize, are you? To put our marriage back together?"

Mark let out a breath and shook his head. "No, I'm not."

"Well, then?" Libby threw her hands up in question. Mark sat dumbly, staring at the countertop. Libby sighed loudly and turned around, tapping her fingers on the counter, waiting for the coffee to finish brewing. "Well, I hope you're happy, Mark, because really, that's what it's all about, isn't it? It's all about you. All about what you want."

"Babe, please–"

Libby laughed sadistically. "You're kidding right? You don't get to call me 'Babe' anymore." She rolled her eyes, and turned around pulling her mug out from under the Keurig spout. "Babe, let's get married. Babe, let's move into this huge house that we can't afford yet. Babe let's buy this huge, ugly bed that no one in their right mind would choose. Babe, let's have a baby." She spun around and glared at him. "Actually, on second thought, since you can't seem to stay pregnant, let's just forget the whole thing. And while we're at it, *babe*, why don't you quit working so that I can start banging your replacement while you pretend to be a writer?" She slammed her coffee cup down on the counter so hard that it splattered hot liquid on Mark's hand.

"Dammit, Libs!" he shouted and yanked his hand towards his chest.

"Get out. Get *out*." She pointed to the door.

"I need to get my things–"

"As far as I'm concerned, you don't *have* any things," she growled.

"Libby, please, I don't want this to be ugly."

"I think she asked you to leave, Mark." Elena said from the doorway, her phone in hand. "I've got Reggie on the phone just waiting to come over here and kick your ass."

Mark sighed in defeat and stood. "I want to settle this out of court. Can we do that?"

"The sooner, the better," Libby sneered.

Elena and Libby followed him out and stood in the doorway while he scooped up his ruined clothes from the front lawn. He carelessly shoved the armload into his SUV, and without another look at either of them, he backed the car out of the driveway and disappeared from sight.

"I swear, you're better off," Elena sighed, staring down the street.

Libby let out a breath so long she might have been holding it for the entire time Mark had been there. She grabbed Elena's hand and squeezed it hard. "I just can't believe this is my life."

Chapter 5

JASON HUNG UP the phone after leaving yet another message for the elusive Elizabeth Abbott. He wondered if his voice had betrayed him–since his initial call, the answering machine message had been changed. Instead of "The Abbotts'," the sweet voice now said, "You've reached the residence of Libby Abbott." Jason had been intrigued by the new message and it had taken him an extra few seconds to recalibrate his thoughts.

"I guess we're playing phone tag. I'll send you an email here in a minute. That might be better for now, but please give me a call back when you're able," he'd said.

Now he turned to his computer and pulled up Libby's information from the email he'd received from *American Woman*. He copied and pasted the email address into a new message and paused with his fingers over the keyboard. Eyebrows furrowed, he looked from side to side, as if expecting someone to be watching him.

"It's just an email, Jason." He rolled his eyes at himself and began to type.

"Dear Ms. Abbott, I hope this letter finds you well,"

He held down the backspace button until the first sentence was deleted. Groaning, he ran his fingers through his hair and began again.

"I'm sorry that we haven't been able to connect on the phone yet. I was forwarded a short story that you had published in American Woman in January, and I absolutely fell in love . . ."

"Seriously?" He wanted to smack himself. He hit the delete button repeatedly.

"I was very impressed," he typed instead. *"I'd like the opportunity to speak with you about your aspirations as a writer and how I might be able to be of some support to you. You can email me at the above address or give me a call at the office number that you have already. I really look forward to hearing from you!"*

He signed off and then sent the email without telling her that he'd already pitched her short story to his friend Andrew Green, and that Andrew had practically drooled over what he'd read. Jason prayed that Libby would call him back ASAP.

LIBBY WAS UPSTAIRS and up to her elbows in bathroom cleaner when the phone rang. She'd reached it too late and hadn't heard the message left on the machine downstairs. She was on a roll in the bathroom—it was almost shining—so she decided to finish her work there and then check the message after. She'd almost forgotten all about Jason Randall and Crane Literary Agency. As she was rinsing the last of the grime off of her forearms, she suddenly remembered the call from a few days prior, and she raced down the stairs, arms still dripping, and listened to the message. As soon as it was over, she raced back upstairs to her office and clicked the email icon on her laptop.

One new message: **Jason Randall Re: Phone Tag**

Her eyes skimmed over the words quickly, and then a second time, more slowly. Libby clutched a hand to her chest, wondering if it were possible for her heart to actually leap out of her body. She stood up slowly, pacing her office, trying to calm herself down, and then found herself jumping up and down, squealing like a three year old with a new Barbie.

When her feet finally stopped dancing, she covered her mouth with her hands and dared to let the reality sink in. She picked up the *American Woman* magazine that lay on her desk and held it to her heart. "I can't believe this!"

For all that she had endured in the past few days and months, this was surely the light at the end of the tunnel. She picked up the phone and called Elena at work to tell her the news.

Elena squealed even louder than Libby had. With her eyes closed and tears squeezing through them, Libby rationalized that it was nothing more than interest from an agent. A publisher was a whole different ball game.

"But Libby, it's a heck of a lot easier to get a publisher when you have an agent backing you up!"

"I know. I know! I just want to be careful about my expectations . . ."

"Whatever. I say we need to celebrate some more!"

"Let's wait until after I talk to the guy, okay? And how about a break from the Mexican fiesta drinks?"

Elena laughed. "I hear you. We're too old to be drunk during the week!"

"I think I'm too old to be drunk at all, but–"

"No more talking! Call the guy back!"

"Okay. I'll let you know how it goes!" Libby turned off the phone and then turned it on again, about to dial the office number on the bottom of Jason Randall's email, but then she stopped herself. What if she couldn't contain her excitement? What if her voice cracked and she got embarrassed and said something stupid? What if the emotional roller coaster she was on went into hyperdrive and she burst into tears on the phone?

"No way," she said firmly and sat back down, pulling the computer onto her lap. She hit 'reply' on the email from Jason and began to type.

Dear Mr. Randall,

I am deeply flattered that you enjoyed my story in this winter's edition of

American Woman. *I'll let you off the hook, just this once, for reading a woman's magazine, since it may potentially benefit me in the long run."* Libby smiled and typed a smiley face beside the sentence.

"I've loved writing since I was a child and have been creating stories and characters ever since. Unfortunately, I had bills to pay, so I didn't pursue writing as a career, but instead became a paralegal and worked in a firm until a few years ago, when my husband . . ."

Libby paused and pursed her lips to one side of her mouth. She deleted the last two words and then continued.

". . . I decided to pursue a more fulfilling life and try writing again. It's been very slow and I've only had a few short stories published, but I am serious about pursuing it as a career. I dream about publishing novels and surviving on the success of my characters and the impact that they have on my readers. I would love to hear about your agency and explore what it would look like for us to work together, if that is a possibility. Thank you, again, for your time and consideration!"

Libby didn't breathe until she heard the whooshing sound of the email being sent. She sat for a moment, resting her head on the back of her chair, staring at the ceiling.

"Please let this be the beginning of something good," she whispered to the empty room.

~e

JASON JUMPED WHEN Libby's name appeared in his inbox. He clicked the new message so fast the sound of the notification barely had time to finish.

He chuckled at her jab about *American Woman* and then his lips closed in a small smile. Jason pulled up his calendar on the computer and stared at it thoughtfully.

"Amanda?" he called.

"Yeah, boss. What's up?" She rolled her chair into his doorway and pushed her glasses up on her nose.

"Isn't there a conference in Dallas soon?"

"Yes, but you said you couldn't go because of Layne Atfield's book launch. It's the same weekend, remember?"

"What day is the launch party?"

"Uh, let me check." She rolled back to her desk and then returned with her iPad in hand. "Party is on the twentieth, and the conference is the nineteenth and twentieth."

"What time is the party?"

"Jason, seriously? What is so important in Dallas? If you miss the launch party–"

"I won't. I'm just trying to figure something out."

Amanda sighed. "The party starts at eight."

"At Emerald?"

"Yes."

"So, if I needed to, I could go to Dallas on Friday and be back Sunday in plenty of time for the party."

"Why would you take that risk though?"

"It's not a risk! I could fly back early on Sunday!"

"But why?" Amanda pressed.

"There is an author I want to meet with, that's all."

Amanda narrowed her eyes at her boss. "Meet with? Is this about that Elizabeth woman you keep asking about? She hasn't called back yet."

"I know. She emailed me. And, yes. It's about her."

"If you want to meet her so badly, why don't you just fly her here?"

"I guess that's an option," Jason said thoughtfully.

"Well, whatever you do, you can't miss Layne's launch. It's our biggest event this quarter."

"I won't miss it. But, just in case, do you think Peter could represent the firm?"

"Jason!" Amanda scolded.

"Okay, okay!" he laughed. "Speaking of Peter, could you have him come in tomorrow morning? I think it's time I upped his workload."

Amanda's expression brightened. "Really?"

"Yes. And I'm going to need to hire another agent. Would you start looking on the job boards?"

"But you just said—"

"He's not quite there yet, Amanda. I admit he's not terrible, but he's still green."

She nodded. "Okay. I'll start looking and I'll have some potential resumes on your desk tomorrow."

"Perfect." Jason turned his attention back to the computer and responded to Libby's email.

LIBBY, WHO HADN'T expected such a quick response from a big New York City literary agent, went on with the rest of her plans for the day, which involved scrubbing her house clean from top to bottom. When she'd started that morning after Mark and Elena had both left, anger had fueled her, but now there was excitement as she used a broom to knock down cobwebs and Mark's toothbrush to clean the grout in the kitchen. Potential swarmed around with the dust particles as she wiped off the wooden shelves in the living room and other surfaces around the house.

She had an agent! Well, she almost had an agent, or she maybe had an agent . . . she really wasn't sure. She had an agent who was interested in signing her – maybe? She was so lost in her daydreams while she worked that she didn't even notice the time and was startled when she heard a knock on the door and saw that it was nearly six p.m. She hadn't even eaten all day.

She pushed up from her hands and knees where she was cleaning the tiles in the entryway and opened the door for Elena and her boyfriend, Reggie.

"Take your shoes off!" she commanded as soon as they lifted their feet to enter.

Elena peered curiously from behind Reggie which was a feat; he was huge and she looked even smaller standing beside him. He was incredibly intimidating to anyone who didn't know him, and he was often mistaken for a football player.

"If a guy's tall, you automatically think basketball. If he's black, you automatically think football. Not all black dudes got game, and not all tall dudes can dribble," he'd say to anyone who'd ask. He was, however, a P.E. teacher at the local high school.

"Have you cleaned the whole house?" Elena said looking around while she slipped off her shoes.

"Maybe," Libby huffed as she pushed some loose bangs out of her eyes. "I had to do something."

"Wow. Want to come to my place next?" Reggie joked, scratching his shiny bald head.

Elena and Libby both cringed.

"Baby, remember you promised to never, ever bring another living being into that cesspool?"

"Oh, yeah," he grinned. "Right."

Libby's stomach growled as she noticed a large paper bag in Elena's hands. "Is that dinner? I haven't eaten since breakfast."

Elena nodded. "I thought if you wanted, Reggie and I could help you purge some things after we eat."

Aside from the suits and the 'rags' in the garbage bag upstairs, the rest of Mark's things remained littered around the house wherever he'd left them. Libby had purposefully distracted herself from the task of packing up his things. It wasn't something she wanted to do alone.

"That would be amazing," she sighed.

Reggie bent forward and put his arms around Libby, crushing her in a bear hug. "You're gonna be okay, Libby. You're gonna get through this."

She smiled at him when he set her back on her feet. "Thanks, Reggie. I'm glad I've got you guys to back me up."

"She looks pretty bad, huh?" Reggie said in a low voice as Libby led them into the kitchen.

"She looks exhausted," Elena agreed.

"I can hear you!" Libby cried from around the corner.

A FEW HOURS later, all of the boxes Reggie had brought had been packed to the brim and lined against a wall in the garage. The master bed had been dismantled (no chainsaw necessary) and now sat beside the boxes, waiting for Mark to come and pick them all up.

"I can bring more boxes tomorrow if you want," Reggie offered as the three of them stood side by side admiring their hard work.

Libby nodded. "There're still a bunch of books in the office and who knows what else in the attic."

"Maybe you should take a break. You've worked pretty hard. I think we should go shopping tomorrow!" Elena said with a hopeful grin.

"Thanks, but this is kind of therapeutic. It sort of feels like I'm purging the house of him."

"Well, is there anything else we can do for you tonight?" Reggie asked.

"Reg, let's go clean up the kitchen from dinner," Elena suggested.

"You really don't have to do that," Libby protested.

"You're right. We don't. But we want to."

"Uh, I don't know if I want to . . ." Reggie winked and then let Elena pull him back into the house.

Libby stood in the garage and continued to stare at the boxes full of her husband's things. If she stopped for too long, she knew the dark cloud she'd been avoiding all day would hover and threaten to overtake her. She took a breath, puffed her chest out and went back into the house, closing the garage door firmly behind her.

Slowly she climbed the stairs for what seemed like the thousandth time that night. She went to the office to shut off her computer and noticed that she had a few unread emails. When she saw Jason Randall's name listed, she clicked on it immediately.

"Oh, my gosh!" she cried while she read.

Elena came running into the office a few seconds later. "What?"

"He wants to fly me to New York!"

"Who does? Mark?" Reggie asked, coming in behind Elena.

"No! Jason Randall!" Libby's eyes grew wide with excitement.

"The agent?" Elena asked.

Libby nodded excitedly. "Oh, my gosh! I can't believe this!"

"Wow, Libby! That's awesome!" Reggie clapped her on the back, a huge grin spreading across his face.

"What about Mark?" Libby asked suddenly.

"What about him?" Elena grimaced.

"I mean, what about this whole mess? The divorce? All of it?"

"Have you signed the papers yet?"

"No. I figured I should have a lawyer look at them. I worked for a law firm but that doesn't mean I know what I'm doing here."

"Well, do it. Do it fast. This is an opportunity that could change your life, Libby. You're going to be a published author!"

Libby shook her head warily. "That's a long way off, El!"

"But it's a definite possibility. Mark has held you back for long enough. Get this taken care of as soon as you can, and then hop a flight to New York!"

Pursing her lips together, Libby nodded slowly. "You're right. There's no sense dragging this on. It's not as if we're going to get back together. I'll call a lawyer tomorrow."

"Yeah, but Libby, you might not want to rush this whole agent thing, I mean, you might want to take some time to really consider your options. What if you tell the guy you have some stuff goin' on and you need a little time?" Reggie suggested.

"Do not show weakness!" Elena gave Reggie a dirty look. "At least meet with a lawyer and see what the time frame looks like for the whole process. Then decide!"

"Yeah. That sounds good. I could probably go to New York sometime in the next month, regardless of what happens here. Reggie's right, too; I don't want to rush through this and make any bad choices. I need to have a clear head. If this guy is really interested in me, he'll wait. . . ."

Elena rolled her eyes. "So you're going to get a lawyer?"

Libby nodded. "Tomorrow."

"Good. Well, I guess we're going to get out of your hair then, if you're all right."

Libby nodded and walked them downstairs. "You are both amazing. Thank you for your help tonight."

"No worries. We've got your back," Reggie said as he hugged her.

"You deserve this, Libby. It's your turn. I just know it." Elena grinned and squeezed Libby's hand.

"I hope so." Libby sighed, waved, then shut the door behind them. She paused for a moment to collect herself then raced back up the stairs to her computer, staring at it thoughtfully for a moment before sitting down to respond to Jason Randall's email.

"Dear Mr. Randall,

I am overwhelmed by your offer to meet in New York. I feel the need to be honest with you, however. I am currently in the middle of some significant "personal issues," as you might call them. To be frank, I was surprised this week with divorce papers along with other sensitive information about the state of my marriage, and I'm just not quite sure when I will be able to get away. I don't think it's really hit me yet. Your phone calls have been a great distraction, but now I'm left balancing the scales of two different life-altering situations. Would it be completely ridiculous of me to request a few weeks to get things in order here before moving forward with you?"

Libby chewed her lip as she re-read her message. Did she give away too much information? Did she seem weak? Would he delete the email and move on to the next person in his queue?

"Here goes nothing," she sighed and clicked the send button.

Chapter 6

"LISTEN, PETER. I think you're talented, and I think you've got potential. I feel like maybe we each had different expectations of what this job should entail, so let's set a few ground rules," Jason said, leaning back in his desk chair. "First of all, and this is simply personal preference, I will never rep fan-fiction. I don't even want it to waste space on my desk."

Peter nodded and scribbled something down on his legal pad from his spot on the other side of Jason's desk. "That's really an easy fix for the most part. We just have to add it to the website," Peter offered.

"Oh, right. The website. Kevin used to handle all of that. Do you by any chance know how to do any of that?"

"I just need the login. In fact, if you'd let, me I'd like to update some other things on there as well."

Jason didn't have to think twice about it. "I'll find that info; Amanda may even have it. Just let me see anything you change before it goes live on the site."

Peter agreed, then he sat forward, his black horn-rimmed glasses pushed against his face and his jet black hair angled up and to one side like Jason had seen on the cover of recent grocery store magazines.

Oh, boy, Jason thought to himself as Peter's eagerness seemed to ooze into the room. Out loud he said, "Second, stop trying to find things that I would like. You don't have to please me; you have to please publishers who have to please readers. We're not looking for *our* next favorite novel; we're looking for *their* next favorite novel." Jason pointed out the window.

Peter nodded again, and this time Jason imagined a light bulb going off in Peter's head. One can only hope, he thought.

"I think that's enough to get you started on the right track. So from now on, if you find something that you think will appeal to the masses, then I want you to research the plot and the subject matter and make sure that it's not plagiarized, for one, and two, that it's completely original. Find the problems in the story and make note of them. Then, and only then, pass them on to me. I'll take it from there. And no more than five a week for the next month until we hire someone else, all right?"

"Yes, sir. Thank you. I won't let you down." Peter stood up eagerly, smoothed out his skinny jeans, and adjusted his argyle cardigan.

Jason waved him out of the room and chuckled to himself when Peter left. "I'm so glad I already lived through the 80's." He opened his laptop and waited for the sound that he'd been anticipating since the previous afternoon.

"There you are," he grinned when the chime went off. He opened the email and started reading. His forehead creased with a frown. "Crap," he whispered. Then he called out to Amanda.

"Right here." Her head popped into view in the doorway.

"Book me a flight to DFW on the eighteenth and get me into that conference on Friday night."

"Seriously?"

"Yes. And don't ask questions. I'm the boss, remember?" He waited a moment and then called out, "I saw those eyes rolling!"

She snorted and he saw the travel webpage pop up on her screen.

Jason picked up the phone and dialed Libby's number. "Please answer, please answer!"

"Hello?"

Finally, her voice in real-time. "Libby? Ah, Elizabeth Abbott?"

"Yes, who's calling?"

"This is Jason Randall."

"Oh, my gosh, hi!" her tone of voice went up a few notches.

"Hey, there. How are you doing today?" He tried to sound business-like.

"Uh, fine. I'm fine. Did you get my email from last night?"

"I did. That's why I'm calling. I was wondering if it would be alright if I came to you instead. I have a conference in Dallas next weekend and I was hoping we could meet for lunch or dinner or something."

"Oh! Really?" She sounded surprised.

"Yeah. I'm going to be there anyway, and I'd really like to sit down with you."

"Yes, absolutely! I mean, I would love to meet with you! What day are you thinking?

"Uh, well, I'm flying in on the," he raised his voice so that Amanda would hear him.

"Eighteenth at noon," she hissed back.

"Eighteenth at noon," he repeated into the phone. "So we could do dinner that night, or lunch the next day. Whichever you prefer. I have to be back in New York early on the twentieth for a launch party though, so unfortunately, those are the only times I could meet."

"Lunch on the nineteenth sounds great!"

"Perfect. I'm not sure where I'm staying yet, but how about I give you a call next week and we can set it up?"

"That's fine. Let me give you my cell number. It'll be a lot easier to reach me there, especially with all this garbage I have going on."

"I'm sorry about that. Divorce is pretty brutal," he said sincerely. He could hear the exhaustion in her voice.

"I've barely gotten my feet wet and I'm overwhelmed," Libby admitted.

"I'm no stranger to it so I can tell you that you're going to come out on the other side of this, and you'll be better for it. And who knows, maybe I'll get to be a part of that–I mean–oh wow, that didn't come out right." Jason sunk his head into his hands and leaned his elbows on the desk.

Amanda snorted loudly from her desk, and Jason looked up and shot a dirty look at her back.

"That's okay. I think I understand what you mean." There was a hint of laughter in Libby's voice.

Jason breathed a sigh of relief.

"Thank you for that, though," she continued. "It's nice to hear that from someone who's been through it. Right now it seems like this will go on forever."

"I hesitate to say that I'm thankful for everything that happened in my own marriage, but I'm definitely a better person because of it. I promise it won't last forever."

"Well, thank you. That's, um, encouraging."

"It's also extremely unprofessional of me, but I figure I've already discredited myself by admitting that I read women's magazines, so . . . ."

Libby laughed good-naturedly. "Really, I appreciate all the encouragement I can get right now."

The sound of her rich laughter raised goosebumps on his skin.

"Well, I won't overstep my boundaries anymore, but if I can at least take your mind off of things for a while, maybe that will help. I'll see you next week."

"Okay! I'm really looking forward to it."

"Me, too."

"Bye, Mr. Randall."

Jason hung up the phone and drummed his fingers on his desk. He didn't notice when Amanda stood up and leaned against the doorway, staring at him with narrowed eyes.

"You were flirting with her," she stated.

"Huh? What? No, I wasn't!" Jason sat up abruptly.

"Yes. You. Were!" Amanda's eyes bugged out of her head and she took slow steps toward him. "You were flirting with a potential client!"

"Amanda, be serious–"

"I'm serious as a heart attack. You were flirting with Elizabeth Abbott." A huge smile spread across her face.

"I'm not listening to this." Jason turned his attention to his computer screen and pretended to be engrossed in something.

"Oh, I think it's great, boss. It's about time you started dating again."

"Dating!" Jason sputtered. "Seriously, Amanda!"

"Don't worry. Secret's safe with me!" She winked at him and left the office with a bounce in her step. Jason rolled his eyes and then remembered the way Libby's laughter had sent shivers down his spine. He stood up quickly and shut the door to his office.

"God, are You doing something here? Am I playing with fire? Because she's right, you know. It's been almost two years. I've let this job consume my life in order to avoid having to put myself out there again. So, are You doing this? Because if not, then I don't even want to mess with it."

All things work together for the good of those who are called according to my purpose, Jason.

His favorite verse spoken straight from the Father's mouth didn't exactly make him feel better. "I remember. But–"

All things. Trust me.

"Sure. Trust *You*. What about everyone else in the world?"

You'll always have me. I'll never leave you nor forsake you.

"That's supposed to be comforting, right?" Jason sighed and ran his fingers through his hair. "Okay, fine. I trust You."

LIBBY SAT OUTSIDE on the bench facing her garden, staring at her phone for a long time before a hummingbird flew by and caught her attention. It settled on the feeder she'd placed in the middle of her hibiscus plant, wings zipping up and down faster than she could blink. An odd sense of peace had come over her while she'd listened to Jason speak briefly about his own experience with divorce. She pulled her knees to her chest and settled against the back of the bench, happy that spring was beginning to blossom. It would be a few weeks before the flowers opened and showed their faces, but just seeing the buds on the rose bush beginning to sprout made her smile. Elena had helped her plant the garden right outside of the backdoor last spring. It was Libby's favorite place to be alone.

She trailed her finger around the iron swirls of the bench. Alone. That was what she was now, completely alone. She said the word quietly, but even at a whisper it sounded like thunder in her ears. She wiped at her eyes as she felt the stinging presence of tears. The peace she'd felt while on the phone didn't overshadow her grief. As the hummingbird flew away, having drank all of the sugar water, Libby sighed. She felt as empty as the bird feeder. Jason's words had given her a little hope, but she knew she had a long way to go to get to the place that he was talking about.

"The only thing I've learned so far is that I fell in love with a liar," she sniffed. "Like mother, like daughter, I suppose." Libby thought back to the only memory she had of her dad: the back of his head, climbing into his car and roaring out of the driveway twenty-six years ago. She and her mom had gone to live with Libby's Grandma Liza after that. Liza Hopkins had raised Libby while her mom worked two jobs to support the makeshift family.

Libby wished more than anything that Grandma Liza were alive. She would know exactly what to do and what to say. A tear slipped down Libby's cheek as she remembered the warm embrace of her grandmother who had been more like a mother to Libby than anyone else had.

"What would you say, Grandma? What would you say to me right now?"

She would tell you that you are strong, but that you don't have to be. She would tell you that God is for you and is watching over you.

Libby chuckled sadly. "That's exactly what she would say." She didn't even recognize that the voice she'd heard had not been her own but the quiet whisper she had known years ago in her youth.

"I am strong." Libby stood up, clutched her phone in her hands, and went inside to find the number for a divorce attorney.

LATER THAT NIGHT, Libby sat at her computer and read through the piece that had caught Jason Randall's attention. She remembered how much she had needed to cut out in order to fit the word count for magazine print. It had been almost painful to leave out some of her favorite parts and hack up the story so that it still made sense.

Libby clicked around her documents folder until she found the original file and opened it.

"There you guys are," she smiled and began to read from the beginning.

Sarah's fingers ached as she scrubbed the tattered fabric of her apron against the washboard. Her failed attempt at baking was simply not washing away. The whole pie had smashed into her chest while she'd tripped on a loose floorboard in the cookhouse, a floorboard that would have been fixed already if her husband had still been around.

The loneliness seemed to have its own heartbeat inside of her chest; she felt it drumming all day, every day. She missed him with every beat and hated him for it.

The setting sun shone brightly on her curly blonde hair and she willed it to sear her skin, set her aflame, anything to rid herself of the pressure, the monotony, and the agony of trying to run the ranch by herself. As dust began to pick up around her, she heard the tell-tale sound of a wagon in the distance, a reminder that she wasn't actually alone. She stood up and stretched her back. Then, shielding her eyes from the sun, she watched as a billow of dust came swirling down the dirt road.

Here come the new ranch hands, she thought to herself. More mouths to feed, but in trade-off, more able-bodied men to help her get through another spring and summer. Jeremy would be driving them in, supervising them carefully, weeding out the riffraff.

When she saw the horses come around the bend, a lump rose in her throat. It was the first time the hands had been brought in by anyone other than her husband.

Even after a year, the ache for his touch had not lessened. The stress of running his ranch was insurmountable, but she'd had nowhere else to go, and the dusty land and dirty animals that surrounded her were her only means of survival. If Jeremy hadn't stayed on when most everyone had written her off, Sarah would have found herself destitute. She could have sold the ranch but for a pittance of what it was worth. Men didn't take women seriously.

You hardly take yourself seriously, Sarah, she said to herself. Yet here you are running this place and not even into the ground.

Jeremy slowed the wagon in front of the bunkhouse and tipped his hat at her. The ache rose in her again. She heaved a sigh as she imagined the feel of Red's gaze washing over her. But Red was gone, and no amount of daydreaming would change that fact.

Libby was so focused that she was surprised when she looked at the clock on her screen and saw that it was after midnight. She rubbed her eyes and saved the file she'd been editing.

Since the other bed had been dismantled, she'd gladly taken up residence in the guest room and, earlier that day, had moved the contents of her dresser and closet over. She continued to use the master bathroom, mostly because of how spacious the counters were without all of Mark's stuff, and only a little bit because of the Jacuzzi tub.

She changed into a T-shirt and jogging shorts and climbed into bed. Her thoughts were on Sarah Parks and her lonely heart. The irony was not lost on Libby. She almost wished that her husband had died instead of what had actually happened. She immediately felt guilty for the thought. It wasn't right to wish death on anyone, even though she was pretty sure Mark hadn't suffered much remorse for his own thoughts and actions. He hadn't even apologized for what he'd done, just that she'd found out. Libby tried to push thoughts of him away and fell asleep, anticipating a day of writing ahead of her.

Chapter 7

OVER THE NEXT few days, Libby found her escape in *Red Parks Ranch*. It was therapeutic to exit reality for the daylight hours and work on solving someone else's problems, even if they were fictional. She took her time reading, revising, and allowing Sarah's grief to swallow her own. She only wished that she had a Jeremy in her life to distract her like Sarah did.

Jeremy sat at the end of one of the large wooden tables in the cookhouse, listening to the new ranch hands chattering on, trading stories and getting to know one another. His eyes, however, were focused on the woman washing dishes on the other side of the room. He'd known Sarah for as many years as she'd been married to his best friend, and up until recently, he'd never once had a questionable thought about her. He'd been questioning himself a lot lately, though.

He could still see the effect of Red's accident in the bags under Sarah's eyes and the tired way she moved from task to task, but she was strong and she never complained. Just this morning he'd walked in on her hammering a floorboard back into place by the stove. She masked her wounds with hard labor. She worked as hard as any of her employees and still had every meal hot and ready when they came in from the fields.

Jeremy felt a sense of guilt for allowing his thoughts to travel in the directions they'd gone recently. What would Red say? But then, Red was gone. Dead. The thought gave Jeremy a cold slap back into reality. How could he just up and take notice of his best friend's widow?

You're disgusting, he chided himself, all the while his gaze never shifted from the golden curls that stuck with sweat to the back of her neck and the button down shirt that bloused around the men's work pants that she wore.

He shook his head, remembering how she had insisted that what was appropriate for women today was no longer appropriate for her. She didn't fancy herself a lady anymore. That stung Jeremy in a way he couldn't explain. If there was anything he could do to remove the pressure from her and let her go back to the soft, happy-go-lucky mistress of the house he'd once known, he would. Even still, she seemed to command the rhythm of his heart, and he wasn't quite sure what to do about it.

He watched as she scrubbed dishes in the wash basin and stirred a pot on the stove intermittently, her rolled-up sleeve sliding down her tanned arm. Her attire did nothing to compliment her figure, but Jeremy had seen her dolled up before. He knew where her curves were, not because he'd taken appreciation before recently, but because she'd been the only woman on the ranch for as long as he'd been there.

The ranch hands were unabashed in their remarks, and though Jeremy would always shush them, especially when Red had been around, in a room full of crowded, sweaty ranch hands, it was hard not to notice her.

Sarah's shoulders sagged a little as she dried a plate. Jeremy grabbed his hat off the table, pushed back his chair, and walked slowly towards her.

"Sarah?" he said quietly as he came up behind her. She jumped at his nearness.

"Jeremy! Don't you know not to sneak up on a woman

like that?" she wiped her hair from her forehead.

"Sneak up? In this racket?" He glanced over at the ruckus happening around the tables and grinned at her. She cast her eyes downward, drying the plate faster.

Even though she'd written it and read it a hundred times, the skin on Libby's neck prickled as she anticipated her characters' connection. She looked down from the screen, trying to push away the impending sadness that seemed on the verge of swallowing her when her mind wasn't distracted by something else.

"Just because I'm not happy doesn't mean they can't be," she whispered and looked back up at the screen.

"Are you okay, Sarah?" he resisted the urge to touch her arm.

"I'm fine, Jeremy. Are you?" she asked quizzically.

He sensed nervousness in her, but maybe he was looking for it. They'd known each other for years and she'd never been nervous around him before.

"You look tired. Can I help you?" He reached for the plate she was scrubbing so furiously. His hands closed around her fingers as he reached for the towel. Her skin burned beneath his hands, and he was sure he saw something amiss in her eyes.

"Th-thank you, Jeremy. I'm going to check the stew for tonight." She pulled her hand from under his briskly and stood with her back to him at the stove.

*   *   *

Sarah stared at the wall as she stirred, fighting back hot tears, demanding control of herself. To be touched again, she'd never imagined how much she would miss it. Just the simple graze of Jeremy's fingers over hers had sent her heart into frenzy. If she could just forget that she was a woman with needs. Or if she could simply conjure up her dead husband once in awhile and find comfort in her imagination, maybe that would suffice.

"At least you have that," Libby said to the computer screen. "I wouldn't want to imagine Mark if you paid me."

She took a deep breath and blinked, but she did not turn to face Jeremy again. She couldn't undermine herself like that or reveal her weakness to him. He was a man, a man that she trusted, but right now, she didn't exactly trust herself.

The cell phone ringing beside her startled Libby; an unfamiliar number blinked at her with the same New York area code as Jason Randall. Her breath caught in her throat as she answered it.

"Hi, is this Libby?" the strong, soothing voice asked.

"Mr. Randall?"

"Please, call me Jason."

"Jason, hi." There was a small, awkward pause. "Uh, what can I do for you?"

"Well, I've got my hotel squared away for this weekend and I wanted to check in with you about lunch on Saturday."

"Oh! Right!"

"Did you forget?"

Was it her or was there a tinge of disappointment in his voice?

"No, no! It's in my calendar. I've just been eyeballs deep in *Red Parks Ranch* this week." She clicked the save button on her document and sat back in her chair.

"That's great! How is it going?"

"It's good. I'm about halfway through with my first round of revisions."

"Great! Do you think you could send me what you've got?"

"Um, I guess I could email what I've worked on. It's still very rough. Sometimes I think it's harder to re-write something than to just start from scratch."

"I bet it's fantastic. Why don't you keep working and then email me on Thursday night? That way I'll have something to read on the plane."

"Okay. I can do that." She picked up a pen from the coffee table and rolled it nervously in her fingers, trying to remind herself that he'd already read a good chunk of the story and loved it.

It's the reason you're even on the phone with him, Libby. Calm down, she thought.

"All right, now about Saturday, I'm staying at the Hilton downtown and from the looks of things, there are a number of great restaurants nearby. Should we just meet at the hotel?"

"Sure, what time?"

"Noon?"

"I can do that."

"Perfect." He paused for a moment and then asked, "How is everything else? Are you okay?"

Libby was a little taken aback by his question, but after all, she was the one who'd originally been so open about what she was going through. "I'm okay, I guess. Our lawyers are trying to work stuff out without having to go to court. I really don't know much of anything except that he's not the man I thought I married. Oh, and that Ralph Lauren fabric reacts as badly to bleach as anything else does."

"Um . . . do I want to know?" Jason laughed.

"Probably not. I have had a few moments of rage here and there."

"Naturally. Well, just make sure you get those out of your system before we meet, deal?"

"Oh, you don't have anything to worry about. I didn't walk in on you and your secretary going at it in your office—"

"Oh, now there's a mental image. Thanks," Jason groaned.

"Oh, geez, sorry."

He laughed it off and then sobered. "You really walked in on them?"

She sighed. "Yes."

"Wow. I'm sorry you had to see that."

"You said it's going to make me a better person, right?" Libby said hopefully.

"Um, something like that. Don't kill me if I'm wrong."

"You can just pick up the bill on my therapy sessions, how about that?" Libby chuckled.

"Uh, let's just see how it goes, okay?" Jason laughed.

"Well, at least now I know who to ask about getting a ridiculous boob job." She clamped her hand on her forehead as soon as she'd said the words.

Great. You're so professional, Libby, she chided herself.

"Uh, well, on that note–" Jason chuckled nervously.

"Sorry. Never mind. I better get back to work. I'll see you Saturday?"

"Okay, I'll see you then."

JASON HUNG UP the phone and stood up. The pile of papers that had been in his lap slid to the floor as he fist-pumped the air. Then he looked around his empty office as though someone was watching him, cleared his throat, and picked up the papers off the floor.

LIBBY WAS MORTIFIED by how much she'd revealed to Jason, especially the bit about Bria's fake breasts.

"I'm such an idiot," she groaned and dropped her head in her hands. After a few seconds, she knew exactly what she had to do.

She picked up her phone and dialed Elena, who howled with laughter when she heard the story.

"This is a disaster! He's probably going to think I'm a total ditz!" Libby shook her head, but soon she was giggling along with Elena.

"If he didn't cancel your lunch date after all that, I think you're in the clear!"

"I am so embarrassed!" Libby sighed, her cheeks burning.

"And rightly so! You're going to have to dress up real sexy-like to make him forget."

Libby rolled her eyes. "Yeah, right. Speaking of clothes though, will you come over and help me pick something out for Saturday?"

"Of course! You know I can dress you better than you can dress yourself!"

"Thanks for the vote of confidence."

"Anytime. I'll come over Friday after work?"

"Sure. I'll make dinner."

"Free food? I'm there."

"Great. I'm gonna go. Jason wants me to email him what I've finished on Thursday, and I want Jeremy and Sarah to get together before then."

"Uh, number one: Jason? You're on a first name basis? And two: spoiler alert," Elena cried.

"Number one: yes. Number two: you've read the short story already!"

"Oh. Right. Never mind then."

"Goodbye El," Libby said impatiently.

"Bye, bye," Elena sang as she ended the call.

Libby turned back to her computer. "Okay, Jeremy. Time to get your groove on."

Jeremy checked the sky nervously, estimating that Sarah had been gone for over 45 minutes. Aside from the fact that his men were thirsty, Jeremy knew it didn't take that long to fill the water canteens and haul them back out to the pasture.

"Boss, why don't you go check on her? Ain't right she been gone this long." Abe, a brute of a man and Jeremy's second in command, approached cautiously.

Jeremy pursed his lips to the side. He'd attempted to be discreet about his concern. "The men need their water," he said as he took off his cowboy hat and mopped his forehead with a blue kerchief.

"They do. It's a hot one today," Abe agreed.

"All right. You got this under control?" Jeremy nodded to the crew of men rebuilding a large portion of fence that had been knocked down in the previous night's windstorm.

"Yes, sir."

Jeremy spat on the ground and grabbed the nearest

horse by the reigns, threw them over its head, and pulled his body into the saddle. "If I'm not back in ten minutes-"

"I'll send someone for ya."

With that reassurance, Jeremy squeezed the horse's belly with his heels and set his sights on the shed that housed the water pump, far in the distance. The closer he got, the more concerned he grew, as he couldn't see any sign of Sarah around the ranch buildings. What if she'd tripped and knocked herself out on the water pump? He urged the horse faster and the animal whinnied in protest; it wasn't accustomed to running back in the direction of the barn.

When he reached the pump house, he called her name and jumped off of the horse's back. He stormed the shed and stopped short at the sight before him.

She sat beside the pump leaning against the wall, her hair spilling out of the pins that held it back, her head facing forward. She was fast asleep.

She was the definition of serenity. Her features were so relaxed that she bore resemblance to the woman that Jeremy's best friend had married rather than the widow he'd left behind.

She was beautiful. Jeremy took one tentative step towards her and then stopped himself. It was Sarah. Red's Sarah.

Red is gone, he argued with himself, and I'm here.

Fueled by passion and a need that grew with each moment his eyes continued to gaze on her, he continued to move forward until he was standing right in front of her.

As he dropped to his knees, she stirred slightly but didn't wake. He reached his fingers forward and brushed a damp curl from her cheek. Her skin was warm against his touch; he exhaled loudly.

What are you doing, man? he berated himself.

Sarah's eyes fluttered and a sigh escaped her full pink lips.

"Sarah," he whispered, resting his palm on her cheek. "What are you doing to me, Sarah?" He leaned forward, and any resolve he'd had to distance himself

from her seemed to slip through the cracks in the
wooden slatted walls. He traced her lips with his
thumb. They were like velvet against his rough,
calloused fingertip.

Sarah woke then, confusion crossing her face before she realized where she was and whom she was
with. She shifted and her gaze softened as their eyes
met, and Jeremy saw her chest heave up and down as
she pressed her cheek into the palm against it.

Tears filled her eyes and Jeremy couldn't stop
himself from doing what he did next.

He took her other cheek in his left palm and
pulled her face to his.

Normally, Libby would have paused to imagine the moment,
linger in it, perhaps even trace her fingers over her own lips, but not
this time. She didn't believe that she had the emotional strength not
to fall head first into an emotional breakdown. It had been months
since Mark had touched her at all, much less in a sensual way.

"Power through it, Libby. It's just a story."

Sarah wanted to tell him to stop, but more than
that, she wanted him to continue. She didn't say a
word but let his hands draw her face closer to his
until their lips met.

Though encompassed in semi-darkness in the closed
shed, Sarah felt as though the sunlight was washing
over her. Energy buzzed through her veins and lit a
fire in her belly.

Slowly, she covered his hands with her own and
pressed back with her lips on his.

This was the man who had been so dutifully watching over her since Red's death. Jeremy had been with
them since they'd started the ranch. He'd become a
part of their family. But now, feeling his hands on
her, his lips moving gently against hers, she felt
something new, or maybe it was something old. Whatever it was, she wasn't sure she should be feeling it
at all, but oh, how she had missed being touched,
being kissed.

Hungrily, she slipped her hands around his neck and dug her fingers into his hair. A soft moan passed between them and he pulled her body even closer, pushing her lips apart with his.

His lips were on fire, or hers were . . . something was on fire between them, and for the life of her, she couldn't even pretend that it was Red she was kissing. She was kissing Jeremy, and she'd never felt so ignited in her life.

Libby took a deep breath and pushed her computer from her lap onto the ottoman in front of her. "At least Sarah's getting some," she said with a sigh. Another long inhale kept her tears at bay, but she knew she needed a break. She wasn't exactly thrilled about exploring the idea of new love at the moment.

Chapter 8

"ARE YOU NERVOUS?" Elena asked as she watched Libby pull outfits out of the closet and dump them on the bed.

"Uh, not exactly . . ."

"Seriously? You're about to meet your agent! And he sounds cute!"

Libby's jaw dropped and she looked at Elena accusingly.

"What?" Elena shrugged. "I listened to his message and I think he sounds cute!"

"You're awful. First of all, he's not my agent yet, and secondly, I'm in no way interested in your opinions about how cute he may or may not sound."

"But you think he sounds cute, right?" Elena grinned and grabbed her iPhone from the bed.

Libby rolled her eyes and reached for a cream colored blouse and black pencil skirt. "What about this?" She held it up to her chest.

Elena scrunched her nose in disapproval. "Too severe. Too business-like. Too . . . unavailable."

"I *am* unavailable," Libby insisted.

Elena giggled and scrounged around on the bed and pulled out a tapered black jacket.

"I like this one."

"That's not too severe?" Libby eyed the jacket with uncertainty.

"Wear it with some skinny jeans and a casual top." Elena grabbed the leg of a pair of jeans she'd been eyeing and tossed them at Libby who held them up to her waist. "And heels," she added.

"How casual? Like, T-shirt casual, or business casual?"

"Let me look." Elena walked in the closet and started to dig. "I think something loose and billowy that you can tuck in." She slid hangers around noisily and then pulled one off the bar. "This is perfect."

She held up a loose-fitting white top that gathered at the waistline.

"Of course you'd pick that one," Libby groaned. "I don't usually wear that because it's so loose up top."

"Show me."

Libby sighed and began changing into the outfit. "See?" she said a moment later, bending over to demonstrate how far the top would gape open.

"It's gorgeous! Stylish, professional, but not too professional." Elena nodded in approval. "And it definitely says, 'I'm recently divorced and temporarily not interested, but please check back in a month or so.' Just don't bend over."

Libby grabbed a shirt off of the dresser behind her and threw it at Elena. "Seriously!"

"I know. I'm sorry, but, I mean, what if he's *gorgeous*?" Elena swooned.

"It wouldn't matter if he were Channing Tatum. He's a man, and therefore, off my radar."

"You didn't switch teams and forget to tell me, did you?" Elena winked.

"Why do I even put up with you?" Libby cried, exasperated. She changed back into her yoga pants and T-shirt and hung the other outfit back in the closet.

"I'm going to make you hang the rest of this stuff up while I check on dinner." Libby tossed her head defiantly and stomped out of the room.

Elena leaned back to make sure Libby wasn't coming back in and then quickly typed a name into the search bar on her phone's browser.

"Well, hello there, Mr. Randall," she grinned at the smile that beamed up at her from the phone. "Just like I thought."

"It's ready!" Libby's voice called up the stairs.

Elena closed the browser and tucked the phone in her back pocket, trying to wipe the mischievous smile from her face.

THE NERVOUS BUTTERFLIES finally began to dance as Libby got ready for her big meeting. She focused on breathing slowly while she applied her make-up and curled her hair in soft waves away from her face. Dialing Elena's number, she put the phone on speaker on the counter beside her.

"Hey, girl! You ready?" Elena answered.

"I'm starting to get a little nervous now," Libby admitted.

"Good! You should be nervous! This is a huge day for you!"

"I know." She puckered her lips and applied a light gloss. "I'm sorry I teased you so much last night."

"It's okay. It kind of helped take my mind off of how big this is."

"Well, good. I just want you to keep an open mind. You never know what's going to happen."

"Nothing is going to happen, El."

"I'm sure it's not, but just don't go in with any walls up!"

"I think I have a right to a few walls," Libby sputtered.

"Of course you do. I just don't want you to miss out on anything because of what Mark did."

"You mean besides the last seven or so years that I've missed out on because I've been living a lie?"

"Libby, I just want you to be able to move on."

"Believe me, I plan to. But it's barely been a week since . . ." she paused and steadied herself on the counter.

"I know."

"As much as I hate him right now, El, those years, that history, they don't just go away. I'm not ready to even entertain the idea of moving on. I feel like I'm still trying to break away at this cement block around my feet!"

Elena sighed, "I know. I'm sorry, Libby. I wish I could just make it all go away. I wish I could erase him from your life."

"I know you would if you could. Hell, I would too. Except for that first year. Our first year was pretty great," she sighed, standing tall again and fluffing her waves one more time. "I *am* going to be okay. It's just going to take time. Lots of time. And at this point I'm not looking for any distractions," she sighed.

"You are amazing, Libby. You have so much strength."

"Ha! Just be glad you're not here when things get rough!"

"Lots of snot and tears?" Elena laughed.

"Buckets."

"That will pass. And besides, you have this amazing opportunity that is a welcome distraction, right?"

"True. A novel would be the only distraction that would benefit me right now."

"Then focus on that. Forget everything I said last night and just get yourself an agent, okay?"

Libby looked suspiciously down at the phone. "Right," she said hesitantly.

"Love you, Libby."

"Mmhm. I love you, too. I better go, though, or I'm going to be late."

"Wait! Text me a picture of yourself! I want to see you before your big meeting!"

Libby shook her head. "All right, bye." She ended the call and pulled up the camera app on her phone, stood back so her body fit into the mirror, and snapped a picture of her giving Elena a thumbs up and an overly confident expression on her face.

"Knock him dead! Or, well, don't. But if looks could kill . . ." Elena responded.

LIBBY PULLED INTO the Hilton parking lot at 11:55 on the nose and hurried to the huge double doors that led to the lobby. When she stepped through them she felt like she'd walked into a Japanese garden. In the lobby, there were small ponds of water surrounded by stone walls and lush greenery, and huge Asian-inspired lamps were staggered throughout the room like pillars. Wooden-slatted walls surrounded the sitting areas, and Libby imagined how much prettier a space it would be if it weren't inside a hotel, but outside, with a touch of Elena's floral expertise.

It was warm in the lobby with the sun shining down through the glass ceiling, and Libby unbuttoned her coat and hung it over one arm, revealing the short-sleeved, white, silky top that she had picked out with Elena's help. She smoothed her hand over her hips, flipped her hair out from her neck, and glanced around the lobby, trying to spot someone who might be trying to spot her.

She was startled when his voice came from behind her. "Libby?"

She spun on her heel, a greeting on her lips, but she faltered as soon as she saw the face that matched the voice. She stumbled forward slightly, trying to recover. Jason reached his hand out and steadied her with a smile.

"Sorry, I didn't mean to startle you!"

"Oh, no! I–that's fine! I, uh–" She stumbled over her words while trying to recover her thoughts. Elena's instincts had been spot on. He was gorgeous. Much more handsome than she'd imagined that one time she'd let her curiosity take her mind on a rabbit trail.

His olive complexion and dark brown eyes told her he had to be of some Eastern descent. Greek or Italian maybe? She wasn't sure, but she didn't mind staring while she tried to figure it out. His black hair was cut short and looked as though he'd simply run his fingers through it once or twice when he woke up in the morning. His eyes were kind, but also searching–oh right. She'd been speaking, hadn't she?

"Um, sorry." Libby set her shoulders and held out her hand. "I'm Libby Abbott." She smiled while her mind played cruel tricks on her. Jason's hand slipped into hers and she had to physically stop herself from inhaling sharply.

"Jason Randall. It's great to finally meet you."

"Likewise," she said breathlessly. "So, where to?"

"Ah, well, if I can just have my hand back," Jason chuckled and indicated that she hadn't let go yet.

Cheeks burning, Libby pulled her hand away abruptly and apologized again. Jason gestured past the Japanese garden.

"There is actually a really nice restaurant here at the hotel. When I booked the room, I thought I'd be closer to downtown, but the concierge said that with traffic on 35, it takes a while to get over there."

"It's true. I think Dallas has the worst traffic of anywhere. Except New York, of course." She refrained from rolling her eyes at herself.

He smiled graciously. "Well, then is it okay if we try the place here?"

"Absolutely. Lead the way." Libby stepped aside and hung back a few steps as Jason moved ahead of her. His dark blue button down shirt fit him perfectly, it only bloused a little at his waistline and his dark, straight-legged jeans smoothed across his backside.

Libby swore at herself silently. What was that she'd been defending to Elena? Her need to heal, her need for time, the fact that she most definitely did not want any distractions; well, it wasn't a crime to admire the goods . . . was it?

Oh, good grief, Libby. Snap out of it, she thought. She shook thoughts from her head, averted her eyes, and hurried to catch up with Jason.

A hostess led them to a booth by the window and handed them each a menu. Jason set his down and clasped his fingers together.

Libby smiled nervously.

They sat in awkward silence, staring at each other for a moment before Jason picked his menu up again and said, "Let's order and then get down to business."

"Okay," Libby nodded and exhaled slowly, her heart pounding.

"Are you nervous?" Jason chuckled as he turned the menu over.

"Uh, yes. A little," she laughed.

"No need to be. I'm the one that's here to woo you."

"Woo me?" Libby asked in surprise.

"Well, yeah. Basically."

The waiter arrived then and took their drink orders. They each turned back to their menus and when their drinks were delivered, they ordered their food.

"So, tell me how you plan to woo me," Libby grinned, leaning forward to take a sip from her soda.

"I'm going to wine you and dine you and show you a world you've never dreamed of," Jason said without cracking a smile.

Libby's eyes doubled in size. What did he mean by that?

"Oh wow," he laughed. "You should see your face!"

She exhaled slowly again. "I'm sorry. I just–wow. My friend was kind of teasing me about meeting with you today and well, to be honest I just didn't expect you to be so good looking and I'm just not really in the space to–" Libby clamped her hand over her mouth. "Oh, my gosh," she mumbled through her fingers, feeling the warmth spreading on her cheeks.

Jason let out a loud roar of laughter and Libby cursed herself in her head, covering her whole face with her hands.

Jason laughed so hard that he snorted. Libby's head snapped up and she stared at him wide-eyed, slowly moving her hands from her face. "Did you just . . . snort?" She began to laugh with him, and soon they were both near tears from laughing so hard.

Jason gripped the table with both hands, trying to recover his poise, and Libby wiped at her eyes furiously.

"How was that for a first impression?" she sighed breathlessly.

"It was perfection," he grinned.

"So embarrassing." Libby shook her head at herself.

"I think mine was worse. But if it makes you feel any better," Jason's expression sobered, "I think you are beautiful."

Libby's breath caught in her throat, and she clasped her hands together in her lap.

"Thank you," she whispered.

"Back to business?" he asked.

Libby nodded eagerly. "Please." She couldn't help thinking that when he smiled, he looked just a little bit like that actor from an old Sandra Bullock movie. She couldn't place the name or the title just then, though.

"Here's the deal. I've already seen that you have talent, so you're getting the best end of the stick here because you're skipping the part that most authors hate."

"Pitching and querying?" Libby said knowingly.

"Yes! You've done your research!"

"Actually, I've avoided it like the plague. That's why I was so surprised when you called."

"So, you haven't pitched at all before?"

Libby shook her head. "I've only ever submitted my short stories. The plan was to get some street cred with magazines or online publications and then have something to brag about. But then life kind of got in the way," she said, her voice trailing off.

He nodded in understanding. "It's unusual for an agent to reach out like this, I admit it. But it's not unheard of. When raw talent hits you in the face, you don't turn away from it."

Libby's cheeks flushed with the compliment.

"I've actually already pitched your short story to a publisher." Jason announced, watching her expression carefully.

"You what?" Her eyes widened and she sat forward intently.

Jason nodded. "He wants to see the manuscript, at least what you sent me last night, which I almost finished on the plane yesterday. The guy beside me couldn't take a clue and kept talking to me about this girl he was about to marry that he'd met online a month ago."

"And?" Libby's eyes grew guarded.

"He proposed over Skype and was on his way to meet her in person for the first time!" Jason rolled his eyes.

"I meant, what did you think about my manuscript?" Libby giggled nervously.

"Oh!" he laughed. "Right. Like I said, raw talent. You write beautifully, and it's no wonder that *American Woman* has kept you such a secret. You have a hungry audience already, did you know that?"

She stared at him blankly. "Huh?"

"Have you ever gone onto the *American Woman* website and seen the comments about your story?"

Libby shook her head. "I mean, I did at first for like a week, but there wasn't much to look at."

Jason grinned and pulled a tablet out onto the table. "There is now." He powered up the tablet and passed it over to her, pointing to the screen. "Scroll to the bottom and read the comments."

"It says there are almost a thousand comments. That can't be right, can it?"

"Read them," Jason urged gently.

Libby read out loud. "Elizabeth Abbott is my new favorite author. Is she going to publish anytime soon?" Her jaw dropped open and she looked up at Jason in shock then kept reading. "My only complaint was that this was a short story. Is there more to it? I need more!" she continued. "Jeremy is so hot. I wish he would come herd my cattle!" Libby laughed incredulously.

"There are more meaningful comments, but Libby, you already have a following. You need to capitalize on this now. The publisher wants your book in editing by October, and with a stroke of luck, he thinks they'll have it on the shelf within a year.

Libby choked on a drink of her soda. "Seriously? October?"

"Do you think you can do that?"

"I'm in the middle of a divorce!"

"I know, and I explained that there were some extenuating circumstances, but they still want to try."

Libby nodded and turned her eyes to the ceiling, breathing deeply.

"You okay?"

"Yeah, just overwhelmed."

Jason leaned forward and put his hand out, palm up. She looked warily at it and then slowly put her hand in his. His fingers were soft as they closed around her hand.

"Can I be bold for a minute, Libby?"

Libby gulped and nodded, her hand warming quickly.

"This divorce could destroy you. The pain could eat you alive, but I don't think you're going to let it. I see a fight in you. I see strength. And with this opportunity, I think that we can create something amazing together."

Libby's hand was sweating in Jason's, and the way he was gazing at her felt like he was seeing into the very core of her soul. She blinked away tears and wiped at them with her free hand.

"Libby?" An unwelcome voice shattered the moment between agent and author. Libby's chest heaved and she withdrew her hand from Jason's immediately, feeling as though she were going to throw up.

Chapter 9

JASON STOOD UP defensively. From the look on Libby's face, it wasn't hard to put two and two together. This was her husband.

"What in the world?" Mark sneered as his eyes darted back and forth between Libby and Jason.

"Hi, there," Jason said, thrusting out a hand. "Jason Randall. Libby's agent."

"Agent? You have an *agent?*" Mark was shocked and ignored Jason's hand. He sneered down at Libby who was staring wide-eyed at the table and looking like she was about to be sick.

"Mark, come on, our table is ready!"

Enter the busty-blonde, Jason thought, and had to guard his reaction to the woman who had just appeared beside Libby's ex-husband.

"Oh," she said in shock when her eyes fell on Libby. Her cheeks turned bright red in embarrassment, while her blouse gaped open, exposing two perfectly crafted mounds of flesh that were hard not miss. Her face wasn't even that pretty; it had the sheen that he was so used to seeing in New York–the plastic surgery glow. Her makeup was so thick he wondered why she even bothered with the procedures. Jason glanced down at Libby and saw that she was as pale as the white table cloth.

Do something, you idiot! Jason thought.

"Libby and I are having a business meeting, and I'm pressed for time, so if you don't mind?" Jason gave Mark a generous smile, but the tone of his voice dared Mark to overstay his welcome.

"Right. Well. Libby, I'll see you next week at the settlement meeting," Mark said curtly and grabbed Bria's arm gruffly as they continued to their table.

The waitress delivered the food then and Libby's face turned green. Jason's stomach twisted at the look on her face, and before she could protest, he pulled her out of her seat and whisked her into the corridor that led to the bathrooms. She was hyperventilating, her whole body trembling.

Jason, at an obvious loss for how to comfort the woman crying in front of him, raised his hand to lay it on her shoulder but hesitated, made a fist with it instead, and dropped it back to his side. Libby covered her face with her hands, and he heard soft whimpers coming from behind them. Ache rose in him and finally he pulled her into his arms and let her bury her face in his chest. He said nothing but simply held her and let her cry.

"I'm so sorry," she whispered after a moment. "This is so humiliating."

"Don't," Jason shook his head as she pulled away. "This isn't your fault."

"I don't know about that," she sighed and looked at the ceiling, blinking repeatedly.

Jason noticed that she was still trembling and took the liberty of guiding her further down the hallway to a door with an exit sign above it. They entered a brightly lit hallway and he looked around, recognizing it as the hallway that led to his room. Libby needed a place to retreat for a few minutes, and he had a hotel room all to himself. It wasn't the best or most professional solution, but he dug in his pocket and pulled out the key card anyway. He hesitated for a split second.

Get over yourself, Jas, he scolded himself. She's in trouble and you can help.

"Here," he said, handing the key to Libby. "My room is just around that corner, number one-twelve. Make yourself at home and I'll be there in a minute."

Libby started to protest, but Jason urged her in the direction he had pointed. "You are pale and shaky and you need to lie down."

Libby hesitated but then took the card and said, "Thank you," her voice barely above a whisper.

Jason waited until he was sure she could get to the room without assistance and then turned back into the restaurant to get their food boxed up.

LIBBY MADE HER way slowly down the hall and turned the corner, looking at the little gold numbers on the dark wooden doors. When she reached Jason's door, she slid the key in and gently pushed the door open, too upset to feel awkward about being in the hotel room of a man she'd just met. She picked the bed that had an open suitcase lying on it and crawled on to the mattress, pulling a pillow to her chest and tucking her knees up around it.

She cursed herself as the tears started again. She had been doing so well at keeping her emotions in check. She'd been writing like a fiend and had purposely kept her thoughts from her failed marriage unless she absolutely had to think about it, like when her lawyer had called to schedule their settlement appointment.

Maybe that's part of the problem.

This time, Libby recognized the voice that echoed in her spirit and she felt an even deeper sense of sadness flow through her.

Ignorance is bliss only until the reality of what you're ignoring hits you right between the eyes.

Her face contorted with the painful truth. She'd simply been ignoring her problems and passing that off as dealing with them, but deep down she knew better than to think she could get away with it for long.

I'm here, Libby. I'll never leave you nor forsake you.

"I can't talk to you," she whispered and rolled her body in the opposite direction, as if she could physically turn her back on the God that she'd been introduced to as a young child. *As if I haven't done that a thousand times already*, she thought.

Jason knocked gently on the door. "Libby? Can I come in?"

She stood slowly and opened the door, keeping her eyes on the floor, embarrassed.

"How are you?" He stepped inside and let the door swing shut behind him.

Libby rolled her eyes. "I should probably just go. I think this was a bad idea."

Jason stepped back in surprise. "What are you talking about?"

"I don't think I can do this right now," she said apologetically.

Jason sighed and dug his fingers through his hair. "I know the last thirty minutes have been a little strange, but can we sit and talk about it first?"

Libby turned her gaze to him, her head tilted to one side. "Why are you so persistent? Don't you have authors knocking down your door? Why do you want me?"

Jason held out his hand, indicating for her to come back into the main room. Reluctantly, she followed him and perched on the edge of the bed where she'd been lying.

Jason pulled a rolling chair from the small desk beside the TV and sat in front of her. "What you're going through right now is going to make you a better writer, a better human being, and a better woman."

Libby stared at him in bewilderment. "You say that, but how can you know?"

"It has to. Because if it doesn't, then it means that he won!" Jason pointed his finger toward the door. "I'm a really good judge of character, Libby. It's part of what makes me a good agent. I can read people through their writing. You are a storyteller, which means that you're not going to let the story get the best of you. You're in control. Now, I know that sometimes characters can surprise us and act in ways that we didn't expect them to." Again, he pointed at the door. "But you're the one who gets to decide how you're going to respond to the twists and turns, and I don't think you're the kind of woman who is going to let this thing rule you. You will recover from this, and this book, and the next one and the next one after that, will be so much better because of it."

Libby closed her eyes and sighed. "You make it sound so easy."

"It's not easy. I won't pretend like it is, but . . . you will be stronger afterwards. I promise you that."

Libby sat silently for a minute, trying to absorb everything Jason was saying to her. "You seem really confident in me," she said nervously.

"Yeah, and I'm probably coming on a little strong. Sorry. I tend to do that. And I tend to speak my mind," he said apologetically. "But I don't normally invite prospective clients back to my hotel room." He grinned, but his cheeks were red.

Libby smiled good-naturedly. "I don't normally wind up in the hotel rooms of guys I just met." She managed a small laugh. "Honestly, it's nice to know that someone believes in me, even if you are practically a stranger." She took a deep breath, anxious to take the focus off of herself. "Did you see her?" she asked, peering up at him from under her lashes.

Jason blew out a breath, his eyes wide. "I did."

"She's gorgeous, right?"

Jason made a snorting sound and gave Libby a disapproving look. "She's completely fake, Libby. That's not beauty. That's money."

"That's what Elena says."

"Elena's right. Who's Elena?" he asked.

"She's my best friend."

"She sounds like a good one."

"She is. The best."

"Well, then listen to her, believe her. There is nothing substantial about that woman, and that of course begs the question, is there any substance to him?"

Libby stared at the wall in front of her absently. "There used to be."

"Well, then he's obviously lost it, and that's all there is to say about that." He shrugged and gave her a pointed look. "Please don't walk away from this."

She turned her eyes back to him and hesitated. "I might need some flexibility on the deadline," she said slowly.

"I can get you more time."

She took a deep breath. "Okay. I'm in."

He sighed in relief. "Good. That's really, really good."

"I'm so sorry you had to witness this. I hope it doesn't color the way you see me–"

"Please," he chuckled. "I've seen it before, in the mirror, and let me tell you, there is nothing attractive about a grown man crying alone in his bathroom."

Libby noticed the relief that washed over his face when she finally cracked a smile.

"It takes time to get over something like this. And it's been, what, two weeks for you?"

She nodded. "Barely. How did you get over it?"

"Ugh," he sighed and leaned back in his chair. "Leanne and I should never have gotten married in the first place. I think we both knew that from the beginning, and so did everyone else. We were always better friends than we were lovers."

Libby blushed and stared at her hands.

"I just mean–"

"It's okay. I get it."

"Well, our situation was different than yours, but the end result was the same. We lost each other, and though we're cordial and talk occasionally, if we'd never married each other, we'd still be good friends. We had chemistry that we mistook for love."

"Who left whom?"

"She left me," Jason stated. "I really did love her, but it wasn't the right kind of love. We wanted spouses, but we married room-mates. She came home one day when things had been particularly bad between us and said that she wanted out."

"So what did you do?"

"I flipped out. I accused her of cheating on me, which she didn't, at least not–well, it wasn't the same. She had met someone, but that's it. I think I was more broken because I knew that I had willingly made the mistake."

"What do you mean?"

"I knew she wasn't the one from the beginning, but I let my judgment get clouded."

"How did you know she wasn't the one?"

Jason puffed his cheeks up and then blew the air through his lips. "Do you believe in God?" He asked cautiously.

Libby laughed nervously. "Yes. We're just not exactly on the best terms these days."

"Well, I'm pretty certain that I heard God tell me that Leanne was not the woman He desired for me. But I chose her anyway."

"Do you think He punished you for choosing her?"

"I used to, but I know better than that now. We were doomed from the start; we just clued in a little too late."

"I used to hear Him speak to me."

"God? Really?" Jason sat forward intently.

She shrugged. "Yeah. When I was younger. My grandma used to take me to church all the time. I loved it. But I was innocent and untainted back then." Libby sighed and then suddenly felt very uncomfortable. "I should probably go." She grabbed her purse from where she'd dropped it on the floor and then chuckled. "I can't imagine what this will look like . . ."

"Don't worry, they didn't stick around. I saw them leave when I was getting our food boxed up." He handed her a white Styrofoam package.

"I'm so sorry that this took over our meeting, Jason."

He shook his head. "We got the important things out of the way, right? I'll be your agent; you'll write me a best-seller?"

Libby smiled and nodded. "Yeah. That's the plan."

"Let's make it official," Jason grinned and stuck out his hand.

She put her hand in his and shook it, feeling a constricting in her chest at his touch.

"It was nice to meet you, Jason," she said quietly.

"You too. I'll have Amanda forward you a contract on Monday."

Slowly she retracted her hand, held her packaged food close to her stomach, and left his room. She exhaled as the door shut behind her, her thoughts swirling. She was too terrified to let them land anywhere and hurried out of the hotel and back to her car, praying silently that she could make it home without having a mental breakdown.

JASON STOOD IN his room, staring at the spot where Libby had just stood. "Oh, God. Help me. I'm not kidding." Thrill mixed with a touch of panic rose inside of his chest. "I didn't expect that. Really, I didn't. Please help me."

He sank back down into the chair slowly. It would not be good for him to fall for the not-quite-divorced-or-healed-for-that-matter Libby Abbott. Not good at all.

You're kidding yourself, son.

"I'm not. I swear."

You wanted her to be perfect.

"But I didn't think she would be."

She is broken, Jason.

"She's *completely* beautiful," he sighed and wondered if God ever regretted the amount of beauty he poured into one single being. "No. Of course you don't. You like watching me squirm!"

Chapter 10

NOT READY TO be alone with her thoughts, Libby drove straight to Elena's store rather than going home. She needed a sounding board. She needed her best friend. Pulling up to the storefront with the big purple awning that said "Floral Occasions" in big scripted letters, she could see Elena walking to the back room and Samantha at the counter ringing up a customer.

The bells on the door chimed when she entered, and Samantha glanced up, giving her a huge smile.

"Hi, Libby!" she called. "How was your big meeting? Was he gorgeous or what?"

Libby shot her a dark look and said nothing, aiming for the back room.

"Hey!" Elena said in surprise when Libby blew through the doorway. "How did it go?" She set down the planter she was carrying, put her hands on her hips, and narrowed her eyes. "What? What happened? Was he awful?"

"Mark," Libby started and then had to steady herself on a table nearby. "Mark happened."

"What?" Elena leaned forward, her eyes bulging in horror.

Libby fidgeted with the hem of her top and gulped. "With Bria."

"No!" Elena rushed forward and wrapped her arms around her

friend. "Oh, Libby. I'm so sorry!"

"Jason got rid of him and then just, whisked me away, and the next thing I know, I'm crying in his hotel room!"

"Jason? Your *agent* did that?" Elena pulled away abruptly and searched Libby's face.

Libby was still in shock from the entire experience. Seeing Mark like that, the way that Jason had rescued her, the way it felt when their hands touched, not once, but twice . . . her head was still reeling. She pushed her hands through her hair and held them on her head, pulling the skin on her face tight. "I don't really know how to explain what happened."

"You were in his hotel room?"

"Yeah, but he just . . . talked me through it. He's divorced, so he knew what to say, I guess."

"What did he say?"

"You'd like him. He said exactly the kinds of things you've been saying to me." She dropped her hands to her side and sat on the corner of the table.

"Li-ike?" Elena pressed.

"That Bria is a fraud, that Mark has no substance, and that I'm amazing." She shrugged her shoulders, still trying to comprehend all that had happened.

"I *do* like him! Jason Randall." Elena grinned and pulled in for another hug. "But I hate that you had to go through that, Libby. I hate it."

"At least I wasn't alone."

"He's gorgeous, isn't he?" Elena asked in a knowing tone.

Libby closed her eyes, but a smile played at her lips. "A little."

"A little! Come on, Libby! He's exquisite!"

Libby stood up and stared at her friend in surprise. "How do you know that? Wait . . ." She narrowed her eyes at Elena.

"Seriously, you need to spend more time online." Elena pulled out her phone and opened up the picture she'd searched for the other night.

"Whoa. How come you didn't show me this before?" Libby pulled the phone closer to get a better look.

"I just figured you needed a little surprise," Elena grinned.

"Well, this particular information would have been extremely helpful beforehand."

Elena pursed her lips to one side. "What did you do?" She narrowed her eyes.

Libby proceeded to tell Elena about the parts of the meeting that happened before Mark had appeared and ruined everything.

"Classic, Libby," Elena snorted at the details of Libby's social blunder.

"Honestly, the entire thing was a complete disaster," Libby slumped onto the corner of the table again and let her eyes graze over the flowers behind the refrigerated doors against the opposite wall.

"Well, this Jason guy sounds like a gem."

Libby covered her face with her hands.

"What? What is it? What aren't you telling me?" Elena crossed her arms over her chest and waited.

"I need you to promise me something, El," Libby said, lowering her hand slowly and resting it on her collarbone.

"Anything. You know that." Elena's tone of voice softened and she took a step closer to Libby. "What do you need?"

"I need you to promise not to let me rebound."

It took a minute for Elena to respond. At first she tilted her head and studied Libby's face, and then she began to laugh. "I knew it!" she cried. "I knew it! You like him!"

Libby jumped up immediately and clamped her hand over Elena's mouth. "Shut up!" she hissed.

Elena swatted the hand away and began to bounce on her heels. "You totally like him! I knew you would. He's gorgeous, and like I said, sounds like an absolute saint!" She continued to giggle.

Libby shook her head. "No, El. Please. Don't encourage whatever you think is going on, because it's not, and it can't."

Elena's grin turned mischievous. "What's going on then?"

"There's just . . . chemistry, is all. There were a few times when we touched,"–she immediately held up her hand to stop Elena's train of thought–"shaking hands, and then when he got me out of the restaurant, just those kinds of things. I felt something," she explained with a defeated shrug. "But that's all, I swear, El. I can't indulge you with this one. I'm not even divorced yet; all it was was . . ."

"Attraction?" Elena asked.

"I don't even want to call it that. Just chemistry."

"I think chemistry is more dangerous than attraction!"

"I'm serious, Elena. Please don't push this. It's the last thing I want right now."

"Okay. I'll drop it. I promise. But the minute I start to see life in those eyes again, I'll be on the lookout." She winked. "For now though, I've got to get back to work. I've got a wedding tomorrow and I'm way behind."

"All right, I'll get out of your hair. Where did I put my jacket?" Libby looked around the room.

"You didn't have it on." Elena was already primping the tree she'd brought back.

"I didn't? Oh, *crap*! I left it at the hotel!" she gave Elena a cautionary glance but Elena couldn't help herself.

"In the room of the guy you're not attracted to?" Elena's eyes were sparkling with laughter.

Libby sighed loudly. "I'm leaving. I have to call the hotel." She saw herself out of the store and once in her car, looked up the number of the restaurant at the Hilton. She was informed that her coat had been delivered to Mr. Randall's room and she would need to contact him to get it back.

"Seriously?" Libby sighed as she threw her phone into her purse roughly. "This day just keeps getting better and better." She slammed her car into reverse and pulled away from the curb, suddenly desperate to be in the safety of her own home where no one would tease her, where Mark had no access since she'd changed the locks, and where she could crawl into her own bed and cry as long as she needed to with no interruptions.

When she pulled into her driveway, she noticed a medium-sized white parcel on her doorstep. She approached it with hesitation. She hadn't ordered anything, hadn't expected anything from anyone. She worried that it was from Mark, but then, what would he possibly send her? Weren't divorce papers enough?

When she reached her stoop, relief washed over her. The box was from the Hilton. How in the world had it gotten to her so quickly? She picked it up and hurried into the kitchen to open it. She found her jacket, along with a bar of gourmet dark chocolate sitting on top of it with a note from Jason.

"Libby, I'm sorry I didn't realize you'd left your jacket in the restaurant," she read out loud. "In fact, I'm sorry for the way things went down today. If there had been any way to prevent the unfortunate events of today from happening, believe me, I would have. And just to clarify, I'm talking about your ex-husband–not anything else. Everything else about our meeting was great. I'm so glad to have finally met you. I look forward to seeing you again. In the meantime, just know that I'm praying for you, and if you ever need a friend, well, you have my number. Jason."

Libby sighed at the kindness of his words. She held the hand-written note to her heart. Who sends notes anymore anyway? She thought. She set the card down and picked up the chocolate bar. Jason couldn't possibly have known that dark chocolate was her favorite indulgence.

"Oh, this is bad news," she sighed and put the chocolate bar down. "Please don't let me lose control," she prayed to no one in particular.

Come back to me, Libby. I'll take care of you.

The response surprised her. "No. This day has had enough drama already. I can't do this right now." She headed upstairs to write, trying to clear her head, but even as she attempted to lose herself in

Jeremy and Sarah's problems, she felt a tugging at her heart.

As she was pulling her salad and some soup out of the fridge a few hours later, weariness hit her. She leaned against the counter and finally answered the voice that had been whispering to her all day. "I trusted You once before. I gave You everything, and You just took it and left. You left me alone. So, please forgive me if I'm not ready to go through all of that again." She opened the microwave in anger and pulled out the bowl of soup so quickly that she spilled some on her hand and dropped the bowl on the stove, cursing loudly.

With half the soup on the stove and the rest seeping out through a newly formed crack in the bowl, Libby slid the whole mess into the sink and sank to the floor against the oven door. She didn't cry; she was numb from her head to her toes. She just stared at the cabinets in the island across from her and breathed in and out slowly.

I'll be here when you change your mind.

Eventually she picked herself up and cleaned up the soup left on the stove. She took the Styrofoam container with her salad in it and sank down onto the couch to eat, barely tasting the food as she chewed it. The only thing that really sounded good was the chocolate bar Jason had sent so she gave up on the salad, broke off a piece of chocolate, and went upstairs to send a reply to Jason.

Dear Jason,

Thank you for sending my jacket back. I'm surprised that I didn't leave my head behind as well . . . what a day. I'm so sorry that our meeting was cut short and that you had to witness what a complete mess I am. At any rate, thank you for your sweet words today and for being a friend when I had no one. There aren't words to express how much that meant to me.

Libby

On Monday while Libby was at her computer looking over the notes an old lawyer friend had made on the contract Jason's secretary had sent her, her inbox chimed with a new email from him.

She bit her lip as she clicked on it.

Libby,

Sorry I didn't get back to you sooner. I'm responding from my personal email address so that you can reach me faster if you need to. The other address isn't connected to my phone, and I didn't open my computer at all once I got home from Dallas. We had a book launch on Sunday so it was pretty crazy out here, but things went well and I'm encouraged by the turnout. I'm glad you received your jacket.

For the record, it's because of how raw and honest you are that I know I'm not taking a gamble on you. You are as real as you seem in your writing; you're not making this stuff up.

I would still like to fly you out to New York when time allows for it, so just let me know how things go on your end and we can set up a meeting with my friend Andrew who is going to publish your novel. I'll give you a call this week.

Talk to you soon!
Jason

Libby forced herself not to respond right away. She had the daunting task of going through the house making a "his and hers" list of all of their belongings to keep her occupied. The dark reality of potentially losing the house had been hanging over her head ever since Monday when her lawyer had called and told her that it looked like it would have to be sold. She knew that even with a book deal, she couldn't keep the monstrosity, nor did she want to live in it alone; it was far too big for one person. It was the place she'd lived the longest though; it was difficult imagining living anywhere else.

On Tuesday night Samantha and Elena arrived, armed with boxes, to help Libby sort through the closets.

"Are you really going to move?" Samantha asked sadly, looking around the guest room from where she sat, cross-legged on the floor beside Elena and Libby.

"It doesn't make any sense to stay. Even if I get the house, I can't pay for it. I don't even have a job!"

"But you have a pending book deal!" Elena reminded her.

"Still. This place," Libby looked around sadly, "this place is full of ghosts now."

Samantha's face paled and she looked around the room anxiously.

"I meant that figuratively, Sam." Libby smiled. "I had plans for this house, plans for my family. And all of that is gone now. I can't stay here any longer than I have to."

"Where are you going to go?" Samantha fixed her hair into a ponytail and grabbed the nearest box, unfolded it, and began taping the bottom.

"Probably an apartment. It really depends on how much we can get for the house and how that gets divvied up. I only have about five hundred to my name right now that Mark has cancelled his direct deposits and cleaned out the account, and I'm investing heavily in ramen noodles right now."

Elena smiled. "You can stay with me if you need to. I only have a couch, but it's a free couch!"

"Thanks, El. Let's just get this closet emptied, okay? I need a break from all of this depressing talk."

Samantha pulled out a box and began digging through it, sorting things into piles: one for Libby to look through, one that could be tossed in the trash per her judgment, and one for obvious sentimental keepsakes.

"Libby! Is this your college yearbook?" Samantha held up a burgundy bound book with the A&M logo on the cover.

"Yep. Texas A&M University, class of let's not remember, shall we?" Libby took the book from Samantha's outstretched hands. As she opened it, an envelope slipped out of it onto Libby's lap.

"What's that?" Elena leaned forward.

Libby turned it over and upon seeing her name scrawled across it, she sighed sadly. "It's from my grandma. It's the letter she wrote me when I left for college."

"You've managed to hang on to it all these years?" Samantha exclaimed.

"All these years. Don't listen to her!" Elena smacked Samantha's shoulder playfully.

"Yeah, my grandma raised me. This was not too long before she died," Libby explained, waving the envelope in the air.

"Are you going to read it?" Samantha asked.

Libby tucked it under her leg for safekeeping. "Later," she said and continued to pull items out of the box she was working on.

When the closets in the guest room, office, and hallway had been sorted, purged, and re-packed with labeled boxes, Elena and Samantha said goodnight to Libby and left her alone in the big, quiet house.

Libby poured herself a generous glass of wine in the kitchen and stared at the envelope on the island. She traced her fingers over her grandmother's elegant cursive. She ached to be able to talk to the older, wiser woman.

"Oh, Grandma," Libby sniffed. "What would you say to me right now?"

Read the letter.

"I'm not sure if I can." She took the crinkled envelope in her hand, wine in the other, and made her way up the stairs slowly. She paused at the master bedroom that was empty but for a few boxes since the monstrous furniture had been moved out.

Libby stepped into the room for the first time in weeks and took an indulging sip of wine. She seated herself cross-legged in the middle of the room where the bed used to sit and opened the envelope, pulling out the aging piece of paper from inside of it.

My dearest Elizabeth,

I can't even begin to tell you how proud I am of you today. College is awaiting your arrival and I've only just minutes ago whispered my last goodbye to you. You have been a most precious gift to me all of these years. i always thought that being a parent was the greatest gift of all, but being your grandmother was one of the greatest blessings of my life. i am so thankful to the Father for orchestrating things in such a way that had you in my home and in my arms, for so long a time. You know i would never wish the circumstances if we had to do them over again, but i find His goodness wherever i can, and i have most definitely found it in you, my dear.

i know you are excited about starting your new life, and i won't waste time with the do's and don'ts. You have a good strong head on your shoulders, though i'm not quite sure what side of the family it came from—obviously not your father's, and well, we're all a little crazy on this side too . . .

But seriously, Elizabeth, my prayer for you is that you never forget your roots, that you re-member all that you have seen and heard with your own eyes and ears: the promises that God has given you, the ways that He has rescued you. Be careful about turning away from those things too quickly. i'm not too old to remember what college is like. Fast girls and smooth talking young men . . . don't be smooth-talked! Oh, shoot. i just gave you a 'don't!' Forgive me?

Life will not be without challenges; you will have moments when you fear that the waves will swallow you whole, but never forget that verse that we memorized together:

1 Kings 8:57 "May the Lord our God be with us as He was with our forefathers; He will never leave us nor forsake us."

Let that be your hope. in all the things that come your way, remember that He is faithful and that He will never ever leave you nor forsake you. You are His beloved, His cherished daughter, and He has such an amazing journey ahead for you. i am tearing up just thinking about it. You will be surprised by how He provides for you, not just financially but for your heart as well. i wish i could be there to see it all happen. i trust Him completely though. i don't have to be present to know that He has his hand on you, that He will do amazing things with your life as long as you continue to let Him.

Well now, reading over this, i see i've taken much liberty with the 'do's and don'ts!' You know me, always full of good intentions.

Darling, i love you more than i can say and even though you're barely two miles from me now, i'm already counting the days till your first break. Be safe and remember, He is always there.

Love, Grandma

Libby wiped the streams that had formed on her cheeks as she read. She lay the letter gently in her lap and turned her face to the ceiling.

"Is this how you meant to provide for my heart?" She asked, covering her face while she wept.

"Grandma, I don't know who I am anymore," she cried. "I wish you were here."

I'm here, Libby.

"I don't want You!" she sniffled.

But I'm here.

Libby didn't respond but remained in the same spot, crying into her hands for a long time before exhaustion took its course and she dragged herself to bed. She read her grandmother's letter one more time before turning off the light.

"I don't know what to do about my life now," she said out loud.

Come back to me. His words sounded like a song, like a lullaby. Over and over He seemed to sing them over her. **Come back to me, come back to me, come back to me.**

Too exhausted to respond or fight, Libby let the melody draw her into a deep and restful sleep.

Chapter 11

LIBBY FELT AS though she'd slept better than she had in weeks, yet she woke with a knot forming in her stomach. Today she would have to spend more time in the same room as Mark than she had since she'd found out he was cheating on her. Granted, there would be lawyers there to keep her from mauling him, but the meeting she'd been anticipating for weeks was upon her. It was time to talk settlement.

She smiled weakly at the mental image of tearing him limb from limb, though she had no plans to get any closer to her soon-to-be ex-husband than the width of the table between them.

Libby ate her scrambled eggs and homemade hash browns, savoring the bites as though she might be stripped of even her taste buds after the meeting that afternoon. She had no idea what to expect from her estranged husband. He had said he didn't want things to get ugly, but she wondered how serious he'd been about that. She kept her fingers crossed that he would agree to split the profit from selling the house.

She glanced around the kitchen, above the cabinets at the empty space between them and the ceiling. She remembered the day she'd come home from the store with a bunch of items to decorate the tops of the cabinets and how adamantly Mark had fought her on them. He wanted clean lines and no clutter, and just like always, she'd rolled over and taken all of her purchases back. The more time she spent in her house alone, the more she realized that she had had very little influence on the décor, other than the guest room. Everything was very much Mark's taste.

The kitchen was sterile, white cabinets and stainless appliances, with zero color anywhere. It now occurred to her how strange that was considering the rest of the house was more similar in style to the bedroom furniture that she'd balked at. At least the big brown leather couch and love seat were comfortable. She didn't mind that the living room looked stately and old world style. She didn't spend much time in there anyway. It was where Mark had watched sports or documentaries. They rarely ever watched television together.

"Wow," Libby sighed as a realization hit her. There were only two places in the house where she really felt at home: the guest room and her office. How pathetic is that? she thought.

"No wonder I don't care that much about losing this place." She took her dishes to the sink, transferred her coffee to a travel mug, and took another look around. "This isn't my home," she said with a shiver, and then left the house, wishing for the first time that she didn't have to return to it.

The settlement meeting was more preliminary than she had expected and took much less time than she'd allotted for it. She sat across the table from Mark, avoiding eye contact, and focused her attention on the lawyer jargon that was going on beside her.

"My client wishes for these proceedings to be as amicable as possible," Mark's lawyer said. He was dressed in a crisp black suit and had a salt-and-pepper colored comb-over.

"We'll see what we can do," was the response from David Daniels, Libby's lawyer, who was older and more stylishly dressed in a grey striped suit and short white hair.

The men went through the list of assets that Libby and Mark had come up with separately and divided them in a manner similar to that of adolescent children drawing a line down the middle of their shared room.

With her revelation from earlier in the morning, Libby wasn't surprised at the lack of argument over items in the house; their styles were so obviously opposite, she wondered how they'd ever managed to live together in the first place. She realized that she had given up way too much of her own personality to be with the man sitting across from her. She began to dream of a place of her own, decorated the way she wanted, though that would take time and money and she only had one of those right now.

The lawyers shook hands and packed up their papers, and they all agreed on the next meeting, two weeks later, to talk about the bigger issues like investments and the house and such. This was where Libby knew things might get dicey. She didn't want the house, but she couldn't walk away from seven years of marriage with nothing. She needed something with which to start a new life. She needed at least half of the proceeds from selling the house, and she wasn't sure Mark would give that to her.

"That wasn't so bad," her lawyer turned to her and smiled. Libby nodded and shook his hand.

"Thank you. I guess we'll talk soon?"

"I'll call you when I have these drafted up and ready for your signature." He tapped his briefcase. "In the meantime, you need to come up with the figure that you need from alimony."

Her eyes widened. "You mean, like, for him to pay me monthly?"

David nodded. "It's standard."

She shook her head. "I don't want that."

David took her arm and steered her down the brightly lit hallway away from the traffic of the elevators. "Libby, this is completely normal; you deserve that money and he deserves to pay it."

She swallowed and bit her lip, letting his reasoning sink in. "I know, but I don't want to be dependent on him. I don't want to be waiting on a check from him every month! I want this over and I don't want to have to think about him again!"

David blinked and nodded his head slowly. "Okay. I understand. What do you think about asking for the house in lieu of alimony?"

"Can we do that?" Libby asked, her eyes darting to the elevators where Mark and his lawyer were disappearing behind closing doors.

"Absolutely. I can't promise we'll get it, but we can definitely try. If he agrees, you can sell the house and all of that money will be yours."

"Then let's do that." The nervous knot that had been bothering her since she woke up twisted violently again and she clutched her stomach.

David put his hand on her arm. "I'm going to get you taken care of, Libby."

She nodded and followed him back to the elevators.

WHILE SHE DROVE home, her cell phone rang in her purse. Thinking it was Elena, she answered without looking.

"Hey. Everything is fine. I'm fine," she said, though her nerves were still pretty wound up.

"Uh, good. I'm glad to hear it!"

Jason's voice surprised her and she jumped in the seat, gunning the gas a little too hard. She reacted by slamming on the brakes so quickly that the person behind her had to swerve in order to avoid rear-ending her. He, in turn, honked and flipped her off as he sped past her.

Libby carefully took notice of her surroundings and started down the road again. "Jason! Hi! I'm sorry; I thought it was Elena."

"No worries," he chuckled. "But did you just get in an accident?"

"Huh? Oh, no," she laughed. "Sorry. You startled me, and, well, I guess that's why you shouldn't text and drive."

"But we're talking. Not texting."

Libby rolled her eyes. "Never mind. What's up?"

"Well, I wanted to check in and see what your next few weeks looked like. My publisher is ready to talk numbers and sign a contract."

"You know what," Libby breathed slowly, "maybe I should pull over." Her heart was pounding as she pulled the car into a parking lot off the side of the road.

"I can call you back if this is a bad time," Jason said quickly.

"No, no. It's fine. I'm parked."

"Great. So when can you fly to New York?"

Libby gulped. This is really happening, she thought. "Um, well, I'm pretty free for the next few weeks, actually."

"Really? No, uh . . . meetings or anything?"

"No. I just came from one actually. Next one is in two weeks."

"Oh! Well, great! How about this weekend then?"

"This weekend? Like in two days?"

"Well, it would be great if you could be here Friday morning. I can send you our finalized contract tonight, and then we'll be ready to take the next step!"

"Next step?" Libby's eyes grew wide.

"Meeting with the publisher, remember?"

"Oh. Right. Um. Friday," she began to think out loud. "There really isn't any good reason why I couldn't get away this weekend, I just –"

"Great! I'll book your flight and send you the itinerary!"

Libby was overwhelmed. "Uh, o-okay," she stuttered. "I guess I'll see you Friday?"

"Absolutely. Oh, and bring something nice to wear."

"You mean business attire?"

"Well, yes, that, but also, uh . . . something a little more dressy. Like, say something you'd wear if you were, uh . . . going to a show."

"What kind of show?" Libby was confused trying to read between the lines of what Jason was saying.

"Ah, let me try something else. Formal, but not prom formal, like–"

"Dinner party formal?"

"Yes! Exactly!"

"You know you could just tell me what this is about; that would make it easier!"

"I could. You're right. But this is way more fun."

Libby laughed and rubbed her hand over her face. "All right. How long do you need me there?"

"How long can you stay?"

The tone of his voice unnerved her a little, but these were lines she wasn't ready to read between yet.

"Uh, well, I do have this really important novel I'm supposed to be writing . . ."

"Okay, okay," he laughed. "Can you stay through Saturday night? Fly home Sunday morning?"

"Yeah, I can do that."

"Great. I'll book it and forward you the details. I'm looking forward to seeing you again, Libby. This time with no chances of your ex-husband ruining things."

Libby shook her head. "Seriously. If he shows up in New York, I might just move to another country!"

"I'm glad that things went well today."

"Oh, did I say that?"

"Yeah, when you thought I was Elena."

"Oh, right," Libby sighed. "It's true. Things went fine today. It's the next meeting I'm worried about." Libby put the car in drive and pulled back on to the road.

"House stuff?"

"Exactly."

"Are you going to try to keep it?"

"Hell, no. The more time I spend there, the more I want to leave and never look back. But I need the money. I need it badly."

"You want all of it?"

"Well, my lawyer suggested that we ask for the house instead of alimony. I just don't want to be dependent on Mark for any longer, you know? I don't want any of his money, but we did buy that house together."

"Doesn't Texas favor the wife in a situation like this?"

"Yes, but we're attempting to settle outside of court. I want it over with as little hassle as possible. The house might be an issue."

"Man, I don't miss this kind of stuff. We did the same thing, settled outside of court. We split everything down the middle and that was the end of it. We never owned a home together, so that made things a bit easier. Still, what I wouldn't have given for a time-traveling Delorean back then!"

Libby laughed as she turned away from the city and into her neighborhood. "Seriously. I could fix so many things in my life if I could go back in time!"

"It's all part of the journey though, Libby. Remember what I said. You'll be stronger on the other end of this."

"I'll buy you dinner when you can prove it," Libby joked.

"Hey, I'll take that bet!"

She could hear the smile in his voice. "Well, I'm almost home and I guess I have to pack for this trip now. Gosh, I've got to go shopping! The last time I wore something formal, I'm pretty sure Bush was president!"

"That's unfortunate," Jason laughed. "I'll let you go. Be looking for my email in about ten minutes. Shoot me one back so I know you got the info."

"Okay. Thanks, Jason."

Libby pulled the car into her driveway and stared at the beige garage door. She felt as though her life were caught in the middle of the most stressful balancing act ever. On one side was her failed marriage, and on the other, an open door she'd only dreamed of. All she needed was for the scales to tip in one direction or another, but each direction was so largely different than the other. One had the power to destroy her, the other could change her life for the better, forever.

"I just want it all over with!" she sighed as she got out of the car. She waved to Mrs. Granbury, the old woman who walked her dog down the street every morning–in a stroller. The absurdity of the image was never lost on Libby, but then she'd always thought how nice it would be to be strolled around for a time rather than having to walk everywhere she needed to go. Then that was always followed by her grandmother's voice saying, "Be thankful that God gave you two good legs to stand on, Elizabeth!" This made her remember her grandmother's letter again.

"So I have something else to balance out now, too. How does that work?" She shook her head and walked inside, ready to spill her guts to her best friend.

"NEW YORK!" ELENA cried over the phone. "Libby! This is so exciting! I can't believe it! Do you know what this means?"

"Yes! It means that–"

"It means we need to go shopping!"

"I knew you were going to say that," Libby sighed.

"Why don't you sound excited?"

"I am! I'm excited that there is actually someone crazy enough out there that wants to publish my book! I'm excited that I get to finally see New York City and Central Park and–"

"About shopping! Why aren't you excited about shopping?"

Libby could practically hear Elena bouncing up and down. "You know I hate shopping, El."

Elena groaned. "But for New York City? Come on! I can meet you at the mall after work! I'll buy dinner!"

Elena was the only person who would wait patiently while Libby hemmed and hawed over outfits, and Libby knew it. She also knew that Elena was the best personal shopper around and that she loved finding great deals.

"Okay. I'll meet you there at five-thirty."

"Oh, this day just got awesome! I have to run. We have one of those Spanish sweet sixteens on Friday. You know I can never pronounce it."

"A Quinceañera? That would be a sweet *fifteen*."

"Yeah. That. So you'll have to tell me all about the meeting to-night, okay?"

"Yep. Will do."

"New York City!" Elena squealed again. "I wish I could come with you."

"I'll take pictures."

"Okay! I'll see you tonight!"

Chapter 12

ELENA DRAGGED LIBBY through just about every boutique store in the mall, while Libby complained about price tags and that sizes were getting smaller.

"Honey, I think that might just be all the wine you've been drinking the past few weeks."

Libby glared at her friend in the mirror where she stood with a horrible pink knit sweater pulled over her T-shirt. "Don't you dare criticize me or tell me I've gained weight."

Elena put her hands up in defense. "I'm just saying–"

"Well, don't!" Libby pouted and pulled the sweater off. "This is depressing."

"Try this one." Elena threw something red and silky at Libby. "I wish he would have told you what you needed something fancy for!"

Libby let the red fabric slip through her fingers slowly, catching it just before it fell to the ground completely. "Me, too. Whatever it is, I think that this will be way too formal and way too expensive for it."

"Just try it on!" Elena gave her a friendly shove back into her changing room where the rest of the clothing rejects were lying in a pile. "Look, if you can decide on one dress, I'll let you off the hook on all the rest and we'll go shopping in your closet tonight for other outfits to wear."

"Fine. That means you just cancelled out more than half of the store!" Libby sounded a little more cheery.

Elena rolled her eyes and tapped on the door. "Hurry up!"

Libby pulled the dress over her head and let it slide down her skin. "It's really soft. Maybe too soft–have I mentioned how much I hate that there are no mirrors in these changing rooms?"

"A thousand times. Get out here!"

Libby stepped through the door and Elena's eyes doubled in size; her hand flew to her mouth. Libby gave her a strange look and then turned to look at her reflection in the mirror. Her eyes grew wide as well.

"No, absolutely not. No way." Libby shook her head vehemently, backing away from the mirror.

Elena cried out in alarm and grabbed her friend. "Elizabeth Abbott, you are stunning. Absolutely gorgeous!" She stepped behind Libby and swept the blonde hair up on top of her head. "Oh, yes. This is it."

"No! It's way too sexy! Look at this! My boobs are practically falling out of this scoop thingy!"

"It's called a cowl-neck, and your boobs look amazing," Elena sighed.

"That's exactly my point. I can't go out in public dressed like this! Not with my agent!" Libby eyed the plunging neckline, knowing that one wrong move would mean disaster.

Elena wasn't listening, though. She had dropped Libby's hair and was pushing her own breasts together and then eyeing Libby's, obviously trying to see if she could make hers more presentable.

An older woman walked behind them and gave them a dirty look. Elena giggled and dropped her hands to her side. "Not kidding, Libby. This is it. If you don't buy this dress, I'll never speak to you again. Now, turn around."

Libby's expression was less than pleased, but she obeyed and looked over her shoulder to see the backside of the dress.

Elena made a high-pitched noise from her throat. The back of the dress plunged similarly the way the front did, but it was deeper and scooped back up the other side just a few inches above where things could get dangerous, and a few inches farther than Libby felt comfortable with. The silk curved over her hips and her buttocks, hanging loosely to the floor.

"It's too long anyway. Look at that!" Libby pulled on the skirt, which was dragging on the floor.

"I'm not stupid, Libby. You're not going to wear this with Chucks!"

"I'm not comfortable with this. It's too much."

"It's not, Libby. It's really not. It's just more than what you're used to. Ten years ago you would have cried about wanting this dress!"

"A lot has changed since then," Libby reminded her friend.

Elena touched the gemstones that gathered the fabric together at the shoulders. "I know that a lot has changed. You've changed. So much. But you're getting a second chance to be you again, Libby, and this dress is so you."

Libby turned around and faced the mirror again. She pursed her lips to one side and did a half-turn. "It does look good," she said regretfully.

"It looks unbelievable," Elena said softly. "And there are ways to keep the girls secure. Double stick tape and all that."

"Oh, fine. But only because it means that we get to go home now!" Libby threw up her arms in defeat.

"Yes!" Elena jumped and hugged her friend. "Quick! Take it off before you change your mind!"

Libby did as she was told and carefully tossed the dress over the door and changed into her own clothes. She breathed easier in her jeans and long-sleeved henley. When she exited the dressing room, Elena was nowhere to be found and neither was the dress. Libby walked out into the store and saw Elena at the cash register, handing over her credit card.

"What are you doing?!" Libby ran up to her friend just as the cashier swiped the card. "Why did you do that?"

"Two reasons," Elena said with a grin as she turned on her heel to face Libby. "One, so that you won't try to take it back later. And two, because I love you, and it's something practical that I can do for you!" She took the bag from the cashier and handed it to Libby and pocketed the receipt.

"I would hardly call this practical, but, thank you. You really didn't have to."

"I know. But I wanted to. Plus, I got to double charge the Spanish birthday lady today because she changed the flowers at the last minute! I have to go in early tomorrow and order a whole new batch of flowers!" Elena grinned.

"Only you could find the good in that."

"More work means more money! Besides, she's going to be so thrilled with how I pulled off her emergency, I'm going to be doing Kinsty Eras until the end of time!"

Libby laughed at Elena's pronunciation of the Spanish tradition and guided her out of the store.

"You have shoes at home?" Elena stopped suddenly as they passed a shoe store.

"Yes. I promise. Can we just go home now?"

"Oh, fine. But I'm checking your closet."

"You have my complete permission." Libby grinned.

Elena linked her arm through Libby's as they started to walk again. "I'm so excited for you. I really wish I could be with you this weekend. I would pay money to see the look on Jason's face when you walk out in that dress."

Libby exhaled and her pace slowed. "I'm seriously rethinking—"

"No you don't. There's no backing out now. The dress is yours, and I refuse to give up the receipt!"

"Then no more talk about Jason and this dress," Libby warned. "I mean it."

"I'll behave," Elena promised with a twinkle in her eye.

FROM THE COMFORT of his own home, Jason Randall had called in every favor owed him in the great state of New York. He had secured a limo, two very hard-to-get tickets to a certain Broadway musical, reservations at a swanky restaurant not far from the theater, and now he was just finalizing the details on Libby's hotel room.

"Geoff, you're the best. Thanks for the upgrade man."

"Anything for you, Mr. Randall. My daughter still talks about meeting Aubrey Winston. Their picture together is in a frame by her bed! When is her next book coming out, by the way? Claudia is chomping at the bit!"

"Well, I can't say officially, but I do know that she's working on it. I'll make sure Claudia gets an invite to the launch party."

"That would be fantastic. Well, everything is set up for your friend's arrival tomorrow. She can just check in like normal. It's all been taken care of."

"Thanks again, Geoff."

He hung up the phone and sat back against his couch with a sigh. If nothing else, after this weekend, Libby would have been wined and dined the way he'd promised.

It sure pays to have friends in high places, Jason thought with a smile.

Chapter 13

ELENA SMILED AT the choices she'd laid out on the bed. Libby hadn't copped out on the shoes. She had a perfect pair of silver heels that sparkled beautifully in the light.

"This charcoal pantsuit is awesome!" Elena exclaimed. "Have I ever seen it before?"

"Probably not. I bought it the week before Mark decided I should quit the firm."

Elena rolled her eyes. "What was the purpose of that again?"

"Who knows? And why did I go along with it in the first place?" Libby sighed and pulled out a garment bag from the closet. She put the fitted charcoal suit into it and then began trying to fit the bag from the mall with the 'evil red dress,' as Libby had dubbed it, on top of the suit.

"What are you doing?" Elena yelped.

"I'm not going to carry two garment bags!" Libby stood back with her hands on her hips.

"Yes, you are! You can't just shove that masterpiece in there! It will get wrinkled!"

"I'm sure there's a steamer at the hotel; it'll be fine."

Elena shook her head. "You have no appreciation for the finer things in life!"

"I don't have energy for the finer things in life! I don't want to check a bag for a two night trip."

"Whatever. Are they even going to let you carry on a garment bag?"

"Well, if they don't, then I'm definitely not paying for two!"

Elena groaned and handed her two more outfits to put in the bag and then flopped onto the bed. "Can I read the email again?"

"Seriously? Haven't you memorized it by now?"

"I just want to read it one more time!" Elena said innocently. Libby tossed her phone over and Elena snatched it off the bed. "Libby there's a new one!"

"Huh?"

"A new email from Jason!"

"That's weird. I didn't hear it ding."

"Me, neither. Want me to read it to you?"

"Fine," Libby groaned.

"Okay. Here goes." Elena sat up straight and tucked one foot underneath her. "Libby," she started in a deep, sultry voice.

"Elena!" Libby laughed. "Stop it!"

"Sorry to bug you again," Elena said again, trying to maintain the voice, but giggling through it. "I was just too excited to wait to tell you–"

"I'm not listening to this!" Libby put her hands over her ears and went into the bathroom.

"Oh, Libby!" Elena cried suddenly. She jumped up and ran into the bathroom, bouncing up and down.

"What? What is it?"

"I was right! You're going to Broadway! He got you tickets to *Hamilton*!"

"No, he didn't," Libby snatched the phone out of Elena's hand and read the email for herself. "Oh, my gosh! How in the world did he manage that?"

Elena squealed again and grabbed Libby's hand, still bouncing. "Who cares? You're going to Broadway! In that amazing dress!"

Libby bit her lip but didn't jump up and down; she was too overwhelmed. "Do you think that dress is nice enough for Broadway?"

Elena laughed. "First you think it's too much, now it's not enough?"

"I don't know! It's Broadway!"

"*Hamilton* is hip-hop, Libby. I think you'll be fine. Let me finish reading the email!" Elena took the phone back and scrolled to the top again, this time reading it in her real voice. "I was just too excited to wait to tell you. I called in a few favors and managed to get us a pair of tickets to *Hamilton* this weekend. I hope that's okay; I thought you would enjoy a real New York City experience. So if you haven't gone shopping yet, that's where we're going. Let me know if this is okay. If you'd rather not go, my feelings won't be hurt."

"Oh, damn, Libby. This guy! He's so cute! His feelings won't be hurt? He's adorable!"

"Let me see that," Libby held out her hand.

"Oh, please, let me?" Elena smiled sweetly and held the phone to her cheek. "I promise I'll be good!"

"Yeah, right. Give me the phone."

Elena handed it over reluctantly and then leaned against the bathroom wall. "You have no idea how jealous I am right now."

"What are you talking about? Reggie is amazing!"

Elena stood up straighter and gave Libby a knowing look. "I was talking about Broadway and New York, you jerk."

"Oh," Libby blushed. "Right."

Elena stared at her friend's crimson face for a moment and then stood a little taller. "Libby, are you sure this is a good idea?" she asked in a more serious tone of voice.

"What do you mean?"

"I know I've been teasing you about this. Honestly, I'm just trying to take your mind off of everything else. But a whole weekend with this guy? Are you going to be okay?"

Libby snorted. "Now you decide to question me? I'm a big girl,

El, and I can take care of myself."

"I know. I'm just checking in on you, for real. I'm not playing around anymore. He's attractive and attentive and you told me to promise not to let you rebound."

"I'm not rebounding, but thank you. I appreciate it." Libby reached forward and squeezed Elena's arm.

"Well, you tell me if anything changes."

"I'll have to tell someone!" They stared at each other quietly for a moment before Libby squealed and finally started jumping up and down. "I'm going to Broadway!"

TOO EXCITED TO sleep that night, Libby geared herself up with a glass of wine, the last piece of the chocolate that Jason had sent her, and sat with her laptop in the middle of the bed. Jeremy and Sarah needed her attention.

Sarah stood in the window of the cookhouse, absently stirring a huge pot of bubbling chili. One might think she was lost in thought, and they'd be half correct, but her eyes were focused on the movement outside, just 10 feet from where she stood. Jeremy, hunched over another fallen fence post, worked tirelessly to repair it before nightfall. Even one missing post could mean a great loss of the herd, whether by coyotes or stray cows. It was the third time this spring that the fence had needed repairing. The whole thing needed to be replaced, but there wasn't money for that just yet. Sarah had other more pressing matters on her mind.

She watched the sweat glisten on his bare back and his muscles heave as he struggled to pull the twine tight across the post. She felt sweat bead across her own forehead as she remembered the kiss they had shared just days ago. They hadn't spoken to each other since then, and he had been avoiding her like the plague. Sarah was tortured over the whole thing. Jeremy's lips had awakened something inside of her soul that was stronger than the loneliness she had been drowning in. When she looked at him, she felt waves of longing and desire crash into shores of guilt and shame, and all week she'd been struggling to find a middle ground.

She couldn't mourn her late husband forever, but could she possibly give in to the battle that was waging against her emotions? When she closed her eyes at night, it was Jeremy who filled her dreams now, igniting a fire so dangerous she woke up every night in a cold sweat.

Obviously he was struggling as much as she was, but was it the same struggle? Or was he reconciled to the mistake and burdened that he had misled her?

Sarah stirred the chili harder, splattering some on her hand. She squealed in pain and wiped it off quickly with her apron. When she looked up again, he was staring into the window, directly at her.

* * *

Jeremy had felt her eyes on him for the last twenty minutes, but he absolutely refused to let himself acknowledge her until he heard her cry out. He dropped his tool and looked up, ready to run to her aid, but she hadn't moved from the window, and she was still staring right at him. He wondered if he'd imagined her voice.

She didn't turn away, as most women would, but stood there, holding his gaze, as if challenging him. He felt as though he'd suffered through enough, though. He took off his hat and wiped his forehead with the handkerchief in his back pocket, never breaking her gaze.

Sarah had been unreadable since the kiss had happened. He had assumed that she was appalled at both of their behavior, and so he had kept his distance. But there had been moments when he had sworn she'd looked his way.

Now there was no mistaking it. She was giving him a look that made his chest tighten. He stood up straighter and squeezed his hands in a fist. He held her gaze and began to take long strides towards the cookhouse.

Abe met him when he was halfway there. "Boss, there's a problem in the north field. Need you to come," Abe panted.

Sarah's gaze left Jeremy's for the first time since he'd looked up. The spell that seemed to have come over him dissipated and he turned to Abe.

"Let's go." Jeremy turned to follow Abe to the barn to grab his horse and his shirt. He took one look back at the window, but Sarah was no longer there.

You're going to lose this battle, he said to himself.

Libby spent all day Thursday writing. It was the quickest way to pass the time. She could write for an hour straight and barely notice the minutes slipping by. She tried to take a couple breaks, but she ended up just watching the time on the clock tick away. She was too nervous and excited about her trip. Because she hadn't slept the night before, she took a sleep aid before climbing into bed that night and prayed that she would fall asleep quickly.

Before she knew it, the alarm on her phone was buzzing and the sun was streaming through her window.

"This is it," she whispered before she even lifted her head off the pillow. A knot of nervous excitement pulled in her stomach. It grew all day and made her slightly nauseous on her flight from DFW to Charlotte. It wasn't until her second flight began to descend into New York that she realized what the real issue was, why she felt like she was going to throw up. She was ten minutes from seeing Jason again. Their last meeting had been so disastrous in her eyes and had ended so strangely that she was worried about what might happen this time. She thought about Elena's questions from a few nights before and the similarities she'd seen between Jeremy and Sarah's saga and her own life. She reminded herself that she wasn't rebounding . . . not yet anyway. She inhaled and exhaled slowly as the plane dipped closer and closer to the ground.

"Don't worry sweetheart, I've been flying this leg for years. We'll be just fine!" The elderly woman beside her said, mistaking Libby's loud breathing for a fear of flying. Libby simply nodded and gave her a fake smile, then turned her eyes forward again, trying to enjoy what had always been her favorite part of flying.

The plane landed and Libby waited as long as possible to get off. A kind man insisted that she go before him after he'd watched her wave countless passengers ahead. She grabbed her backpack from the overhead compartment and forced herself to put one foot in front of the other to get off the plane.

When she got to baggage claim where she had to pick up her garment bag (they'd made her check it because the flight was so full), Jason was already there looking around for her. Her heart caught in her throat.

Please, please, don't do anything stupid, she begged herself. You're still recovering from the wounds of one betrayal. Why set yourself up for another one?

Her throat constricted and she ducked behind a large man and made her way to the bathroom before Jason could spot her.

She locked herself in a stall and dropped her backpack on the ground, swearing in her head. "Oh, God, what am I going to do?" she whispered. She felt vulnerable and wished desperately that she'd brought Elena along.

You could trust me.

I wasn't actually talking to You! she said silently.

When you call, I answer. Trust me, Libby. Trust in me to work this out for you.

I'm not super impressed with Your track record.

I love you, Libby. Remember that even when you feel like I am far away, I've never left you. I've never turned away from you.

Libby shuddered. "You can't stay locked in this bathroom forever, Libby," she said to herself. "He's waiting for you. You are strong. You can handle yourself. You can do this on your own. You are in control."

The pep talk did little to ease her nerves, but she let herself out of the stall anyway and washed her hands. She took a deep breath and stepped out of the bathroom. Jason's expression was concerned as the last of the passengers had come through the rotating doors. She stepped into his view quickly and his face brightened.

"Crap," she muttered to herself while smiling at him. "He's so gorgeous."

Jason rushed to her. "For a minute there I thought maybe you didn't catch the flight!"

"Sorry, I had to use the restroom. I didn't see you," she lied.

"No problem! You're here now! How was the trip?"

"It was fine, thanks."

"Good, well, the cab is out here. Do you have luggage to pick up?"

"Um, actually, yes it's right there–" she pointed as her bag passed them and went around the carousel again.

"Oh, that black one? I'll get it."

Libby watched as Jason chased down her bag. He tripped over a suitcase on his way, but he came up swinging, her luggage in hand.

"Are you okay?" Libby giggled as he returned.

"Just a flesh wound," he grinned and held up her garment bag proudly. "Got it! Shall we?" He pointed to the door with his free hand.

"I'll follow you," Libby said and let Jason take the lead.

He stopped at the curb where a cab was waiting for them and loaded her luggage into the open trunk. "You travel light for a girl," he teased.

"Flattery will get you nowhere!" she warned and then immediately wished she could stop herself from flirting with him.

"We'll see about that," he winked.

Dang it! He's flirting right back! Libby thought as she climbed into the back seat. Something inside of her said that she should enjoy the attention while she had it. Though he was gorgeous, Libby truly believed Jason to be harmless. Time would tell though. She would know by tomorrow night just how harmless he was. That dress seemed to have a siren attached to it, one that Libby could already hear blaring from the trunk.

Chapter 11

JASON CLIMBED INTO the cab beside her. The anxiety that he had felt as he'd waited to see her face in the terminal was eased, and he was more than a little thrilled that she was finally in New York with him.

She's not with you, idiot, he told himself. He fought the urge to look over at her again and instead replayed the moment he'd finally found her in baggage claim. Her hair was pulled up in a loose ponytail, and a few strands hung around her face. The burgundy of her dancer-style sweater sharpened her eyes, which looked healthier, in his opinion, than when he'd seen them a few weeks ago. She wore tight-fitting jeans with knee-high black riding boots. Jason hoped that his smile hadn't betrayed him. He'd thought about seeing her again hundreds of times since the last time they'd met, but he'd figured that the real moment would be exponentially better than anything he could imagine. He couldn't reason himself out of what he was feeling. The only thing he was sure about was that he was incredibly attracted to Elizabeth Abbott, and he wasn't sure how much of a problem that would be in the days and weeks to come.

Jason settled into the seat and directed the cab driver into the city. "Are you hungry? It's almost five thirty. Did you eat in the airport?"

Libby shook her head. "There wasn't time in Charlotte and they only gave us pretzels on the plane."

"How does some deep dish sound?"

"Authentic New York pizza? Sounds fantastic," Libby said with a smile.

Jason didn't let his thoughts reach his face. He would have to prepare himself to see that smile more often. It was a thought that brought little comfort to him.

"So tell me, in your whirlwind tour of the big city, what is the most important place you want to see?"

"Easy. Central Park."

"Really?" Jason grinned. "That just happens to be one of my favorite spots, tourist or not."

"Yes. I want to see the Alice statue and the castle, and then I want to check out the boathouse and Tavern on the Green–"

"Whoa," Jason laughed. "You know that it's over eight hundred acres of land, right? We'll have to rent bikes or scooters!"

Libby's eyes grew round. "Oh, I guess I didn't think about that."

"We totally can; it's just that our time is kind of limited on Sunday."

"Right. I forgot. Sorry. Is the castle far from Alice?"

"It's a long walk, but it's doable."

"Okay, then that's my number one."

"I'll make sure we get there," he promised.

There was that smile again. Jason turned his head slowly to gaze out the window and scolded himself silently.

LIBBY DIDN'T NOTICE Jason's discomfort; she was too busy trying to act natural while staring in awe at the skyline outside the car window as they neared the city. She'd always thought New York City would intimidate her, but for some reason, the enormous skyscrapers took her breath away.

"Wow," she mouthed silently.

"There's the new World Trade Center tower." Jason pointed in the distance toward the peculiarly-shaped building.

Libby sucked in a breath. "Wow. If I had more time . . ."

"The memorial is pretty intense; you'd need a whole day to see it and process it. Maybe next time."

She smiled at him and then quickly turned her attention back out the window, hoping that the shudder of nerves that just ran down her spine when she'd looked at him hadn't been obvious.

As hungry as she was, what she really wanted was to get room service in the safety of her hotel room, alone, and cuddle up with a pillow in a big hotel bed while watching HGTV.

That's such a cop out, Libby. You're with your agent. You should be soaking this in! She rolled her eyes at herself.

The cab pulled up to a pizza place after a twenty minute drive into the city and Jason hopped out, ran around to open Libby's door, and offered his hand while she climbed out onto the sidewalk. She told herself that she didn't notice how nice his warm hand felt against the crisp March air. She told herself that it wasn't particularly sweet that he'd opened the door for her after slinging her garment bag over his shoulder, and as he came up behind her to tell her what the best pizzas were, she told herself that the goosebumps that rose on her neck were simply a sign of her body reacting to the change in temperature inside the restaurant.

They ordered a deluxe pizza to share and then sat in a red vinyl-covered booth for two while they waited.

"Oh, I checked you in already." Jason fished in his pocket and handed her a keycard.

"Thanks."

"I also booked you a massage in the morning, but you can cancel that if you want to. I just thought you might want to relax before our meeting with Andrew Green tomorrow."

"Andrew Green?" She felt the blood in her face drain.

"Yeah, Andrew Green. He's the CEO of Em—"

"Of Emerald Publishing. I know who he is, but you never mentioned–oh, my gosh." Libby's heart was pounding. "No. You can't be serious!"

Jason's lips spread in a wide grin. "I never told you who we're meeting with? Didn't you get the proposal I sent you??"

"I haven't actually looked at it yet, everything happened so fast, and I ended up having to check the bag I put it in." She stopped herself from rambling. "You're not joking? Don't tease me about stuff like this; I have a sense of humor but–"

"Libby," Jason stopped her and put his hand on top of hers. "I can't believe I didn't tell you. *Red Parks Ranch* is going to be published by Emerald."

Libby pulled her hand away quickly, unsure of how to respond. She searched her lap dramatically for something to grip or hold on to. She ended up covering her face with her hands praying that the tears would stop short before they began to fall.

Help me, she prayed silently. Please keep my tears under control. Her eyes filled but didn't overflow and she looked up at Jason's happy grin.

"I take it you're happy?"

Libby had no words. Emerald Publishing–if anyone wanted to be anybody in the literary world, they signed with Emerald. With Andrew Green. Some of her favorite books were by Emerald authors.

"I can't wrap my mind around this. Jason, how did you do this?" She searched his face for a giveaway. He had to be messing with her.

He held his hand out for hers again and when she gave it to him, he squeezed it gently. "Well, he is my friend, but I had so little to do with this. Libby, your work stands on its own. Andrew wants to see everything you've ever submitted to anyone before. He said that we've been sitting around just waiting for you to show up."

The tears couldn't be fenced in then. It was even more embarrassing than the last time. Andrew Green's next breakthrough author was sobbing in a pizzeria in New York City.

"I promise I'm not going to cry every time you see me," Libby half sobbed, half laughed.

Jason, still holding her hand, leaned forward. "I can't believe you didn't know."

"Obviously it's the first I've heard."

"I didn't mean to catch you off guard. But honestly, this might be the best reaction I've ever gotten to this news."

"Seriously? People don't normally freak out? Andrew Green!" She sniffed and wiped her cheeks with a napkin from the steel dispenser by the wall.

"Oh, they freak out, but there's more screaming and jumping up and down."

"I'm doing that inside," she said as a new wave of tears came on.

"I can tell," he grinned. He released her hand as a waiter brought their pizza and set it on the table between them. "You deserve this, Libby."

"I don't see how, but I'm not complaining."

"Let's toast." Jason lifted a piece of pizza in the air, and Libby grinned through shining eyes and followed his lead. "To a second chance at the life you always deserved."

"To random strangers who believe in people with blind faith," Libby said quietly as they touched their pieces together.

"To no longer being random strangers!" Jason grinned and took a bite.

Libby nodded and let her teeth sink into the gooey pizza and closed her eyes in pleasure while she chewed.

JASON ENJOYED WATCHING her respond to everything. When she had questioned him about Emerald, he'd seen such an uncertainty in her eyes; she didn't trust him, or she just didn't know him well enough to know that he would never bait her like that. Watching her eyes turn from such fear to disbelief and then absolute shock had been priceless. Never before had he been able to read a woman so well. But then again, he'd never met a woman who wore her feelings so openly. Now she was staring out across the city street and he was content to simply stare at her while he was supposed to be hailing a cab.

"What time are we meeting him tomorrow?" Libby asked nervously.

"Eleven. I'll have to pick you up at ten to get there on time." He waved a cab down and opened the door for her.

"That's good, then I won't be driving myself crazy with anticipation all day! And then *Hamilton* is tomorrow night?" Libby asked before she climbed into the backseat.

"Yes, and I have a few other surprises up my sleeve."

Libby looked at Jason curiously. "I don't know if I can handle any more!" She slid into the car and folded her hands in her lap.

"Trust me, they pale in comparison, just some fun things I have planned for you."

A smile played at Libby's lips. "You should be careful, Mr. Randall. If you spoil me too much, I may never leave!"

A guy can dream, he thought to himself, and then shut the door.

WHEN LIBBY FINALLY got her wish and snuggled into the huge bed inside a very elegant room with metallic gold wallpaper and cream-colored furniture, she was far too excited to sleep. For a split second, she wished that she had a husband she could share the joy with, but she wouldn't even let that thought spoil her mood. She called Elena instead.

"Hey, are you there? How is New York?" Elena answered excitedly.

"It's fantastic. It's amazing. It's—"

"What happened? You sound like you're on cloud nine!"

"I am, El! I totally am!"

"Jason?"

"No! Andrew Green!" Libby sighed dreamily and rolled over on to her back, letting her arm flop to the side.

"I'm sorry, who?"

"Andrew Green is the CEO of Emerald Publishing."

"Emerald–they do a lot of big names, right?"

"Yes. The best."

"Okay, so did you meet him or something?"

"No, but I'm going to. Tomorrow. At eleven." She waited to see if Elena would catch on. She heard a sharp intake of breath on the other line. "Are you there?" she said after an extended silence.

"Libby," Elena breathed.

Libby could hear the emotion in her friend's voice.

"You're going to be famous! Libby! You're going to be a best-selling author," Elena cried. She began to shout and whoop loudly into the phone. Libby's eyes welled with tears again and she laughed while she listened to her friend relay the news to Reggie. Reggie began to holler in the background.

"I'm so proud of you!" Reggie called out while Elena sobered herself.

"We both are! I am so excited for you, Libby! I can hardly believe it!"

"Me, neither. I'm still in shock. I'm not sure I'll believe it until I actually meet him!"

"So that's the plan then? Tomorrow morning?" Elena asked excitedly.

"Tomorrow morning," Libby confirmed.

"And when is *Hamilton*?"

"In the evening."

"Tomorrow is a huge day!"

"I know. I'm not sure I can handle it all. Jason said he has a few more surprises in store for me, too!" Libby bit her lip and prepared herself for what was coming next.

"Really?" Elena sang. "What kind of surprises? The kind that he keeps in his–"

"Elena!" Libby scolded. "You're sick!"

"Okay, okay. That's the last one, I swear," Elena laughed and then composed herself enough to ask, "How are you really?"

Libby considered her answer carefully. "Scared, I think."

"Of?"

"Of this whole weekend. Tomorrow's meeting, tomorrow night, being with Jason during all of it."

"What do you mean?" Elena asked cautiously.

"He's giving me my dream life, Elena! He's become like a–a–"

"Knight in shining armor?"

"Kind of." Libby wasn't certain she wanted to label him like that.

"Do you feel like he's rescuing you? Because that is definitely rebound material."

"I know," Libby sighed.

"Do you need rescuing?"

"I don't know."

"Well, I think that's an important question to answer, dear. If you need to be rescued, then that knight in his sparkly armor is going to rescue the heck out of you. But what happens when you don't need rescuing anymore?"

"Rebound."

"Exactly. But hear me: There's no shame in needing to be rescued. It's okay to rebound, Libby," Elena said softly.

Libby rolled her eyes. "Not if you know it's what you're doing!"

"Sure, it is. It's a distraction. You just have to remember that you're not always going to be a damsel in distress; eventually knights get bored and armor gets rusty."

"I know. You're right about that part. I don't need to be rescued. I'm not rebounding."

"Good. Then just enjoy your weekend! And call me as soon as your meeting is over!"

"I promise, I will."

"I really am so happy for you, Libby. This is the best news I've heard in like a year."

"Thanks, El. Me too."

"Call me tomorrow!" Elena said again just before they hung up. Libby let the phone lay on the bed beside her and she stared at the ceiling, deep in thought.

I don't need to be rescued, she chanted to herself.

You don't need to be rescued by a man.

Seriously? Do You ever go away? Libby groaned and rolled onto her side.

You need to be fought for. Let me fight for you, Libby.

What does that even mean? I need to be fought for?

You've been fighting for years to stay afloat, to maintain a tight grip on who you are, and in the meantime, you've completely lost yourself. But I know who you are, and I can carry you through all of this. I can fight for you so that you can rest. Let me be your rescue. Just let go.

"I don't know how," Libby whispered as her eyes began to droop.

Chapter 15

LIBBY COULD HAVE let Eduardo knead out the knots in her back forever if it wasn't for the major life event she had planned for that morning. Now she let the hot water in the luxury shower stall in her bathroom continue the massage as it pounded in streams against her back. The steam filled the stall with the scent of lavender and she breathed deeply, willing the peaceful qualities of the leftover massage oil to calm her pounding heart. She had one hour before Jason was to meet her in the lobby. She lingered in the shower, choosing to simply blow-dry her hair straight for the day and then fix it up later for the evening's activities.

As she stepped out of the shower and wiped a section of the mirror clean from condensation, Libby whispered a prayer.

"God, I know it's not fair to ask anything of You, but please don't let me screw anything up today. I'm begging You."

She proceeded to dry her hair and change into the suit that Elena liked so much. She pulled the belt around the tightly fitted jacket and tied it in a knot at her stomach. The outfit was smart and stylish; she almost wished that she wore glasses to further sophisticate the look. Smiling at her appearance, she practiced her greeting for the infamous Andrew Green.

"It's a pleasure to meet you, Mr. Green," she said, holding her hand out. Then she laughed out loud at herself. "No one really does this, do they?" She shook her head at her reflection and gave up on the greeting. She tucked her feet into a pair of black heels and smoothed her hair one last time. "This is it, Libby. First day of the rest of your life." Her nerves began to rise and she closed her eyes trying to calm herself.

I will be here with you. Today is my gift to you. You deserve today.

"Thank You," she whispered reluctantly, and then grabbed her purse and went to meet Jason in the lobby.

JASON WAS WAITING by the front desk, people watching, when Libby appeared from the elevator hallway. He wondered if he would ever get so used to the sight of her that his heart wouldn't halt abruptly anymore. He decided that he hoped he wouldn't. The woman seemed to demand an audience just by walking through the lobby. Jason noticed that more than a few men looked up from newspapers or turned away from conversations as Libby strode towards him.

That's right, she's with me, he thought as she came up beside him. Then he scolded himself. She's not with you. She's your client. Oh God, please don't let me screw this up!

I've got it covered. Just keep your thoughts in check, son.

Jason admitted silently what a difficult task that would be and then greeted his client. "You look great," he said, leaning forward to hug her very briefly.

"Thanks, I'm really nervous!"

Jason laughed heartily. "I bet you are. You'll feel better once you meet him. He's the least intimidating person in the universe."

"Less than that guy?" Libby giggled and nodded to one of the bellboys at the door who was looking around the room like a scared puppy.

"Well, maybe not. I think it's his first day. I saw someone walk out with him a few minutes ago and position him there."

"Then let's be extra nice to him, shall we?" Libby said sweetly.

"This is going to cost me money, isn't it?" Jason laughed.

Libby scrunched her nose at him and pulled a ten-dollar bill out of her purse.

"Oh-ho, no, you don't! I was kidding!" Jason pushed her hand back into her purse and pulled out his wallet.

"I can tip my own bell-boy," Libby said indignantly.

"Not this weekend, you can't! This weekend is on me–er–the company. You're not allowed to spend a dime."

"What about souvenirs?"

"Oh, okay. You can buy your own souvenirs, but that's it."

Libby rolled her eyes dramatically. "Fine. Tip the man then!"

"For opening a door?" Jason balked.

Libby began to reach into her purse again and Jason quickly pulled a bill from his wallet. "All I have is a twenty!" At the look on her face he sighed playfully. "I didn't realize you were so high maintenance!"

"I may have a few surprises up my sleeve as well," she winked at Jason and smiled at the scared looking young man who opened the door for them. Jason held out his hand and transferred the money through a handshake. "It's your lucky day, man." Jason said under his breath and followed Libby onto the street.

His eyes couldn't help but travel the length of her body, but they darted quickly back up as she looked back at him for direction.

Scared that she'd caught him, he avoided her gaze and scanned the oncoming traffic for a vacant cab. When one finally pulled over, he opened the door for her again and then jogged around the other side to get in.

Jason gave the cab driver their destination and then turned his attention to Libby, who was staring at him curiously.

"What?" he asked, suddenly feeling very conspicuous and at the same time, thankful that telepathy wasn't real.

"Nothing," she said quickly and turned away, though he saw her cheeks redden instantly. "You look nice is all."

"Oh," he sat a little straighter and smiled proudly. "Thank you."

"You're welcome."

LIBBY TURNED HER head to watch the street while they navigated their way through the city. There was something about Jason that had a calming effect on her. That's what she'd been considering while she stared at him in the cab. That and how good he looked in his black dress shirt and grey slacks.

I might not need rescuing from a man, but it couldn't hurt to wonder what it might be like to be rescued by this particular man . . . could it? she wondered. Catching his eye while she'd walked across the lobby had eased her nerves instantly, which didn't calm her thoughts. She had noticed the way his frame had seemed to come to attention when he'd seen her. She told herself to let the speculations go and do as Elena had said: simply enjoy the weekend. Then she remembered the words that had been spoken to her heart the night before—that she needed to be fought for and rescued by a Savior instead of a man. She sighed out loud.

"Everything all right?" Jason was quick to ask.

"Oh, yes. Sorry. I'm just thinking."

"Not overthinking, are you?"

She turned her head to face him. "What do you mean?"

He shook his head quickly. "Nothing. Just relax. Don't worry about today."

Libby nodded and went back to gazing out her window.

"Here we are," the cabbie said in a thick accent after many stops and turns through the city.

Libby gulped and stared out the window. It looked like every other street they had just driven down, and she wondered if maybe the driver had misunderstood the address. Jason opened her door for her and again, held his hand out to help her out. He didn't let go after the cab had left them though. He stood in one spot, squeezing her hand.

"You're going to be fine. Andrew's a pro and he's smitten with your book. You don't have to sell it to him. Just be yourself and don't be surprised if he hands you a check today."

"Today?"

Jason nodded. "If you sign the contract, he'll cut you a check on the spot."

"Contract? Today?"

He nodded. "It's all finalized. The only difference from the proposal that I sent you is that I negotiated a little percentage boost if you hit best-seller within the first six months."

"Is that even possible?"

He laughed and rubbed his thumb on her hand. "Libby, the reason you know of Andrew Green is because of people like you and me."

Libby breathed deeply and nodded, wishing that Jason would let go of her hand. It was starting to sweat and she wasn't sure if it was because of him or the impending meeting. Jason finally released her and stepped forward to open a plain glass door that led into a narrow hallway with equally narrow stairs.

"Uh, are you sure this is the right place?" Libby asked warily.

"Yes, ma'am," Jason grinned and stepped aside to let her go first.

"You're extremely gentlemanly," Libby grinned and started up the stairs.

Jason narrowed his eyes at her. "That's a new one, but I'll take it."

"I just mean, you open doors, you let me go first, that kind of thing."

"Isn't that normal behavior?" Jason asked, following her into the dimly lit staircase.

"Maybe once upon a time, but not so much these days."

"Well, I guess you can call me traditional then. Turn left."

Libby reached the top of the stairs and followed his directions.

Before her stood a frosted white glass door with the familiar green gemstone logo that lined the spines on her bookshelf in her office back home. She inhaled deeply and reached a shaky hand forward to open the door.

Jason slipped behind her, opening the door wide for her to walk through. She looked back at him, alarmed by how close he was to her.

"Thank you," she whispered and slowly stepped into the brightly lit office. "Wow."

Stark white boxy couches with deep emerald green throw pillows surrounded a steel-topped magazine table and a shag carpet in the same shade of green. Three walls were pure white with silver light fixtures and the last was done in tiles alternating hues of green and white.

"It's a little overwhelming," Jason whispered in her ear, still close enough that she could feel his breath on her neck. "Whatever you do, don't refer to any of this as green. It's about the only thing he's sensitive about."

"My ears are ringing, Jason," a voice sang through the room. A large, bald man approached them with green-rimmed glasses, a black suit, and a tie the same color as the pillows on the couch.

"Never mind what he says, he'll make me out to be an ogre if there ever was one!" Andrew Green waved his hand flamboyantly and then held it out towards Libby. "You *must* be Elizabeth Abbott. I'm so pleased to meet you."

Slightly shell-shocked, Libby gave him her hand and stared at his bald head while he bent over to kiss it.

"Libby, this is Andrew Green, President and CEO of Emerald Publishing," Jason said proudly.

"I, uh, it's my—um, I'm just a little overwhelmed, Mr. Green," Libby's tongue seemed to trip over her words.

Andrew Green stood up quickly and smiled at her. "Overwhelmed? By me?" he teased. "I like her already!" He winked at Jason. "Shall we?"

Andrew transferred his hand to the small of her back and led her from the lobby into what appeared to be a conference room with the familiar green covering the walls. A shiny white table sat in the middle with twelve chrome chairs around it. Andrew led Libby to one, pulled it out, and then strutted around the table to take a seat directly across from her. Jason settled beside her and laid his satchel on the table.

"Is there anything I can have my assistant get you? Water? Soda?" Andrew cleared his throat. "Adult beverage?"

Libby smiled and said, "Just some water please."

He assured them he'd return swiftly and then left the room. Libby blew out the breath she'd been holding and turned to Jason.

"He's gay!" She whispered in surprise.

"What?" Jason responded, aghast.

Libby rolled her eyes. "Come on!"

"I'm surprised you didn't know that!" Jason snickered.

"I've never actually seen him! If I'd known he was gay, I wouldn't have been so nervous!"

"Huh?" Jason looked confused.

"Gay men are so much more generous and forgiving! Accepting, even! I've always felt more at ease with them." Libby sighed.

"Oh, so you like *gay* men," Jason laughed. "That's the problem!"

Before either one of them could react to that statement, Andrew's assistant came in with Libby's water and a soda for Jason.

"Thanks, Lana," Jason said and stood to kiss her on the cheek.

As she left, Libby started to turn to Jason to ask something, but Andrew was already coming back through the door.

"All right, then. Let's get down to brass tacks, shall we?" He swirled a dark colored liquid around in a snifter. "Don't mind me," he said as Libby eyed his beverage. "I've just gotten off the phone with my mother and she literally drives me to drink. I always have to come down after she's told me how despicable my lifestyle is."

Being that Libby knew Jason was somewhat religious, she wondered if the statement had offended him at all, but he hadn't flinched.

"Well, Andy, what'd you think?" Jason pressed.

"Of my mother? She's a lunatic! Oh, but that's not what you were talking about, is it?" He gave a sly smile as he sat down and wagged his finger at Jason. He crossed his knees and turned towards Libby. "Are you ready to publish a novel, dear?" He grinned and took a sip of his drink.

"Yes! I'm ready." She nodded vigorously. She felt like a third grader staring at a counter full of candy. She could hardly keep from bouncing in her seat.

"Good, because I'm ready to publish it. Is it finished now?"

Libby shot Jason a look of panic. He gave her a reassuring look and leaned forward.

"She's working on revisions right now; it'll be ready for editing in October."

"Let's see if we can move the time frame up a bit. I'd like to have your first draft in by August fifteenth."

Jason took a sharp breath and looked at Libby, whose jaw was dropping.

"What do you think, Libby?"

"Uh, yes! Absolutely. I can do that." She continued to nod like a bobble-head. She would work nonstop until then if it killed her.

"That's what I like to hear." He slid a stack of papers over to Libby. "I just need you to sign on the dotted line," he said with a smile. "I'll leave you two to go over it. Jason, you hold her hand and make sure she's happy, all right?" Andrew winked and left the room again.

Jason chuckled and pulled the stack of papers between them, leaning in with his pen to point out the details that she'd failed to read ahead of time.

After fifteen minutes of perusing and questioning, Libby pulled the stack closer and nervously accepted Jason's pen. She wished she could have five minutes of privacy to process this moment, to take the time to record every last detail of the past thirty minutes into her brain forever. Instead she twisted the pen in her hand and pressed the ball to the line that already had her name typed underneath it.

"This feels too good to be true," she whispered.

Jason put his hand on the back of her chair and grinned. "I promise it's not."

She swallowed and didn't waste another second. She scrawled her signature on each page with a sticky tab and then slid the papers back to Jason, who was beaming.

Andrew returned a few moments later, his hand outstretched. Libby watched with knots in her stomach while Jason handed the contract over.

"I feel like I just signed over the rights to my first born," she said quietly.

Andrew laughed and held the papers in the air. "We'll take good care of you, Libby Abbott. Our reputation depends on it."

"I'm aware of your reputation, Mr. Green, and I'm humbled to have this opportunity."

Andrew cocked his head to one side and clicked his tongue. "Aren't you precious? Next time you're here, I want to take you out on the town. I think you and I could do some damage to Manhattan." He grinned.

"I'm taking her out tonight," Jason piped up. "She may be spoiled by the time you get the chance."

Andrew's eyes sparkled. "Ah, yes. I heard about your plans for this evening. Everything is set, by the way." He winked at Jason.

Libby looked between the two of them, feeling like the odd one out. "What's set?"

"Never mind that. I've got to run now. Libby, it was fabulous to meet you, I can't wait to introduce you to the rest of the gang, but unfortunately, I'm due at the airport in an hour." He started to leave the room and then stopped abruptly. "Oh, I almost forgot! Here's your advance." Andrew pulled two folded check-sized papers out of the inside of his suit jacket and handed one to each of them and then left the room with a smile on his face.

Libby held the check with trembling fingers. Jason pocketed his own and immediately took Libby by the arms, sitting her back down in her chair.

"I can't look at it."

"You already know the number, though."

"I know. I just . . . I need a minute."

"Do you want to be alone?" Jason asked.

"Yes," she said and then as soon as he stood up, she grabbed his arm. "No!"

He smiled knowingly and sat back down beside her. As though of the same mind, he opened his hand and accepted hers as it slid down his arm. "How about I open it, and you look when you're ready?"

She nodded and slid the check over to him. As soon as he had unfolded it and laid it in front of her on the table, she stared into his face.

"I have a book deal," she said breathlessly. "I'm going to be a published author."

"You are," he said quietly, then pressed his lips together in a thin line, his expression unreadable, but his eyes were fixed on hers, unmoving, unblinking.

Libby gulped and finally sat forward, her eyes still on him.

"Just look, Libby," he whispered.

She did and immediately a sob caught in her throat. She withdrew her hand from his and placed it over her eyes. "Look at all those zeroes!"

Jason chuckled, "Did you think we were just joking?"

"Am I good enough for this?" She finally sat up and looked at him with questioning eyes.

"Stop doubting yourself. It's time to celebrate." Jason stood, took both of her hands again, and pulled her up. Before he could say or do anything, Libby threw her arms around him and hugged him tight.

"This is because of you!" she exclaimed. "Thank you so much!"

He cleared his throat and hugged her loosely. "Actually it was my ex-wife who discovered you, so—"

"This was you," Libby whispered as she pulled back and lifted her gaze to his. "I don't know how to thank you."

"Don't forget that I got paid, too," he said in a gravelly voice, looking away from her quickly.

Libby quickly dropped her arms to her side. "Sorry," she whispered. "I'm just so overwhelmed. After the past few months of hell, this is just . . . unbelievable."

"Well, I believe that God's timing is perfect, and I think this is proof of that."

Libby smiled and stepped back from him, picking up the check off the table. She chuckled and said, "I don't feel safe carrying this around!"

"We'll go straight to the bank. Just put it in your purse and don't wave it around or anything," Jason chuckled.

"Okay, let's go." Libby took one last look around the room. This room would go down in her memory as the happiest place on earth, and she would never forget how Jason Randall had impacted her life.

Chapter 16

AFTER LUNCH AND a brief stroll through Times Square, Jason dropped Libby back at the hotel and promised to be back for her at six pm on the dot. In the privacy of her hotel room, Libby pulled out the receipt from her bank. She was in awe, first, that her cash had dwindled so quickly to a mere eighty-eight dollars before she'd made her deposit, and second, that she felt like she really had been rescued. According to her contract, this was just the beginning. After she'd delivered the completed manuscript, she would receive another check and eventually, royalties from book sales.

"It's like I've stepped into someone else's life," She told Elena over the phone. "I don't know where this came from!"

"The universe is paying you back for years of servitude to that scumbag!" Elena giggled.

"The universe, God, Santa Claus, I don't care who! I'm so grateful!" Libby lay down on the bed, exhausted from the emotional roller coaster she'd been on that morning.

"Nah, Santa's too cheap for that!"

Libby smiled. "I could be done with today right now, I think. I'm so tired!"

"No way! Broadway tonight, Libby! Broadway!"

"I know. I think I need to take a power nap first, though."

"That's a good idea. Then you can be totally refreshed for tonight and alert enough to text me details all night long!"

"Um, I'll be busy watching the show."

"Then afterwards?" Elena asked hopefully.

"Of course. I'll tell you everything."

"Okay, good. Just know that I'll be waiting anxiously by the phone!"

"You have nothing better to do, El?" Libby joked.

"Not tonight! I wish your life were a reality show so I didn't have to wait for details."

Libby rolled her eyes. "That would be horrible. I'm going to sleep now."

"Bye, Libby. Have fun tonight!"

As Libby rolled over and tucked a pillow under her head, she was surprised that the thoughts rolling through her mind weren't about her book deal or her huge check, but instead were of the moments when Jason had grabbed her hand in support, when she had jumped into a thankful embrace without thinking, and the way it had felt when he'd hugged her back. She felt goosebumps prickle across her skin and she squeezed her eyes shut tighter, trying to push the thoughts away.

When she woke up an hour later, her eyes focused on the red dress that was hanging in the closet across from the bed.

"I am seriously rethinking that dress." She sighed and rolled onto her other side to see what time it was. Four-thirty. She had an hour and a half before Jason was meeting her again. She sat up and rubbed her eyes, feeling groggy and as though she'd slept too long. Coffee was her only thought, and she eyed the room service menu on the nightstand.

She picked up the phone and ordered a triple shot latte and then let her head loll back against the headboard, eyelids drooping. She was excited about seeing *Hamilton*, but she was so tired, the last thing she wanted to do was fix her hair and makeup and put on a pretty dress. She wondered if there were a cast recording of *Hamilton* that they could listen to instead and then immediately chided herself for being so selfish. Jason had gone out of his way to plan a fun night for her. Suddenly she sat up a little straighter, her eyes not quite so tired anymore.

He can't possibly do this for every author he represents, she thought. The knot that had settled in her stomach on the plane the day before began to twist again, and Libby groaned out loud.

Trust me, Libby.

I don't trust anyone right now, God!

I'm going to take care of you. I'm going to protect you.

Libby leaned over the bed and pulled her grandmother's letter from her overnight bag. She'd read and reread it a few times every day since it had been rediscovered. It was ironic to her that the letter talked about her being rescued, and now that topic was coming up again.

"If I need to be rescued from anything, it's myself," Libby sighed and let the letter slide to her lap.

There's nothing wrong with you, Libby. Just some old wounds that need dressing.

A knock on the door startled her until she remembered her coffee order. Grateful, she grabbed some change off of the table and answered the door. She tipped the waiter and brought the mug back to the bed, perching gently on the mattress.

"I'm screwing this up with Jason," she admitted to the empty room. "I'm letting this attraction get too much playing time. I'm dwelling on the feelings too much. I need to be more in control. If I do something stupid–"

If you do something stupid. But you haven't yet. I will be with you. Don't worry so much about what you're feeling. It's not wrong to be attracted. I created you to feel that.

"I'm still married," she whispered.

That's true. Acting on the attraction would be dangerous. There is a time for everything, Libby.

"Why are You here now? Why, all of a sudden, did You show up in my life again?" She took a sip of her coffee and blinked back tears.

Because I promised that I would never leave you, nor forsake you.

She shook her head. "I don't know if I believe that."

Libby took her coffee into the bathroom and plugged in her curling iron. She stared at herself in the mirror while it heated up. "A time for everything," she told her reflection. "This is not the time."

WHEN JASON ARRIVED at the hotel to meet Libby, he was as unsure of himself as he'd ever been. He'd spent the afternoon arguing with himself over his intentions with her. Even before they'd met in person, he'd felt a connection; her writing had drawn him in, and her picture had transfixed him. Meeting her in person had been the icing on the cake. The more time he spent with her, the more he'd become caught up in the idea of being with her and the desire to know her better. She was so genuine and real; she said what she felt and thought, even if it ended up embarrassing her in the end. She was refreshing and beautiful, and he simply couldn't ignore the stirring going on inside of him.

Too many times that afternoon he'd had ample opportunity to act on his feelings, but he'd done the right thing every time. While she walked beside him in Times Square, arms swinging at her sides, he'd refrained from taking her hand and tucking her arm under his.

When she'd tripped on a steel grate in the sidewalk and barreled into him sideways, he'd fought the urge to take her into his arms and kiss her passionately. He was glad that *Hamilton* would bring a distraction and that he wouldn't have to fight through those three hours as hard as he had all day. He hadn't prepared himself for what he was about to experience, though.

This time, when Libby stepped into view, Jason felt as though he'd been sucker punched. His breath whooshed out of his mouth and he took a steadying step backwards. If only a few heads had turned that morning when she'd emerged, this time, all across the lobby, newspapers and jaws alike were dropped. Even women stopped and turned to watch Libby walk towards him. She seemed to notice this time, too, and she adjusted her dress slightly as she glanced around nervously.

Jason simply stared, unable to help himself. The dress dipped dangerously between her breasts, fabric swaying precariously with each step. As she walked, the dress slipped in and out from between her legs, hugging her thighs on either side. Jason felt woozy from the lack of oxygen and breathed in deeply as Libby approached him.

Move! he told himself and stumbled forward. He had to force his gaze to her eyes, which seemed to look right through him. Her hair was pinned back loosely, her bangs pulled back and pushed up slightly, and a few thin wisps of hair curled gently against her face. Her eyes looked more dramatic than normal as well; they seemed to beckon him but warn him at the same time.

Jason couldn't help himself. He let out a slow, descending whistle.

"Hi," she said nervously.

Jason didn't trust his voice and didn't say anything; he just shook his head slowly.

"What? Is this okay? Is it too much? Not enough?" She crossed her arms over her stomach nervously.

"Libby." He finally found his voice, though it cracked as he took another step towards her. "You're beautiful." He couldn't resist touching her bare arm and placing a kiss on her cheek. "You're stunning, and every person in this room is jealous of me right now," he whispered in her ear.

Libby's cheeks flushed and her skin prickled under his touch. "I'm sure not every person–"

"Every. Person." Jason grinned and released his hold on her arm.

Her cheeks flamed and she clasped her hands together.

"Do you have a coat?" Jason asked suddenly. "It's going to be cold tonight."

Libby stared at him, wide-eyed. "Of course I don't have a coat," she groaned. "It's practically summer in Texas already!"

"And still winter in New York. Don't worry, you can use mine. Come on, our ride is waiting," Jason held his arm out for her to lead the way and when he fell into step behind her, a noise caught in his throat at the sight of her backside.

Are You trying to kill me? he prayed. Seriously?

The back of the dress scooped far down her back with a wide piece of fabric that hung like a swing above her behind. He felt as though any resolve he'd had to pursue a strictly agent/client relationship was defeated as the fabric of her dress swished in the wind. The bellboy caught his eye and gave him an approving nod.

Jason shook his head, forgetting all about the mode of transportation he'd arranged for them.

"Is this for us?" Libby turned to him in shock.

"Yes," he said weakly.

"A limo!"

"Yes," he sighed again. Get a grip, man, he told himself. God, You could have prepared me for this!

I've been preparing you for this for a lifetime.

Jason hadn't anticipated such a response. He had the good sense to look away while Libby bent to get through the door that the chauffeur had opened for her. When she was safely seated and she had made sure her dress was still covering everything appropriately, Jason slid in beside her.

"How did you manage this?" Libby took in the limo excitedly. "Wait. Don't tell me. This is Andrew Green's limo isn't it?"

"What gave it away?" Jason grinned and pulled a green pillow off of the seat that ran along the inside of the car.

Libby chuckled and sat back. "You don't do this for everyone, do you?" she asked cautiously.

Jason leaned forward and pulled a bottle of champagne out of a small fridge disguised as a cabinet.

"No, I don't." He left his answer at that, uncorked the bottle, poured two glasses of bubbly liquid, and handed her one.

Libby didn't press him further but took the champagne immediately to her lips.

A short while later, the chauffeur announced that they'd arrived, pulled the limo to the side of the street, and then jogged around to let them out. Jason got out and let Andrew's chauffeur help Libby out. He wasn't sure he could control where his eyes landed. He waited until she was on the sidewalk and fully upright before looking at her and thoughtlessly placing his hand on her bare back to lead her into the theater. As soon as their flesh touched, electricity passed between them. Libby jumped and laughed nervously, and Jason dropped his hand.

"Sorry," he said quietly. He walked to the box office, had their tickets scanned, and then he let her go ahead of him up a massive staircase that led to the foyer surrounding the theater.

The crowd was heavy and Libby held back for Jason to catch up at the top of the stairs. She grabbed his arm gently.

"I don't want to lose you," she said over the din.

He simply nodded and scanned signs to find their section. Finally he located the right door and together they maneuvered through the crowd and into the theater full of people milling about, searching for their seats.

Jason led her down the middle aisle to the twentieth row.

"These are great seats!" Libby exclaimed as they climbed over the row of people already seated.

He stopped at their seats and turned to face the stage, sitting down slowly. Libby, still standing, turned her gaze down to him before she sat.

"Are you alright?" She asked.

"Huh? Oh! Of course. Sorry. Just thinking."

"About?"

He shrugged nonchalantly. "You don't wanna know."

"Is something wrong?" she pressed.

"No, not at all," he smiled at her, determined to enjoy their evening, even if it meant more to him than it did to her. By the time the music started, Jason was feeling somewhat more like himself and he settled into his seat, loosening the tie at his neck a little.

"You look really nice, by the way," Libby whispered. "I really like that suit."

Jason smiled and fought the strange urge to laugh. "Thanks," he whispered back.

As amazing as *Hamilton* was, Jason enjoyed watching Libby experience it more than the show itself. She was mesmerized by the performance and mouthed the words to the few songs that she knew. Her chest rose and fell quickly when darkness fell on the stage, signaling intermission.

Jason grinned. "Do you want anything? They have drinks and snacks out there."

"Maybe just a bottle of water?"

"Sure. I'll be right back." Jason stood and made his way out of the theater.

LIBBY WAS THANKFUL for the effects of the champagne from the limo, which helped hold her insecurities at bay. She was self conscious in the sexy red dress, especially since she had noticed the turning of heads in the lobby of the hotel, but most importantly because she had seen Jason stumble at the sight of her and the pained expression that had crossed his face. She made a mental note to murder Elena at the next opportunity.

"You two are cute," an elderly voice behind her said.

Libby looked back at the woman who was sitting behind Jason's empty seat. "Oh, we're not a couple," she said politely.

The woman raised her eyebrows, giving Libby a dubious look.

Libby smiled and turned back to face the stage. The woman's expression continued to nag her though. "Excuse me." she leaned over to get the woman's attention. "What made you think we were a couple?"

The lady paused her conversation with the man beside her and turned to face Libby again. "Ask him what happened in the first act, honey. He'll have no clue. He was watching you the entire time!"

Libby pursed her lips to one side and sat up in her seat again. It was a few moments before Jason returned with two bottles of water in his hands.

"It's crazy out there! And these? Seven dollars each!"

"That's insane!" Libby exclaimed. "I'll drink it slowly and savor every sip."

When Jason sat down, Libby turned to him, eyeing the woman behind him. "So, what was your favorite part of that act?" she asked.

The woman gave Libby a knowing look and tilted her head closer for his answer.

"Uh, well, I uh, I love the way the stage turns . . ." The lights lowered and the music began to play again. "Oh look! It's starting again!" Jason turned his head quickly to the stage and appeared to be completely engrossed in the action taking place on stage.

The woman cleared her throat and Libby sighed as she sat back to try and enjoy the rest of the show, which actually wasn't that difficult to do. She found herself completely engrossed in what was happening on stage. When the second act finished, Libby had completely forgotten the old woman with the Jersey accent, and had tears streaming down her cheeks.

"I think I'm in love with Broadway!" she swooned, wiping her eyes as they waited for their row to clear out.

"I have to admit, that was pretty amazing, but I'm so sorry about the affair thing." Jason cringed. "I had no idea."

Libby was touched by the sincerity in his eyes and remembered how Jason had stiffened during the song, "Say No to This."

"I knew about it before so I was prepared. It wasn't easy to watch, but I made it."

"I don't think it should be easy to watch. Infidelity is not a natural behavior."

"At any rate," Libby was ready to move off the subject, "they did a fantastic job. If history had been this exciting in high school, I probably would have gotten better grades!"

"No kidding," Jason laughed. "So you're really okay?"

Libby nodded. "I'm really okay. We *are* going to eat now, though, right? I'm starving!"

Jason grinned. "Just wait and see!"

"Thank you for this, Jason. This has been the most amazing day!"

"I'm glad you're enjoying it."

"You've officially ruined me for the ordinary. I don't think I'll ever be satisfied with normal life again!"

Jason grinned happily and as they made their way slowly out of the theater, once again he placed his hand on her back, gently leading her. She made an effort not to react to his warm hand on her skin and was surprised to feel relief when he left it there until they reached the sidewalk instead of pulling away quickly like earlier. He slipped off his jacket and draped it around her shoulders.

"There's a restaurant just a short walk from here. Is that okay?" She nodded and looked down at the hand that had been touching her back.

"May I?" he asked with his hand out.

She gave him her hand, and immediately their fingers intertwined while he led her around groups of theatergoers who were taking up the sidewalk. He pointed out the restaurant ahead.

"21 Club?" she shuddered at the chill in the air and pulled the jacket tighter with her free hand.

"That's the one. Do you know it?"

She shook her head. "Should I?"

"It's got quite a history. Back in the 1920s, during prohibition, it was a speakeasy. The cops tried to shut it down numerous times, but they could never find any liquor in the place. The owners had a whole system for getting rid of it, which involved sending it down some chutes and into the sewer."

"Really? Wow. That's such a waste!" Libby exclaimed as they neared their destination.

"You'd think so, but the demand for liquor back then was so high, they could charge an arm and a leg for the stuff. Whatever they lost was easily recouped in the next night's sales, and any amount of money is worth avoiding going to jail, I suppose. It's a hot spot now, and they have an amazing wine selection."

He pulled open the door, gave the host his name, and they were promptly shown up the stairs and to a table in the corner of the yellow-lit room. Murals of the city streets filled the walls, and the tables were set with crisp white linens and crystal-clear wine glasses. Libby drew in a sharp breath at the beauty of the room. After Jason had ordered a bottle of wine for them, Libby remembered the old lady from the theater.

"Jason, I–"

"Libby–" he said at the same time. "Go ahead," he insisted.

She hesitated a moment and then said, "I just wanted to ask you a question."

"I'm listening."

"Why did you go to all this trouble for me? I know you can't possibly treat all of your clients like this; you'd never make any money. So please, tell me the truth. Why me?"

Jason sighed and sat back in his seat. "You found me out, huh?" he smiled.

Libby tilted her head to the side. "I'm not sure what you mean."

"You're right. I couldn't possibly do this for the rest of my clients. I called in a lot of favors this weekend, Libby. Partly because I felt like you needed to be spoiled a little bit, and partly because I wanted to be the one doing the spoiling."

Libby swallowed and pulled her hand into her lap. The waiter arrived then, poured a small amount of wine into a glass for Jason to test, and at his approval, filled both glasses and left the bottle on the table. Libby grabbed hers quickly and took a small sip.

"It's completely unprofessional of me, but there's something about you…"

"This stupid dress." Libby rolled her eyes and adjusted it again.

Jason laughed and shook his head. "That's not what I mean, though truth be told, the dress doesn't help matters." He turned his gaze out towards the rest of the diners as his cheeks pinked. "The first time I read your story in the magazine, I knew there was something special about you. I just wasn't sure what it was or what impact it would have on me."

Libby took another, longer drink of wine and asked tentatively, "What kind of effect do I have on you?"

He didn't answer right away but stared at his wine glass, tracing his finger around the bottom of it. "The kind that keeps me up at night," he admitted without making eye contact.

Libby drew in a sharp breath and froze.

"Listen," he said, sounding apologetic. "I know this isn't the time. I know everything is changing and you're probably not sure which way is up or down. So I'm not telling you any of this because I'm asking for anything. I just want to be honest with you. All I want right now is for you to enjoy a carefree evening on the town, hopefully with some good company. That's it, I swear." He leaned forward and stared into her eyes with an intensity that betrayed his words.

"You affect me too," she admitted quietly. "But I'm still legally married. Even if my marriage has basically been over for the last year, I'm still reeling from the shock of it all. But you do have an affect on me."

"I knew it," Jason teased, causing her to blush and turn her gaze to the table.

"Don't make it easy on me or anything." She fidgeted with her napkin and then laid it back in her lap. "What I'm trying to say is that there might be chemistry here, but that doesn't mean that I can or should do anything about it. Besides that, I hardly know you."

"I know," Jason said good-naturedly. "That's why I'm putting all the cards on the table. So that you know I'm not trying anything. I'm not even looking for anything, and I wanted to put you at ease in case I had done anything to make you feel uncomfortable." Jason sat back and put his wine glass to his lips.

Libby shook her head. "Today has been amazing. But thank you for being honest with me."

"Always."

They ordered their food and then Libby excused herself to go to the ladies room. She locked herself in a stall and pulled out her phone. She called Elena and relayed the conversation she'd just had with Jason.

"Whoa, Libby." Elena said slowly.

"What am I supposed to do?"

"Is this where I tell you not to rebound or to dive in with both feet?" Elena asked seriously.

"You haven't even met him, El!"

"I don't have to. The guy has totally won me over!"

"I'm married!"

"Come on, Libby. Your marriage has been over for a long time. Your divorce is weeks away. You're basically a free woman."

"What happened to my friend who wasn't going to let me fall–"

"I'm still here, I just–I'm just not sure that you should overlook this guy! What if he's not around when you are ready?"

Libby rolled her eyes. "You're so not helping! Look, I've got to go or he'll think I've freaked out and left."

"Okay. Call me when you get back to your room!"

"I will, I promise." Libby left the bathroom quickly and returned to the table.

Chapter 17

THE FIVE MINUTES she was gone from the table felt like hours. He should never have been so candid with her. He convinced himself she'd found a back exit and was running down an alley trying to escape him. When the flash of red caught his eye from the direction she'd left, he breathed a sigh of relief, though his hands were a little shaky.

"I ordered some bruschetta as an appetizer," Jason said nervously, watching as Libby sat down.

"Great! I'm starving!" She picked up a piece and nibbled on it. She appeared unaffected and totally composed after his embarrassing revelation.

"So, how does it feel to have signed your first book deal?" Jason asked, trying to steer the conversation in a new direction.

"I'm still in shock," Libby admitted. "I can't believe this is happening."

"Well, just wait until Andrew calls for a second installment." Jason grinned, his nerves easing themselves.

"Second installment? You mean a second book?"

"Don't look so surprised! Isn't this what you wanted?"

"Yes, of course! I just never dreamed it would actually happen!" she said in awe.

"So let me get this straight . . . you quit your day job to write books, but never thought you'd publish any? What have you been doing with your time?" Jason asked curiously.

Laughing nervously, Libby rolled her eyes. "Have you ever heard of Netflix?"

Jason laughed loudly. "Oh yes. It's where creatives go to die. I didn't take you for a binge-watcher," Jason teased.

She grimaced. "I just got so bored when the writer's block set in."

"Why didn't you just go back to work?"

"My soon-to-be former husband didn't want me there. After the miscarriages, everything—"

Libby's mouth snapped shut. Jason saw the discomfort pass quickly over her features.

"I had two, back to back." She shifted in her seat and straightened her shoulders.

"Oh, Libby. I had no idea," Jason said apologetically.

She shrugged. "It's in the past, but if I had to pick something, I'd say that they were the catalyst for the downfall of our relationship. That was when he began to pull away. I can see it clear as day now."

"Did you both want kids?"

She nodded again. "Yes, badly."

"So do you think his actions were retribution or just a knee-jerk reaction?"

"Probably a little of both. When he pulled away, I didn't chase after him. I wonder if things might be different if I had."

"Well, did you try again? Do fertility tests? Anything?"

Libby shook her head. "He wouldn't. He didn't want to go through the drama of it all. He's an all-or-nothing kind of guy. Besides, I was pretty broken after the second one. I didn't want to put my body through all of that, either."

Jason blew out a breath. "I'm so sorry, Libby."

"I suppose it's better that we're going through the divorce without the extra stress of having custody to deal with. I couldn't handle that. Mark was always capable of cheating. Hell, for all I know, he could have been cheating the whole time. I don't care enough to find out though. It's over now and I just need to move on."

Their food arrived then and the waiter set their plates in front of them. Before Libby could touch her fork, Jason opened his mouth and began to pray.

"God, I just want to thank You for the amazing day that we've had today, I'm thankful that You've brought Libby into my life, for whatever reason it may be. I've asked You this before, and I'll keep asking, would You continue to strengthen her and comfort her as she walks this road ahead of her? Thanks for this food and for great company. Amen."

Libby stared at him.

"What?" Jason asked as he picked up his knife and fork and dug into his steak.

"You pray for me?" she looked taken aback.

"Of course!" He took a bite. "Is that weird?"

"I guess not. The only person in the world that ever prayed for me was my grandmother. She died just before Mark and I got married."

Jason raised his eyebrows and kept chewing.

Libby eyed Jason curiously as she cut into her chicken. "I have a question."

"Shoot."

"You're a Christian, and Andrew Green is obviously gay, but you work with him, talk about him like he's your friend, and yet you didn't even flinch when he mocked his mother's beliefs."

"Is there a question in there?" Jason asked teasingly.

"Are you okay with homosexuality?"

He set his fork and knife down and smiled. "Andrew is my friend. Just because we don't share the same beliefs doesn't mean we can't have a functional relationship. We agreed to disagree a long time ago and our friendship works because we don't try to convince each other that the other person is wrong." Jason shrugged his shoulders. "I do, however, pray for him. I pray for him a lot.

"If I can love Andrew for who he is, then that's the best example of Christ that I can be. He knows how I feel, but he also knows that I don't need to throw my beliefs in his face all the time."

"That's really cool, Jason. I know a lot of Christians who don't see things so clearly. My grandmother's church split over some stuff like this when I was in college."

"I'm as big a screw up as the next guy, but I try to live better than that. I fail a lot, but I still try."

"I think you probably do better than you think," she said softly.

He cleared his throat and fidgeted with the fork in his hand. "So, uh, were you close to your grandmother?"

"Very," she said with a smile. "At least until college. When my dad left us, my mom and I went to live with my grandma. She raised me while Mom worked two jobs to provide for us."

"What about your mom?"

Libby shrugged. "Mom was never around, and I think she preferred it that way. We don't keep in touch. I don't blame her for being gone; she did it for me, after all, but my grandma was the one I was closest to."

"What was she like?"

"She was a Christian, like you. She was kind and funny, and she loved me better than I've ever been loved in my life. I miss her all the time."

"So did you grow up going to church, then?" Jason speared the last of his steak and put it in his mouth.

"Yes, I went to church camp every summer and Sunday school every weekend. I sang in the choir–"

"Wait. You sang? In the choir?" Jason chuckled.

"Yes. Horribly," Libby laughed. "It didn't last long!"

"So then if you grew up in the church–"

"I know what you're going to ask. Do I go to church now? The answer is no. I haven't been to church in a very long time."

"Did something happen?"

"College?" Libby shrugged.

Jason nodded, knowingly. "Ah yes. The tumultuous years of higher learning that require us to find ourselves anywhere other than where we've already been found!"

Libby laughed heartily. "That's pretty accurate. Without my grandma there to drag me along, I enjoyed getting to sleep in on Sundays. I felt guilty at first, but then the newfound freedom of another weekend-day was too much to pass up. At that point I was also being pursued by a couple of different guys, and I wanted to have fun, so I told God He was off the hook, that He could look the other way and I'd call Him up when I needed Him."

Jason was taken aback. "You know that's not how He works, right?"

"Yes, I do now, and I'm pretty sure I did back then, but it made me feel better to believe that I'd given Him a pass, that He didn't have to worry about me anymore."

"Are you sure there isn't a small piece of you that still believes that He took you up on that pass?"

"I took my grandmother's death pretty hard. I guess I've always felt like that was God getting back at me for pushing Him away."

Jason cringed. "Remember I told you that I used to think God was punishing me for marrying Leanne? It took a long time for me to realize the truth. I made a bad decision and had to reap the consequences of it." When Libby didn't say anything, Jason floundered. "So, do you still feel that way? Like He's punishing you?"

"I'm not sure. Obviously Mark was a mistake, but I blame him alone for his actions. It's been long enough since my grandma's death that I think maybe it was just something that happened, but I'm still not sure I'm ready to let God off the hook, though I feel like He's been a lot more present lately."

"Yeah?" Jason sat forward, listening intently.

"It's strange, but lately I've just been thinking more about that part of my life and wondering what really happened to it."

"Hmm. Well that's not a bad place to be."

Libby stuck a piece of asparagus in her mouth. "This food is really good, by the way. Like, insanely good."

"I know. I don't come here very often, so when I do, it's a real treat. Which reminds me, I hope you saved room for dessert." Jason wanted to talk more about where she was spiritually, but he could tell she wasn't as open about that subject as she'd been about the rest of her life, so he let it drop.

Libby looked up in surprise as a busboy cleared their plates and a waiter brought out an enormous slice of chocolate cheesecake.

Jason smiled. "Prepare to be amazed." He handed her a fork and watched as she took a small, tentative bite.

"Oh, my gosh," she swooned. "I could bathe in that!"

Jason cringed. "You wouldn't want to eat it after that," he laughed and reached his fork toward the plate.

"We're not sharing this, are we?" She looked up abruptly.

"Uh, did you notice how big the thing is? If it's that big of a deal, you can have most of it." He dug his fork into the side closest to him.

"Most of it? You've never seen me eat chocolate before, mister."

Jason laughed. "If you can eat this whole thing by yourself, I'll sing in front of the whole restaurant."

"Challenge accepted!" Libby grinned and began to chip away at the enormous slice in front of her. It only took about four bites before she laid her fork down, defeated and disappointed.

Jason laughed and took a few bites for himself. "We can get it to go and finish tomorrow on our picnic at the park."

"Picnic?" Libby asked.

"Central Park, remember?"

"Oh! Right! That'll be fun!"

Jason signaled the waiter and asked for a box for the cheesecake and handed off his credit card. "I'll take it home and put it in the fridge."

"Can you be trusted with that?" Libby asked him suspiciously.

"I promise. I won't touch it without you." Jason put his hands up in defense.

"All right, fine. I know I'll probably be craving this thing at midnight though."

"Libby, are you a chocoholic?" he asked, his tone mocking.

She rolled her eyes. "Maybe. Maybe not."

The waiter brought back the check and the box.

"You ready?" Jason asked while he signed the receipt.

Libby stood up and immediately groaned. "Oh, wow".

"You okay?"

"Yeah, just stuffed. I'm glad I didn't finish that cheesecake!"

"Do you want to walk for a bit? I can have the driver meet us anywhere."

"Sure, but not too far; I'm in heels!" She kicked up her foot to reveal her silver heels.

"Okay. I'll call him right now." Jason followed Libby down the stairs to the lobby while on the phone. He stopped at the hostess stand quickly and exchanged some words with the girl there before meeting Libby at the door.

"What was that about?" she asked.

"Oh, I was just thanking them for doing a great job." Jason shrugged.

They stepped outside and immediately Libby squealed at the chill in the air. She began rubbing her arms together against the breeze. Not missing a beat, Jason pulled off his suit jacket and held it out for her again. Libby slid her arms in the sleeves and pulled the jacket tight around her torso.

"Thank you!" She smiled sheepishly at him. "I can't believe that I didn't bring a dress coat."

"Well, I should have warned you about how cold it can get up here."

"It's okay. This dress is ridiculous anyway—"

"I beg to differ," Jason said in a playful tone and fell into step beside her. He felt a strange sense of relief now that they'd talked about what was going on between them. He felt more free to be himself.

The light from the street lamps lit their path on the sidewalk that was much less crowded than it had been before.

"So, I've done a lot of talking tonight," Libby pointed out. "What's your story?"

Jason sighed. "Ah, I thought I was off the hook!"

Libby shook her head. "No way. It's not fair that you know so much about me and I know nothing about you!"

"Not nothing! You know about my divorce!"

"Yes, that's a fantastic thing to base my opinion of you on. Your divorce."

He sighed again. "All right. What do you want to know?"

Libby continued to walk and after a few steps asked, "Why did you become an agent?"

"That's a great question," Jason nodded. "I went to school to be a journalist, actually."

"Really?"

"Yep. My friend Kevin Crane–"

"As in Crane Literary Agents?"

"One and the same. Well, he decided that he wanted to start an agency and asked me to partner with him after college. Kevin had already spent a lot of time in the publishing world. His dad is a business writer in DC, so Kevin grew up with it. He taught me everything I know, and lo and behold, I turned out to be pretty decent at it."

"So how come I didn't meet him this weekend?"

Jason chuckled mischievously. "Because Kevin met an actress about a year ago, tossed the business in my lap, and moved to Los Angeles."

Libby's jaw dropped. "Seriously? So you own the company?"

"Technically. But honestly, I expect him back any day now. You know how Hollywood relationships go." He winked.

Libby giggled. "If the business is yours, why don't you change the name?"

"I just haven't gotten around to it. I also need to hire another agent. I don't have a lot of time for that stuff."

"But you have time to eat pizza and go to Broadway shows and picnic in Central Park with me?"

He paused in his steps. "Touché, Ms. Abbott. Touché. I guess I only have time for the things I want to do."

"That doesn't sound like very good business practice," Libby teased.

"I know. It's really amazing that the place hasn't fallen to pieces yet. I guess I owe it all to Amanda."

"Amanda?" Libby asked, a hint of jealousy in her voice.

Jason chuckled. "She's my assistant. You've spoken with her before. And her lover, Peter, is my intern. That's another situation I should deal with that I've just let go on."

"So you have an office romance going on, too?" Libby raised her eyebrows. "Your life is almost as dramatic as mine!"

"Not by a long shot," Jason laughed. "That sounded awful. I'm so sorry!"

Libby took the jab good-naturedly. "It's fine. Honestly, laughing feels good."

They continued toward the limo where the driver was waiting for them. Jason climbed in after Libby and they rode in a comfortable silence back to the hotel, each lost in their own thoughts.

LIBBY MARVELED AT how much more relaxed she felt at that very moment than she had in a month. It wasn't the wine; she'd tried to dull her aches in the past with plenty more wine than she'd consumed at dinner. She knew it wasn't the city with its busy sidewalks and noisy streets. Jason was the only factor that made sense, and even though her nerves were abuzz when he was around, she felt strangely at ease at the same time. She didn't venture to ponder what it all meant; she just enjoyed being with him.

When they pulled up to the hotel and the chauffeur helped her out, Jason followed her, much to her surprise.

"I'll walk you in," he said.

Libby nodded and stepped into the empty lobby with Jason by her side.

Chapter 18

THE ELEVATOR LIFTED them in silence and opened onto her floor. Libby turned awkwardly but Jason held his arm out, indicating that he meant to see her to her door. She clutched her purse tightly as they walked down the hall. When they got to her door, she slipped his jacket from her shoulders and handed it back to him.

"So, picnic tomorrow?" Jason broached as he slid his arms into the sleeves of the jacket. It smelled like her and he blinked to keep his wits about him.

"I'm really looking forward to it." She nodded.

"Okay, I'll pick up food and meet you here at, what? Eleven a.m.?"

"Sure. Don't forget my cheesecake," Libby grinned.

"I wouldn't risk that. Are you picky about sandwiches?"

"Not really, just no mushrooms."

"Got it. Cheesecake, no mushrooms."

Libby reached into her purse and pulled out her keycard, waving it awkwardly. "Thank you for tonight, Jason. It was definitely one of my top nights ever." She reached out to give him a hug and he stepped forward, pulling her close.

"You're welcome," he said quietly, breathing her in. "I'm glad you had a good time." She fit into his arms perfectly, and the skin on her back seemed to burn against his hands. He wasn't ready for the night to be over yet. If only the timing was different. Reluctantly, he began to loosen his arms from around her.

"Ow!" Libby squealed and grabbed on to him again.

"What?" Jason tried to step back, but felt a tug at his shoulder and Libby held fast to him.

"My earring! It's caught on your jacket!" she cried.

"Okay. Don't move. I'll see if I can unhook it." Libby stood still while Jason tried to free her earring. He inhaled quickly when he realized how close her face was to his. He was a foot taller than her, but she was wearing heels, putting their faces inches apart. Her hands collided with his as they both tried to free the earring.

"There! Got it!" she exclaimed triumphantly, holding the earring up for him to see.

When their eyes met, Jason knew he was in serious trouble. The relief on Libby's face melted away as she stared up at him. Her lips parted just enough for her breath to come out and wash over his face. He couldn't read her expression, but she wasn't pulling away from him. She wasn't reminding him that she was technically still married or even recovering; she was simply staring up at him, and as he placed his hands on her hips, she lifted her chin just enough that he knew she wouldn't refuse him. The underlying tension that had been building between them all day seemed to explode now.

They stumbled backward and he pressed his hand against the wall beside her head. He stared into her eyes, searching one more time for something that would either shut him down or urge him forward.

Slowly, Libby's hands twisted around the lapels of his jacket and she pulled his face closer to hers.

Jason closed the distance between them and pressed his lips gently against hers. A moan caught in his throat as his hand slid around her again, his fingers twisting around the fabric at her back.

It was that red flag, that touch, his fingers around her bare waist that he ignored first. Jason felt her hands slide around his neck and pull him deeper into the kiss, all the while warning bells were blaring in his mind.

Sometimes a guy just has to be a guy, he reasoned and he pressed himself hard against her as her lips opened to his. They were soft and there was still a hint of wine on her tongue.

Her skin was silky smooth against his touch, and he had been so set on leaving without touching her again. He'd mustered up the strength to to leave, but with one look his resolution dissolved. If only she had pushed him away, he would never have made another move, but she kept tightening her arms around his neck, kept kissing him back as if she too had lost all of her resolve. Up until now, he thought he'd been kidding himself that she would reciprocate his attraction.

She dug her hands in his hair, and he liked the possessiveness of that move.

As soon as he had the thought of taking her key and opening the door, the warning in his head was impossible to ignore. Abruptly he pulled his lips from hers and swore, taking a step back.

Immediately Libby let go of him and covered her heaving chest with her hands. She looked terrified.

"I'm sorry, Libby. I'm so sorry." He stepped further from her and began to turn towards the elevators.

"Jason, wait. Don't leave like this." She reached out and grabbed his arm. His eyes were dark when he turned back to her.

"I lost control of myself. It won't happen again," he muttered.

Her eyes seemed to plead with him. "Don't say that," she whispered.

His expression softened, his heart pounding in his chest. "You don't hate me for what I just did?"

"I'm here, too! I kissed you back!"

Jason sighed heavily and raked his fingers through his hair. He slumped against the wall across from her. "I don't know what to say."

Libby gazed at him sadly. "I don't either." She took one step toward him, but he stopped her with one look.

"Please, don't come any closer."

Her shoulders fell, but she nodded and leaned against the door.

"I think I'd better go now." He stood up and stared down the long hallway. He should have let her walk in alone. He should never have come up here with her.

"Okay," She whispered, though neither one of them made any signs of moving.

"Libby, I'm so–"

"Don't. Don't say it." She shook her head vehemently. "It was . . . nice," she sighed.

"Nice?" He looked at her in surprise.

Her cheeks were already flaming red. "It was amazing," she whispered. "But I can't–"

"I know." Jason started down the hallway.

"Will I still see you tomorrow?" Libby called after him.

"Yeah. I'll see you at eleven," he said without looking back.

JASON SENT THE limo away and chose to walk eight blocks in the cold to get to his town home. He needed the chilly breeze to help him simmer down. He argued with himself the whole way home, argued with God, even.

You can stop punishing yourself now, Jason.

Yeah right. That was the dumbest thing I think I've ever done.

It wasn't your wisest move ever, and it was a bit premature, but I can still work with it.

Work with it? I don't want You to work with it! I want You to take this thing away! Take her away! If I can't be with her–

You don't know what I'm doing, Jason. I need you to entrust this whole situation into my hands, and depend on me for patience and self control.

There is absolutely none of that where she is concerned! Jason laughed out loud at the thought of being in control of himself around Libby. He was falling for her, big time. He wanted to be punished for it, to be yelled at. But God had never yelled at him. God had always spoken to him with grace and love. He shook his head and jammed his hands into his pockets.

Ask for help, and trust me. I won't leave you to your own devices if you ask for help.

Then help me! he begged silently.

All right, now we're talking.

Jason shuddered against the cold and took the stairs two at a time to reach his front door.

The ranch hands seemed to linger longer than normal over their meal. Ready to retire for the night, Sarah was anxious for them to leave so she could clean up and head back to her cabin. She was weary after her long day spent driving into town, and the task of unloading the supplies into the pantry had taken its toll on her. Jeremy's admonition from last month flashed to the front of her thoughts as she rubbed at the stiffness in her neck.

"Sarah, there is no need for you to do the work of two men. I don't care if you put your pants on one leg at a time, same as me; this sack of flour," he'd kicked at the huge bag she'd struggled to drag into the pantry, "it's too heavy. You are paying these men, me even, to do this kind of stuff."

"I'll thank you to remember that we agreed that while you'd keep things in order out there," Sarah motioned towards the window, "I'd keep things in order in here. I got the flour in here; I'm a capable woman."

"No argument there. I just wish you'd let me do the heavy lifting."

Sarah had rolled her eyes and then promised to ask for help next time.

As the tension in her neck failed to ease under the pressure from her fingers, she wished that she'd held up her end of the promise and hadn't hauled in this month's supplies.

"Night ma'am. Thank you again." The last of the men tipped his hat to her and left the building, heading back to the bunkhouse where they all stayed. Believing that she was alone, she undid some of the buttons that were cutting into her throat and pulled a few wayward pins from her hair. Sarah began to hum an old tune her mother used to sing and washed up the last of the dishes, stacking them neatly on the shelf. Suddenly she heard a familiar voice.

"Neck botherin' you?"

Startled, she dropped the towel she was holding and turned around to find Jeremy standing at the back of the room. She felt her heart flutter and her blood boil as he walked over to her with that look in his eyes, the one he'd had when they'd kissed.

"Only a little," she said, her voice hoarse.

"Turn 'round," he ordered.

Her heart caught in her throat as she turned back to face the window.

His hand was warm on her skin. He rubbed his thumb and forefinger against her neck gently, searching for the tender spots while his other hand anchored on her shoulder.

"You unloaded all of the supplies by yourself again, didn't you?"

She flinched when he found a knot and cringed against the pressure that he applied slowly.

"I told you, I'm capable. And besides, I thought you were just talking about flour. I didn't buy any flour this time."

His hand stopped moving and rested on her neck, her skin prickling underneath the warm breath of his defeated sigh.

"This doesn't look very appropriate," she whispered.

"Ain't nobody looking," he said quietly.

Sarah turned around, facing him.

He sighed and dropped his hands to his sides. "Sarah, I've tried."

"Jeremy," her voice trembled.

"I've tried and I've tried, but I can't turn this

off. I can't help but think Red'd want you to be
happy. That he'd want you to be loved again. Now I
know I'll never be the man he was, but Sarah, I'm
about done for. If I can't be with you, then I can't
be here anymore. You gotta tell me what you want.
Because if it ain't me, then I'll go right now."

Sarah bit her lip so hard it nearly bled. It only
took her a minute to give in to her desires and tell
him exactly what he wanted to hear.

"I want you," she whispered.

He wasted no time pulling her into his arms. The
familiar scent of horses and sweat overwhelmed her
and she hugged him back, wishing she could hold him
tighter.

"Are you sure?" he whispered into her ear. "Are
you really sure?"

Sarah pulled back from him, started toward the
door, and with one glance and a tug on his hand,
beckoned for him to follow her through it.

Libby closed her eyes as she shut the laptop. She'd hoped that
working would distract her a little, but it had only made things
worse. That one brief moment in the hallway had been the most
passionate moment she'd ever spent in someone's arms. Not even
Mark had ever made her feel that kind of fire. If Jason had held her
any longer, he might have sent her over the edge of the cliff she felt
she was nearing–either that or she would have jumped willingly. She
felt lost and out of control, excited and ashamed at the same time.
There was an odd sense of camaraderie between herself and the
woman she had created on paper, as if the character's story had
foretold the author's. She closed her eyes and trailed her fingers
where Jason's lips had been and then dropped her head into her
hands.

"Oh, God. What am I doing?" She hadn't meant it as a prayer,
but as soon as the words left her mouth she felt a calm course
through her veins. She lay down on the bed and wept quietly.

When tears had finally stopped, she allowed herself to relive
those last moments in the hallway with Jason one more time. Her

heart was beating like a drum inside of her; she wouldn't have been surprised if the occupants of rooms around her complained about the noise. She put a hand over her heart as if to still it, but it pounded on as she remembered the taste of his mouth and tickle of his fingers on her skin. She'd felt the fullness of his body against hers when he'd pressed her against the wall and she had trembled beneath the pressure. She'd never met a man who could retreat at that point, and she was amazed that he had. She was in *awe* that he had, and thankful, too. Her meltdown afterwards had proved to her that she wasn't ready for that, or any of it for that matter. She sighed and pushed her hair off of her face again. She heard a text message beep on her phone.

"Elena!" she cried.

Elena was probably pacing around her apartment freaking out. Libby grabbed her cell phone and called Elena on speakerphone. Suddenly desperate to get out of the evil dress, she changed into her pajamas while the phone rang.

"Libby! Where've you been?" Elena cried when she answered.

"I know. I'm sorry." Libby carried the phone into the bathroom and stood at the mirror, pulling pins out of her hair.

"What in the world happened? Do you know how long I've been waiting?"

Libby sighed and supported herself on the counter with her hands. "He kissed me," she said.

Elena gasped. "He what?"

"You heard me."

"I knew it!" Elena squealed. "What did you do?"

Libby scrunched her eyes closed and hung her head. "I kissed him back."

"*You what?*" Elena yelled.

Fearing that the neighbors could hear her, Libby shushed her friend.

"You what?" Elena repeated just above a whisper.

"I kissed him back, El."

"Shut up!" she hissed, "He *kissed* you? You kissed him back?"

"I know," Libby sighed. She didn't know what else to say.

Elena seemed at a loss for words, too, but finally blurted out, "What was it like?"

"I don't want to relive it again, El."

"You're not getting off the hook that easily, sister!"

Libby grabbed the phone and sat down against the wall beside the sink. She pressed the speakerphone button and held the phone to her ear instead.

"It was a mistake. A very unfortunate, amazing mistake," Libby said sadly.

Elena groaned sympathetically. "I know you didn't want this to happen."

"But I did, El. That's why I kissed him back. That's why he was the one to finally pull away."

"What do you think it means?"

"Exactly what I didn't want to happen."

"What if you're not rebounding, Libby? What if this is just an awesome guy who deserves a chance?"

"I'm in the middle of a divorce, Elena! Why do I have to keep reminding everyone?"

"You don't. I know it, but does that mean you can't be happy? That you can't move on? Things have been over between you and Mark for a long time, Libby. It's just taken the last few months for you to realize it."

"I know. But it's too fast, El."

Elena sighed. "Okay, forget about the kiss for a minute. How was the rest of your night?"

A small smile curved on her lips as she remembered the other events of the evening. "It was incredible. *Hamilton* was incredible," she sighed. "And we went to this amazing restaurant and ate the most delicious cheesecake I've ever had–"

"Better than Cheesecake Warehouse?"

"Totally. Then we walked for a bit outside."

"How did you feel during all of that?"

"Conflicted," Libby said, leaning her head against the wall and stretching her legs out on the floor.

"What do you mean?"

"When I was with Jason tonight, there were moments when things felt so right and so calm, like my universe had finally recovered its axis."

Elena snorted.

"It's lame, I know, but that's the best I can do."

"You're a writer, that's all," Elena teased.

"But then there were moments, like when he'd touch me, when it felt like my blood was going to explode out of my skin." Libby's heart fluttered as she recalled those moments.

"I knew that dress was the right choice," Elena sighed happily.

"I know you're proud of yourself, Elena, but this isn't exactly all fun and games for me over here," Libby pouted.

"You can only deny it for so long, lady."

"Deny what? I'm not denying anything!"

"All of those things that you described to me just now, how you felt all night, how you got goose bumps every time he touched you, why you kissed him back—those are all signs that you're falling for this guy!"

"They're signs that I'm attracted to him. That's it!"

"Oh, Libby. The harder you try to fight this, the harder it's going to be to win!"

"So I'm destined to lose? Is that what you're saying?"

Elena was quiet for a moment. "I want to meet him. Is that a possibility?"

"Well, I'm certainly not going to be inviting him to Dallas anytime soon. I can't deal with this right now!"

"I think I'd be able to figure this out better if he could come and spend some time with us. Just have him come out for a weekend or something!"

"Elena! No! That would just make things worse! He's supposed to be my agent, not my boyfriend!"

"Okay, okay. Fine. Don't invite him out. But I'm going to figure out a way to meet him so I can tell you what I think."

"You're not going to need to think anything because nothing is going to happen. I'm not going to let it."

Just then, there was a knock at the door in the other room. Startled, Libby jumped up and checked that her pajamas were decent. "There's someone at the door. Hang on."

She tossed the phone on the bed while she crossed the room to the door. Her heart was pounding and she hated herself for hoping that it was Jason. She opened the door and was surprised to find a bellboy there with a Styrofoam box in his hands.

"What's this?" Libby asked, confused.

"It was just delivered from 21 Club, ma'am." Libby wondered if Jason had left their box of cheesecake at the restaurant, but then they wouldn't actually deliver it, would they? She took the box, thanked the bellboy and then closed the door. She opened the box quickly and her breath caught in her throat. It was cheesecake all right, but it was a brand new piece, never touched by her fork or Jason's. She looked at the clock on her bedside table, remembering her own words. *I'll probably be craving this at midnight.* The clock read 12:01 am.

"Libby?" she heard Elena yell from the bed where the phone was. Libby snatched it up quickly and sank to the corner of the bed.

"Who was it? Was it Jason?"

"No," sniffed Libby. "It was cheesecake."

Chapter 19

Sarah lay on her stomach, staring out the window across from her bed. With the sheets pulled up under her arms, she let out a shiver as she listened to the quiet night. She could feel the gentle rise and fall of the body breathing beside her. She squeezed her eyes shut and tried to push away the memories of his touch, wanting guilt to overcome her, but try as she might, Jeremy's touch seemed to have seared her skin; she could still feel where his hands and lips had been.

She turned her head slowly to the other side and watched his peaceful sleep. Jeremy said he was convinced that Red would have wanted her to be happy. She knew it was true, but what would her husband have said about the fact that his best friend was the one who was doing the pleasing? She'd never considered Jeremy in any way other than a friend before Red had passed. She'd never needed to let her mind wander; her husband had fulfilled every need she'd ever had.

Her eyes moved from the relaxed face to his chest where dark swirls of hair covered him. She gently placed her hand on his chest and twisted the hair around her finger loosely. Red's chest had been bare. She was surprised that she liked the look of a hairy chest and the feel of it on her skin.

The sheets covering him rustled as he stirred at her touch.

Sarah froze, his chest hair still twirled in her fingers. Jeremy's hand reached to swat at what was tickling him and his hand met hers. Slowly his eyes fluttered open and he turned his face to hers.

She met his gaze, remembering the exhilaration of making love to him. It had awakened something in her that she thought had died alongside her husband in the fields of their ranch. To know that she could still be a real woman, to pleasure and be pleasured—it was more than the widow had believed she would be capable of again.

"Are you okay?" Jeremy whispered, holding her hand to his chest and turning on his side. He propped his head on his arm and pulled her hand to his lips.

"Yes," she whispered hoarsely.

He released her hand and traced his finger down her cheek, pushing away strands of hair that had fallen out of her braid.

"I'm in love with you," he whispered. His hand trailed down her neck and over her shoulder and arm then back up the same way.

Sarah's eyes stung as Jeremy pulled her closer to him and kissed her softly on the lips.

"Tell me again," she whispered and slid her arms around his waist, closing the distance between them.

WHEN JASON WOKE up, the events of the previous evening flashed through his mind and he rolled over, face down in his pillow, and groaned.

"How can I see her today?" He beat a fist into his pillow. He stayed in bed until he absolutely had to get up.

Trust me, Jason.

"I'm trying, Lord. I'm just afraid I'm going to get ahead of myself again and screw this all up!" He was standing in front of the mirror, freshly showered, trying to talk some sense into himself.

Well, if you do, I'll fix it.

Jason chuckled as he ran some product through his hair. "At least I keep You busy." He gave himself a once over in the mirror and then closed his eyes. "I don't know what the plan is here, Lord, but You know my heart. I care about her. Please do what You need to do."

I'll take care of you both. I promise.

Jason took hope in those words, pushed his embarrassing actions from his mind, and left to finish getting ready for his day-date with Libby.

When he arrived at the hotel, a paper bag on one arm and some flowers in the other, Libby was already waiting for him so there would be no grand entrance that day, and he was thankful. The drama of it all–watching her walk in and every head in the place turning to stare–he needed a break from it. Even still, his heart stuttered when he saw her. She was casual in a pair of jeans, Converse shoes, and a salmon-colored hoodie.

How is it that she's gorgeous in regular clothes, too? This isn't fair, Jason thought.

Keep your head, and wait on me.

He smiled as he approached Libby. She eyed the small bouquet of flowers in his hand suspiciously.

"Are those for me?" she asked biting her lip.

Jason sighed and handed them over. "A peace offering?" he said apologetically.

Her expression was forgiving. "That wasn't necessary, but they're beautiful." She brought the flowers to her nose and breathed deeply. "Thank you."

"You can have the concierge put them in water in your room for you."

Libby nodded and walked over to the desk, plucked a pink daisy out of the bouquet and handed it to the woman on the other side. She smelled the daisy again and then tucked it into the ring on the side of her purse as she returned to Jason.

"Ready?" he asked.

Libby held her purse protectively to her chest and nodded, following him through the door. They walked in silence for a few blocks, navigating their way around the people walking briskly in their path.

"Are we walking all the way there?" she asked, glancing wide-eyed at the buildings, billboards, and construction zones that loomed around them.

"Yeah, it's just up there a few blocks. See all those trees?"

"Oh. Okay. Well, I can carry the bag if you need a break."

Jason smiled and kept his eyes forward. "If I don't hold it I'm going to try to hold your hand," he admitted.

Libby bit her lips together and looked the other way, but he could see the color rising in her cheeks.

Finally, Jason worked up the courage to address the issue. "I don't regret it," he said, choosing his words carefully. "But I'm sorry that it happened. Does that make any sense?"

Libby nodded. "Yes. I understand completely."

Jason sighed in relief. "I let the moment get away from me and—"

"Jason, you don't have to explain, really. We were both there; we both experienced the same thing."

Jason nodded and they walked the rest of the way in silence, both of their hands occupied with pockets, purses, or paper bags.

"Here we are," Jason said as they crossed the last street in a throng of people. "Central Park."

Libby paused and looked down the street. Cars and high-rises lined one side and on the other there was nothing but trees and stone fixtures lining the boundaries of the park.

"It's so beautiful," she breathed.

Jason led her on a walkway through the park in the direction of the *Alice in Wonderland* statue, and more than once, she had to ask him to slow down so that she could take in her surroundings.

He tried not to observe her as she marveled over the sights; he was already having a hard enough time keeping his head screwed on tightly. He sighed when she asked him to slow down for the third time.

"Did you have somewhere else to be? Because you certainly don't need to entertain me," she said defensively.

Jason stepped toward her quickly. "No, Libby. I'm sorry. There's nowhere else I need to be."

"Then can we please just take it a little slower here?"

"Yes. Absolutely," he said, even though he wanted to do anything but take things slow where she was concerned. He tried to push the thoughts away and focused his mind on seeing the park through new eyes, as she was. Finally they reached the Alice statue and Libby's smile was infectious. There were children climbing on it, sitting in Alice's lap, and hanging around her neck. The expression on Libby's face was worth the agony it had caused Jason to get her there.

How can I care so much about a woman I barely know? he battled in his mind.

You know her better than you think. Better than she thinks.

"Do you want a picture?" Jason asked, pulling out his phone.

"No," she shook her head. "I just want to be here."

Jason gave her a questioning look. "Are you crying?"

"Sorry," she whispered and wiped her eyes and shrugged.

Jason set the paper bag on the ground and put his hand on her back, thankful that this time there was ample fabric covering it. "What's wrong?"

"It's stupid," she smiled sadly. "I was going to bring my kids here someday." She took a deep breath. "I always felt like the first baby was going to be a girl. I was going to name her Alice, after my favorite children's book, and I was going to bring her here when she was old enough to remember it." Libby shook her head and looked up to the sky, blinking back more tears.

Jason's heart sank. Suddenly his desires took a back seat. "I'm sorry, Libby."

She shook her head again.

"No, I am. I didn't realize this would be so painful." He slid his arm around her tighter and pulled her into his side.

"I'm okay. Just a momentary breakdown," she laughed nervously and wiped her eyes.

"Are you sure?" he asked.

She let out a breath and squared her shoulders. "Yes, I'm sorry. There are just some things that will always hurt I guess."

Jason released her and picked up their lunch again. "Well, I was going to suggest eating here, but if you'd rather find another spot . . ." he trailed off.

"Yeah, I'd like to walk a little more, I think."

Jason nodded and led her away from the statue, back to the path. "So, Alice, huh?"

"Yes. She was my favorite. Alice got to escape from her life for a short time, to this crazy, magical world—"

"But it wasn't always good there. She was in a lot of danger in that place as well."

Libby considered that. "But she overcame. She slayed the dragon and defeated the Queen of Hearts. She won."

"And then she woke up," Jason chuckled. "But it's a hopeful story. You never know what life is going to throw at you. What you will get to enjoy and what you will have to overcome." Jason tilted his head to the side and looked at her curiously. "Do you realize how similar those qualities are to your own life?"

Libby rolled her eyes. "Yes, I know."

Jason pointed to a spot off the path near a pond for them to eat and Libby nodded.

"This is Turtle Pond and that is Belvedere Castle." Jason pointed to the stone building jutting out behind the pond as they sat down.

"It's beautiful. Different than I expected."

"How so?"

"It's smaller," she chuckled. "In a park this size, I thought it would be a bit bigger."

"Oh, it's tiny. Trying to get up the stairs in that place is a nightmare if you're claustrophobic. There are people coming up and going down at the same time, and there is really only room for one person at a time. The view is worth it, though."

"Well, we don't have to go all the way inside, but I'd love to go to that lookout." Libby pointed to the landing of the castle where a number of spectators were taking pictures.

"Sure, we can do that."

Jason set out some plastic containers with sandwiches and chips in them and then sat back and gazed at her with a strange look on his face.

Libby returned the look and picked up half of a sandwich. "What?"

"I'm just wondering what is it that you will get to enjoy in this life and what you will have to overcome."

Libby raised her eyebrows. "I think that's pretty obvious right now!"

"At first glance, yes. Your joy in your book deal, and overcoming betrayal, but I wonder what else there is for you."

Libby squirmed under his watchful gaze. "I don't know what you mean."

Jason shrugged and picked up his own sandwich. "I don't either. I was just thinking."

"Right now, I'd just like to enjoy being here with you."

He took a deep breath and looked away from her.

"Oh! I forgot! The cheesecake!" she exclaimed suddenly.

"Dang it! That was my fault!" Jason slapped his hand on his forehead. "I forgot it!"

"No! I mean last night! The cheesecake, at the hotel," she reminded him.

In all of the excitement before he'd left her at the hotel the previous night, he'd completely forgotten about the cheesecake that he'd had sent to her door. "Oh," he said in a choked voice.

"Thank you."

"I wouldn't have done that if I'd known—"

"I ate half of it," she blurted out before he could finish.

Jason laughed, relieved.

"Look, Jason, I know this is weird. And it seems to get weirder no matter what we do."

"You don't have to—"

"No, just listen. I don't know what is going to happen here," she gestured between them. "I don't know what I want, I don't know . . . there is just so much going on right now. Just like you said, I don't know which way is up or down. I feel like I'm in the middle of a tornado, watching my life spin around me."

"I know," he said quietly, picking at the lettuce on his sandwich.

"But I don't want this to be weird. I like being with you. I don't know what that means professionally or personally. I just know that I don't want what happened last night to be the difference in our relationship."

Jason took a deep breath in. "So do you want to pretend it didn't happen?"

Libby chuckled quietly. "No," she said sincerely. "I don't think I could if I tried."

"But it can't happen again."

Libby nodded. "Not now."

"Yeah, I get it. I got it before, I just—"

"Gave in?"

He raised his eyes in agreement.

"That makes two of us."

"Libby, this isn't normal for me."

Libby grinned. "I didn't think it was. You don't strike me as that guy."

"Well, that's a relief. But even still, I know how painful divorce is, no matter what the circumstances, and it's clear that the timing of all of this is off, but—" he paused and waited for a feeling of assurance in his heart before he spoke his next words. "I'll wait until the timing is right."

Libby's shoulders fell and her face twitched as her already red-rimmed eyes filled with crystal liquid again. "I can't ask you to do that. It could be years–"

"You didn't ask me to." Jason held her gaze. He hadn't set out with any plans to make such promises to her when he'd left his house this morning, but the more time they spent together, the more he wanted to ensure that he would get even more time with her. The promise to wait felt like a no-brainer. Now he hoped he wasn't scaring her away.

Libby broke eye contact after a moment and looked out at the rollerbladers passing by. She laughed suddenly and pointed at a woman pushing a familiar-looking stroller.

"That's not a baby," she told Jason.

"Huh?" He sat forward and peered at the lady. As the sidewalk brought her closer, Jason started to chuckle. "It's funny, isn't it? I've seen that in Times Square before. That's not my idea of walking a dog!"

"There's a lady on my street who does that. Sometimes I look around my city and wonder how I've survived there for so long."

"Explain."

Libby leaned back on her arms and tilted her face to the sky. "I'm not Dallas. I've never been Dallas. It's not all the same, mind you. There are plenty of stereotypes that are true and plenty that aren't. But I don't feel like I fit any of them. I don't know why I'm still there. I mean, obviously Mark was there, but that's almost over now, and the only thing keeping me there is . . . Elena, I guess."

"That's your best friend, right?"

Libby grinned. "Yes. And she'd kill me if I ever considered moving."

"Have you?"

"What? Considered moving? Sure."

"Where to?" Jason asked, hoping that New York had made an impression on her.

She sighed dreamily. "The beach. One of the coasts, I don't know which one."

Jason didn't let his disappointment show. "My parents have a house in Myrtle beach. It's really pretty over there."

"Wow, that must be nice."

"It's nothing fancy. They bought it when they retired. It's got a great view though, and I can go whenever I want—not that I ever do."

"Why? Is it still weird with your parents because you married Leanne?"

"No, not at all. They accepted her as family regardless of all of that. I don't know if they still talk to her or not, but they never distanced themselves from us over that. I'm just too busy to take the time off."

Libby looked thoughtful for a moment and said, "I think I just want a slower pace of life."

"So New York is definitely out," Jason laughed.

"Oh, I could do New York for a bit, but not permanently, unless I could build a house right here," she looked over at him and smiled.

"You could squat at the castle, I suppose. I'm sure there's a nook or cranny somewhere that they don't check regularly."

"Would you bring me turkey sandwiches and cheesecake every day?" Libby asked.

"Sure. You bet." I'd serve it to you on a silver platter if you promised to stay here, he thought to himself.

Libby sighed lazily and lay down on the grass. "What about you? Will you live in New York forever?

Jason's eyes traveled the length of her body and landed on her crossed legs and black Chucks. "I grew up in Colorado, actually. But I've been here since college. I went to NYU."

"Did your wife come with you from Colorado?"

"Yep. Something else our parents weren't thrilled about."

"Is she still here?"

"She is. She works for a fashion photographer."

"Are you guys still friends?"

"Depends on how you define that word. We wouldn't avoid one

another if we met on the street, though."

"I feel like I should thank her," Libby said out of nowhere.

"What? Why?" he asked in surprise.

"Because she sent you my story, right?"

"Oh," he laughed. "That. Sorry. Yes, she did. I thought you were going to say for leaving me and making me available to the rest of the women of the world."

Libby laughed and rolled over onto her side. She propped her head on her elbow and grinned. "I was wondering why all those women kept following you everywhere."

Jason rolled his eyes. "You're one to talk. Every time you make a move every man within a half mile radius freezes and looks your direction."

Libby laughed loudly.

"I'm not joking! Twice yesterday I got the pleasure of watching every man in that lobby stop what he was doing, even if it was talking to his wife, mind you, and watch you walk through the room . . . to me." He finished with a proud tone.

Libby snorted. "You're being dramatic!"

"I'm not! I swear, when you walked out in that dress last night, I thought I was going to have to beat some of them off with my own two hands!"

Libby touched her hand to her heart and fluttered her eyelashes. "My prince!"

Jason shook his head. "I'm surprised you didn't notice."

"Whatever," she sighed.

Jason's hands were sweaty just recalling the vision of her walking towards him in that dress. "No joke, Libby. That dress was hot."

"Too hot," she said, rolling onto her back again, staring up at the sky.

"I wouldn't go that far," he teased.

"You almost did," she said, and then looked over, watching his reaction. She burst out laughing again. "I'm sorry," she giggled. "That was mean."

Jason looked away. "Are you done? We need to go find you a new home up there in that castle," he said, slightly wounded.

Libby smiled to herself and began to pack up her trash. "I was only kidding, just trying to make light of it. Too soon?"

He answered her with a disapproving look.

LIBBY FOLLOWED HIM through a sketchy looking trail, sure that he was leading her away from the castle because there was no sight of it ahead. All she could see were brambles and gnarly trees.

"I promise, it's just up here," he panted.

"Well, at least we're going up," she chuckled. "I'm pretty sure we're lost."

"No, we're not. Although, I have been lost in here before. You just have to remember that every trail leads *somewhere*."

"That's really encouraging." Libby rolled her eyes and waited for Jason to push a branch out of the way and move forward.

Finally they emerged from the trail and the castle was just before them.

"Okay, well, I didn't lose complete faith in you," Libby laughed.

"Your castle awaits!" Jason stepped back and swept his hand toward the brick building behind him.

Libby made her way to the stone railing that looked out over the pond and the spot they'd just been sitting, with Jason following close behind. She felt him brush against her side as he took his place.

"This place is amazing," Libby sighed. "I think I really could live here in this castle."

Jason laughed. "You'd get tired of people traipsing through your home every day."

"Well, naturally I'd have it closed to the public." She turned slowly to enjoy the panoramic view of the city skyline. "I bet this place is beautiful when it snows."

Jason groaned. "You have no idea. I saw a picture of the castle on a winter night once—it's eery and beautiful."

Libby looked up at the tower that loomed over head, the wheels in her brain spinning. "I wish I had my laptop right now."

Jason turned to her, raising his eyebrows. "Are you inspired?"

"Always. There is always a story at work in my brain."

"What is it today?"

"That window," she said, pointing up at the tower. "The east tower window. Except, I don't actually know what direction it's facing but, the window, the castle, snow . . . and a lonely girl . . ." she trailed off as the story of an orphaned royal began to form in her mind.

"Would you two like me to take your picture?" A woman's voice broke through Libby's thoughts. She looked back at Jason, who was staring at her with the strangest look on his face. It was the kind of look that reminded Libby of their indiscretion the night before and made her weak in the knees.

"Yes, thank you," Jason said, breaking their gaze. He handed his phone to the older woman who stood behind them, and then he turned Libby around to face the camera.

"Oh, don't be shy," the woman smiled, "get a little closer!"

Libby drew in a sharp breath as Jason's hand slid around her waist and drew her closer to him. She looked up at him with uncertainty.

"Just smile, Libby," he whispered.

She nodded, turned her head, and plastered on the biggest smile she could make.

"Beautiful. Do you mind taking one of me?" the woman asked after handing Jason back his phone.

"Of course not," Jason replied.

Libby wandered into the bottom level of the castle, trying to collect her thoughts. She moved from wall to wall, looking at the images and historical placards without actually seeing them.

With each minute that passed, Libby found herself wishing she could add five more to their time together. She wished she could stay and spend more time walking through the park, talking with

Jason. That was enough for her common sense to tell her that the best thing she could do was to, in fact, go home.

"You want to go up?" Jason's voice startled her.

She shook her head. "No, I'm good."

"It'll take a while to get out of the park, so we should head that direction."

She nodded and followed him out of the castle and they hiked back down to the main path in silence.

As they approached the entrance they'd walked through on their way in, Jason paused and turned to her. "I hope this has been a good day," he said sincerely.

Libby smiled and reached for his hand. "The past two days have been some of the best I've ever had, Jason." She squeezed his hand, pressing it against her cheek. "Thank you."

Jason took a deep breath, his eyes never leaving hers.

"I wish it didn't have to end. I wish I didn't have to go back. I wish the timing were different."

Jason held up their joined hands. "Is it okay if I hang on to this for a bit?" he asked.

She closed her eyes and nodded. Jason let their hands fall, locked his fingers through hers, and led her out of the park.

Chapter 20

JASON LEFT LIBBY at the hotel to pack while he ran an errand, with the promise of returning within the hour. She quickly zipped her clothes into the garment bag, red dress included, and then sat down on the bed with her hands pressed between her knees.

She had put on a very brave face at the park. She'd tried lightening the mood between them in spite of wanting to plunge headfirst into the darkness she had tasted the night before. She hated how she was feeling, drawn to Jason by a force that she couldn't seem to control, yet terrified of what the future might look like. What if she hurt him? Or worse . . . what if he hurt her?

When he'd asked to hold her hand it made her heart pound, but her chest had tightened in fear as well. She tried to stick with her head on the issue. She needed time; she needed to learn to trust again. Jumping into something with Jason wouldn't allow for any of that, but that was what her heart kept telling her to do.

"Jesus, help me," she whispered finally when her thoughts offered her no refuge. Tears spilled over her eyelids and down her cheeks as she begged. "I'm so tired of this roller coaster! I don't know what to do!"

I'm here. I've never left. I'm right here.

"I feel so out of control. I don't know what's right or wrong, I'm scared of everything that's going on right now! I can't do this on my own anymore!"

You don't have to. Just let go.

"How do I do that?"

Practice trusting in me and know that if you fall, I will pick you up. Remember the way we used to be?

Libby smiled sadly and nodded. She remembered precious moments at camp and retreats, even in the privacy of her room as a child, when goose bumps would prickle on her skin and she would feel the warmth of a love she couldn't describe. She remembered the sound of her grandmother's shaky voice reading the Bible after dinner and how captivating it was to hear her older woman's voice choke up on certain passages.

Let me back into your life, Libby. I love you.

The words were soft and she felt that familiar warmth spread through her skin. She leaned forward over her knees, tears still streaming, and pictured herself holding tightly to everything that was weighing her down. Her fears, Mark, *Red Parks Ranch*, Jason, losing her home—she saw her hand squeezing those things so tightly that her knuckles were white and her fingernails dug into her palms.

Just let go. The words were like a whisper in her heart. **Just trust me.**

I'm trying.

Practice makes perfect. As long as you are trying, I can help you.

I'm trying. I'm terrified, but I'm trying.

I will never leave you, nor forsake you, Elizabeth. I've got you. I'm protecting you.

JASON WAS HAVING his own private conversation while he made his way back to the hotel to pick Libby up.

She needs time, Jason. You gave her that today.

I said I would wait, but that's not going to be easy.

You might be surprised.

It's not that I think I'm going to meet someone else; it's that I'm not sure I can keep myself from pursuing her.

I know that. When you love, you love deeply.

Jason sighed and leaned his head against the headrest of the cab he was in. "I didn't say I was in love," he muttered under his breath.

He wished that the cab driver wouldn't drive so fast. The faster he got to the hotel, the sooner Libby would leave him. If the cab was late, maybe she would miss her flight and have to stay another day.

Jason shook his head at himself and prayed for help again.

LIBBY ANSWERED THE knock quickly. She'd been pacing the room, waiting for Jason to return, tired of being alone with her thoughts. She hadn't considered the fact that after he left her at the airport, she'd be even more alone than she felt now. To her there was no place lonelier than a five-hour plane ride with a bunch of strangers.

"Hi, you ready?" he asked.

She nodded silently as he stepped into the room and picked up her luggage. She hesitated when he stepped back into the hallway and looked at her expectantly.

"What? Did you forget something?"

She shook her head and swallowed and then followed him all the way to the sidewalk.

"Go ahead, I'll load the trunk," Jason said when they'd reached the cab.

Libby slid into the cab and waited for Jason to join her. As soon as he did, she put her hand inside his and refused to meet his glance. They sat silently, hand in hand, all the way to the airport. Libby's heart pounded the entire time, and she prayed that anything would happen to keep her from leaving him. She prayed for a wreck on the freeway, for a malfunction with the plane, for the engine in the cab to explode ... anything to keep her from returning to her reality.

She'd had the best time with Jason and she wished that she could just stay in her wonderland forever. Her return to reality would be much more devastating than Alice's.

They arrived at the airport far too soon. Libby let her fingers slip from Jason's as he got out to retrieve her bags. She battled within herself to make the right choice.

You're not a teenager, Libby. You can't run from anything, and you can't hide out here with him. It'll never work, she told herself.

Jason slung her garment bag over his shoulder, handed her the carry-on, and reached for her hand again. She gave it to him and together they walked into the airport. He waited while she checked her bag and got her ticket and then walked her to the security line where she stopped before entering.

They held each other's gaze and seemed to speak volumes to each other without once uttering a sound.

Kiss me! She pleaded silently. Kiss me and don't let me go!

Jason took a deep breath and pulled her into his arms, squeezing her tightly to him. He tipped her chin up and met her lips softly with his own, holding her face in his hands.

"I'll see you soon," he whispered.

"Thank you," she whispered and kissed him one last time, trying to commit the feeling of his lips against hers to memory.

THE ACHE THAT she felt as miles spread between them was unfamiliar; it was as though she'd left a piece of her heart behind in New York City, just like the T-shirts that had screamed at her from street vendors on the way back from Central Park.

As her plane carried her above the clouds, Libby stared listlessly out the window, letting her tears fall freely. She no longer believed that this was a rebound. Jason was special, and even if her divorce wasn't final, even if it had been such a short time, she no longer cared about anyone but him. Mark was a formality that had to be dealt with. Jason was her future. She knew it as sure as she knew that she was flying in mid-air.

How is this possible? she wondered.

Anything is possible. But you have to be careful with your heart, Libby. It's still fragile.

It's not like I'm going to be seeing him every day. He lives in New York.

Distance can't protect your heart, but it can destroy it. Trust in me. Only I can truly save you.

Libby sighed and watched the clouds beneath the aircraft. "I'll try," she whispered.

JASON WAS SOLEMN as he traveled home. He prayed quietly in his head, asking for wisdom and comfort. There was something extraordinary about Libby that he couldn't call by name, yet it gripped him so firmly that he felt the twinge of it late into the night.

Marrying Leanne had just seemed the appropriate thing to do, even though their families had fought it from the first mention of it. It had seemed like the next step he was supposed to take. But this was different. He ached to have Libby back. He even looked up plane tickets to Dallas online before settling for a cold beer from his nearly-empty fridge.

Jason, you've got to give this to me. You've got to trust that I have this under control. It's the only way it will work out for the best.

"Can you give me a hint about what's going on? Can you tell me if this is it or not? If she's it or not? Can you just do that?"

He was met with silence. "It's so irritating when you do that," he sighed and took a gulp of his beer.

LIBBY'S GRUMPY DEMEANOR surprised Elena as they waited at the luggage carousel in the DFW airport.

"Clearly, that's not it because I'm right here," Elena said abruptly as she grabbed Libby's bag.

"Huh?" Libby looked at her, dazed.

"I was just thinking that you looked pathetic enough to have just lost your best friend."

"Oh," Libby sighed, following Elena out to her car. "That's not it."

"Like I said. So what's up then?"

"I don't want to talk about it. Just take me home, please." Libby's mood continued to baffle Elena. She'd been waiting all day to get more details about Jason, to hear about their day at Central Park, but clearly Libby wasn't in the mood to dish about any of it.

Elena drove in silence, occasionally stealing glances at her friend, wondering what could have gone so horribly wrong.

Libby said a simple thank you when Elena dropped her at her house, and with that, turned her back and walked inside, shutting the door firmly behind her.

Elena sat in the driveway, her jaw open for a good three minutes, half expecting Libby to come back out and tell her everything. When it became clear that Libby wasn't coming back, Elena snatched the keys from the ignition and stormed up to the front door. She tried the knob; it was open so she let herself in.

"Libby! What the hell?" Elena shouted as she ran up the stairs to the guest room. She stopped short in the doorway. Libby was on the bed, facing away from the door, sobs racking her body.

Elena rushed over and crawled onto the bed, putting her hand on Libby's arm.

"Shhh," she soothed. "It's going to be okay."

When Libby calmed enough to speak, Elena broached the question carefully. "What happened?"

Libby sniffed loudly. "Exactly what you wanted to happen."

Elena said nothing but tried to figure out what Libby meant.

"I fell for him. I'm *falling* for him." Libby groaned. "But I can't have him because I'm *broken*. Because I'm tainted and I will always be broken and tainted."

"Whoa!" Elena leaned over and pulled Libby's hair out of her face. "Where is this coming from? Did he say all of that?"

Libby rolled onto her back. "No. He didn't say anything like that."

"Then what in the world?"

"I like him, El. A lot. And that makes me gross because I'm still married and yet I'm kissing another man. And I can't possibly like him for real because I still haven't really begun to deal with the Mark thing, or the baby thing, and I–"

"Baby thing?"

Libby's tears streamed down the sides of her face. "We went to see Alice."

"I'm confused."

"The statue, El. We went to the statue of Alice in Central Park." Libby's face contorted and she began to sob.

Elena's heart fell to her stomach. "Oh, Libby. Why? Why did you do that?"

Libby shrugged and covered her face with her hands. "I was there. I had to."

"Did you tell him?"

Libby nodded.

"Geez," Elena whispered. Of all the intimate things Libby had to share, that was the deepest one. She didn't know what to say. It had been devastating to watch her friend suffer through not one but two miscarriages. Elena had watched Libby close up inside of herself during that time, and she remembered that that was when Mark had really begun to distance himself, as if he didn't know how to comfort his wife. Elena wondered now if he had even wanted to.

"Libby, listen to me. You let him have access to a piece of you that maybe you should have guarded a little bit more," she said carefully. "I think that's why you're feeling so fragile right now."

"I know you're right," Libby sniffed. "But it's more than that. In another life, he's the man I was supposed to end up with. He's the one. How did I miss him?"

Elena shook her head. "It's not too late, but you said something a minute ago that I agree with completely. All teasing aside; you haven't dealt with Mark, or the miscarriages, obviously. And you have to. You have to, Libby. You can't go on like this. It's over and you have to deal with it."

Libby turned over and held on to her friend. "I don't know how. I don't want to be here forever. I want to move on. I want to be happy," she cried.

Elena settled herself into a pillow and squeezed Libby's hand. "I don't know how either, but I don't think this is a bad idea. Cry it out. I won't leave. I'll stay as long as you need me too."

Libby's tears soaked through Elena's shirt, but neither of them noticed. Elena stroked her friend's hair and was patient to let her cry out every last tear.

When Libby's sobs died down and her breathing slowed, Elena slowly slid out from under her friend. Libby adjusted herself and pulled a pillow into her chest. Elena left the room, shut the door quietly behind her, and leaned against it.

"God, I know You and I aren't the best of friends, but this is the most important thing I'll ever ask you: please fix her. Please take care of her. Please give her someone, even if it's not this Jason guy; give her someone who will value her and always call out the best in her, who won't squash who she is. That's all. That's all I want from You."

She sighed and pushed herself off the door, hoping that there was a God up there and that He'd actually heard her prayer.

WHEN LIBBY WOKE up, hours later, the room was dark and the house was quiet. She felt groggy and she had that nap-hangover feeling. She lay in bed for a long time waiting for the fog in her head to clear. Soon the words she'd fallen asleep to began to repeat themselves.

I want to take the broken pieces of your heart and put them back together. I can make it beautiful again. I can make it

new. You asked for help, and so I am here, never leaving you, never forsaking you, but you have to trust my words. You have to believe that I mean what I say. Trust that I'm not going to leave you, that I won't pass you up for someone else, and that you are my favorite.

You've blamed me for years of pain and it's true that I could have stepped in; I could have stopped the wounds from being inflicted, but I promised to give free will. No matter what man chooses, though, my love is unchanging. I want you to have everything. I didn't steal those babies from you, Elizabeth, and I didn't abandon you when you were a little girl. That wasn't me driving away from you. That wasn't me passing you off to your grandmother. But that was me inside of her, teaching you and providing for you, loving you, calling out to you. That was me, loving you through her arms. I've never stopped longing for you. I've never stopped caring. You've always been mine. I promise that I will protect you. Just trust me. Believe me. I love you.

"I know that none of this is Your fault," she whispered to the dark room.

It's not your fault either, Elizabeth.

Libby could have sworn her grandmother was in the room with her, echoing the words that were being spoken into her heart.

"I feel like I've been doing this alone for so long. Even with Mark, I've been alone the whole time."

Think back. When did that feeling start?

Libby traveled backwards in time in her mind. "When I left for college. When I left Grandma's."

Did you think that I'd really leave you? That I'd take you up on that "pass" you told Jason about? Do you really believe that I took your grandmother away to punish you?

Libby was surprised that the answer was yes. She knew better than that, but still, she'd acted as though she'd completely severed ties with the God of her youth, and she had believed that He'd given back what she'd deserved.

When you left and expected me to stay behind, I followed you, as closely as you'd let me. I was always there, always wanting to be closer to you. I was with you when your grandmother came to me. I was there, right beside you, Libby.

"I didn't know that," Libby sniffed, clutching a pillow to her chest.

I want to show you how much I think of you. How I can take care of you. Will you trust me?

"With Jason? With the divorce? The book?"

With everything.

Libby exhaled slowly. "I can't make any promises."

Promise that you'll keep trying.

"I'll keep trying."

THE PHONE RANG early the next morning. Though she'd slept in the early evening the day before, Libby had been more exhausted than she'd realized and had slept the whole night like a baby. The ringing of the phone startled her and she reached over groggily, smashing things around on the nightstand looking for the phone.

"Hello?" she croaked.

"Libby? It's David Daniels. We have a problem."

Libby shot up in bed, wondering what in the world her lawyer could be talking about.

"What's wrong?"

"Can you meet me in thirty minutes?"

"Um, yeah. Where?" She fumbled around for a pen and paper to take down the address and then hung up the phone and scrambled to get dressed and brush her teeth. She didn't have time for breakfast so she shoved a piece of bread into her mouth after tying her hair up in a messy ponytail. She sped to the address he'd given her and pulled into the parking lot of a coffee shop where she recognized her lawyer's black Lexus. Libby jogged over to the car and tapped on the window. He motioned for her to get in on the passenger side.

"This is a little dramatic, isn't it?" she asked suspiciously.

"Did you sign a contract this weekend, Libby?" He asked in an authoritative voice.

She gulped. How did he know that? "Yeah, so?"

"I got a call this morning from your husband's attorney. They know about the book deal and the money. This could be very bad news, Libby." Libby's eyes grew wide and immediately she pulled out her phone to log into her banking website.

"Relax. He didn't take the money, but he saw it and he could take this from you, Libby."

"The book deal?"

"The money."

"But I don't even care about the money!"

"You don't understand. I'm not just talking about the advance. I'm talking about alimony and the house. You could potentially walk away with nothing."

"Oh, my word."

"The question is, how did his lawyer know about it before I did? Total disclosure, Libby! You're supposed to tell me this kind of stuff! Why didn't you show me the contract?"

"What difference does it make?" Libby was scared and confused. "I'm your lawyer!"

"You're my divorce attorney! You charge hundreds of dollars per hour! I had a friend look over it, I–I– " She faltered over her words, not sure of how to adequately defend herself.

"I would have advised you not to sign that contract until your divorce was finalized. This jeopardizes our position. He could take us to court and prove that you are self-reliant and don't need his money."

Libby felt as though someone were sucking the life out of her. "I didn't know that," she whispered, her hand pressed on her stomach.

"This is in his favor, Elizabeth."

Libby felt like a rock had been dropped in her stomach. She still didn't understand exactly what her lawyer was saying, but she knew it was bad. She took a deep breath and clasped her hands together tightly in her lap. "Can you explain this to me, please?"

"It's easy. Because you've signed a book deal that guarantees you a certain amount of royalties, and you've signed with the number one publishing company in the country, Mark could walk away from this marriage with everything."

"But this is Texas! Don't I get a break just because of that?"

"Texas is a no-fault state, Libby. Even if you could prove his affair, didn't you quit your job to stay home and write this book?" Daniels raised his eyebrows at her.

Her jaw dropped. "I didn't think it was going to get published! I wrote a short story for a magazine! I got paid twenty-five bucks for it! Then Jason saw it and– "

"Jason Randall, your agent right?"

"Yes!"

"You should have told me all of this immediately," he scolded her.

"I didn't know it was relevant! It was Mark's idea for me to quit! He didn't want me at the office anymore. He didn't want to see me any more than he had to!" Libby sniffed and leaned her head back against the headrest. "I can't believe this. Finally, something good happens in my life and now it's gone. Just like that!"

"We'll fight it, but I just can't guarantee that we'll win."

"So, we have to go to court?" Libby sighed.

"I don't know yet. I'll call Mark's attorney back and we'll see what he says."

"So, what, I should just turn down job offers because my husband had an affair? I'm just supposed to sit back and be dependent on him?" Righteous anger swelled up inside of her so strongly that she wanted to hit something.

"There's a right way to go about this, but you didn't ask me."

"He could really get everything?"

"Yes. Everything."

"Dammit," Libby hissed.

Chapter 21

DAVID DANIELS LEFT Libby standing in the parking lot of the coffee shop by herself, fuming. She gripped the steering wheel so hard on her way home that her hands were white and aching when she arrived. She stormed into her house and pulled up Jason's cell number.

"I'm so glad you called," he said softly instead of saying hello.

"Jason, did you know?" Libby snapped.

"Uh, what?"

"How could you let me sign that contract?" she fumed.

"What are you talking about?"

"Why didn't you warn me? You've been divorced! Why didn't you tell me to wait?"

"Libby, slow down. What's going on?"

"My lawyer called me this morning, practically screaming at me about our contract with Emerald because Mark already knows about it. How? No idea, but he does. And my lawyer said that because of the contract and the money, Mark could get away with everything. Everything!" She sat down on the third step and dropped her head into her hand.

"Libby, I had no idea– "

"I'm going to lose everything because I got suckered into this deal by a flashy smile and a few butterflies in my stomach." She refused to let herself cry anymore over this man or the one who was trying to ruin her life.

"Wow," Jason said, obviously wounded. "I know you're upset, but—"

"Of course I'm upset, Jason! I'm about to lose everything! Absolutely everything!"

"I get that, but Libby, it's not my fault. I didn't do this!"

"Why didn't you tell me to wait?"

"I didn't even know it was a possibility! Do you still have a bank account together? I mean, I don't know what I could have done to prevent this!"

Libby swore under her breath and dropped the phone into her lap. She knew it wasn't Jason's fault. In all of the excitement of signing a book deal, she had deposited the check into the account she still shared with Mark, rather than the new one she'd set up a few weeks ago. That had been one hundred percent her stupid mistake.

Overwhelmed with shame by the way she'd accused him, she groaned loudly and put the phone to her ear again. "I'm so sorry. Oh Jason, I'm so sorry," she cried.

Jason sighed in relief. "It's okay. I understand."

"No, it's not. I'm sorry. I didn't mean what I said," she trailed off, biting her lip so hard she was afraid it would bleed.

"Are you sure?"

"Yes. It was thoughtless and mean, and my anger just went to you because you're the only person who really has the power to hurt me right now."

"Geez, no pressure or anything," he sighed.

"It's just proof that I'm not ready for this. The first sign of trouble and I blame it all on you."

"I'm not Mark. I would never treat a woman like that, even if I didn't love her anymore. And aside from that, I'm a businessman, Libby. This is my job. I don't play."

"I'm so sorry, Jason. I feel horrible."

"Don't worry about it," he said, but his tone was guarded.

"What am I going to do?" she sighed.

"Have you talked to him yet?" Jason asked.

"I just came back from meeting with my lawyer."

"Mark. I meant, have you talked to Mark?"

"No way," Libby said adamantly.

"I know that sounds like the worst thing in the world right now, but just think about it."

"If I never speak to him again, it'll be too soon."

"It won't be easy, but it might help. You decide, but if you're asking my advice, that's it."

"What if it doesn't help? What if it makes things worse?"

"Then you have your advance money to get you through until the book goes on sale."

"I might be three hundred pounds the next time you see me," Libby sulked.

"What? Why?"

"Because I'm going to be surviving on ramen and macaroni and cheese."

"You sound more like yourself now," he chuckled.

"Jason, I'm so sorry."

"Stop apologizing. It's okay. You're allowed to overreact at least once a week right now. Just don't pick me as your punching bag every time, okay?"

Libby smiled sadly. "You forgive me? I swear I didn't mean–"

He sighed. "I know. And I know that you're not ready for this. Sometimes I even wonder if I'm ready for a relationship. There's no harm in waiting."

She shook her head. "Sometimes I think you're too good to be true, like you're a dream or something."

His tone perked. "Oh, I like the idea of you dreaming about me," he teased.

Libby's smile finally returned and she shook her head. "You're kind of relentless, huh?"

"I don't mean to be," he said sincerely.

She took a deep breath. "You really think I should try to talk to him?"

"I really do."

"I'll think about it," Libby sighed, defeated.

"Keep me posted?"

"Yeah. I've got to go figure out what to do now."

"Okay. I'll pray. It'll be okay, Libby. I know it."

"Thanks. I hope you're right."

Libby sat on the stairs for a long time after hanging up, questioning the promise she'd made late last night before falling asleep for the night.

"If this is what Your plan is, I'm out!" She looked to the ceiling accusingly.

Trust me, Libby. Just trust me.

She sighed and closed her eyes, waiting for the answer to come to her. Jason's suggestion played on repeat in her head.

Libby reluctantly pulled up Mark's phone number and hit the text message button. "Can we talk?" she typed. She held her finger over the send button for a moment. "Here goes nothing," she sighed and pressed the button. She stood up, not willing to sit around and wait for his response. She went upstairs and began to unpack her luggage from the weekend. While hanging up the red dress in the very back of her closet, she heard her phone chime twice.

The first message was from Daniels. It read: "Next meeting has been pushed up," and he listed the time and the meeting place. Libby's stomach knotted. She didn't know if the change in time frame was good or bad. The other text was from Mark and said: "Yes. Our appointment has been moved up. Meet me there thirty minutes early."

She didn't like the way he took control of the situation, but at least he'd agreed to meet her. She typed the details into the calendar on her phone and then went back to unpacking, trying to come up with a decent defense for her meeting with Mark, which was now only a week away.

"At least maybe this will all be over with after that," she said as she checked the zippers in the garment bag one last time before returning it to the back of her closet. Something crinkled against her fingers. Puzzled, she pulled on the material and was surprised to find a small package in her hands. She unwrapped the white paper to find a chain with a pendant on it. She turned it slowly in her hands and gasped. In her palm sat a bird's nest made out of craft wire with two round beads in the middle and a small bird attached at the top. She touched the beads gently and a tiny piece of paper slipped out of the wrapping. She bent to pick it up and unfolded it slowly, her eyes prickling with new tears.

"Libby, I saw this and immediately thought of you and your babies. I believe the Father's promises are true, and that He has a plan. He has never left you. –J"

Libby closed her hand around the pendant and squeezed her eyes shut as she sank to the edge of the bed.

"Oh, God," she whispered. She held the necklace to her heart and remembered back to that horrible day in the bathroom, all by herself, losing her first baby.

I was there, Elizabeth. I was there with you. You weren't alone. You were never alone.

"He wasn't here when I needed him," she sobbed. "He was never here when I needed him!"

But I always was. Even when you didn't know it, I've always been here. I'm here now and I'm holding you in my arms. I'm here.

"I need You," she cried. "I need You more than I ever have."

I will always be right here.

Libby wrapped her arms around herself and slid down to the floor, leaning against the bed, envisioning herself opening her hands and releasing the memories of the babies she'd lost years ago, releasing the pain and disappointment.

She opened her eyes after a long time and looked up at the ceiling, feeling as though her lungs had stretched. She breathed in deeply and touched her chest as it rose with life-giving oxygen.

"Thank You," she whispered.

Eventually she pulled herself up off the floor and then examined the pendant again, overwhelmed with Jason's thoughtfulness. She picked up her phone and dialed his number.

"Hey," he said hesitantly.

She hiccuped before a word left her lips. "I found the necklace," she whispered.

His sigh was long and thick with meaning.

"I'm so sorry I yelled at you," she said, her voice cracking.

"You don't have to apologize anymore, Libby."

"I feel terrible though. How could I think—"

"Hey," he said, interrupting her. "Don't think about it again. I'm glad you found it when you did. I hope you like it."

"I love it."

"Good." He sounded relieved. "I thought it was perfect for you."

"It is. It means so much to me."

After a pause, Libby cleared her throat. "Well, I just wanted to say thank you, and let you know that I'm meeting Mark next week before our settlement appointment."

"I think that's the right thing to do."

"Okay, I'm going to let you go. It's been a really exhausting day."

"Bye, Libby."

"Bye," she whispered.

She slipped the chain around her neck and left the luggage on her bed. She needed the peace of her garden.

A few minutes later, with a fresh cup of coffee in her hands, Libby stood in front of her precious roses, staring at buds that were just beginning to birth beautifully-colored petals.

"I wish life were that easy. Wake up in the spring, look beautiful for a few months, and then die."

Now you know there is much more to it than that. Those bushes have to be watered and fed and pruned and cared for.

"Yes, but I do that. The flower doesn't have to do anything but exist. I take care of it."

That's what I want for you, Libby. I want you to simply exist and let me take care of you. You've been so busy trying to fend for yourself, to take care of yourself, when it's really my job.

Libby lifted her steaming mug to her lips and closed her eyes as she sipped. "I let go of the babies today. That's a start, isn't it?"

It's a beautiful start. But there is more.

"It's hard to have to keep letting go. This is my life. These are the things that hold me together." She took a few steps back until she felt her bench behind her calves and then sat down slowly.

These are the things that I dreamed for you, things that I put into motion for you. But I am the one who holds you together.

"I don't understand how any of this could have been in Your plans for me," she sighed.

The pain, the hardship, that's not what I want for you, but the beauty in it all is when you allow me into those wounds, and you let me heal you, you let me make something beautiful from the rubble. My promise is that I am here, always. Nothing you can do will turn my love and my eyes away from you! I'll never leave you–

"Nor forsake, I know. I remember."

None of this is beyond the realm of my goodness. I can use all of these things to give you the best life, the life that I want you to have.

"But he ruined that life." Libby sniffed and cupped both hands around her mug, seeking comfort in the warmth of it.

A layer of grey clouds started to roll in above her, and she was struck with the absurdity of her last sentence. I guess one man can't ruin Your plans, can he? she asked silently.

Not even a thousand men. My desires for you are insurmountable.

Libby felt a squeezing in her chest where a small seed of hope sprouted. She grabbed hold of the nest around her neck and rubbed the beads with her thumb. She had a question; one that she was afraid might undo everything the Lord had just spoken into her heart.

"Was I supposed to marry him?" She felt a drop of rain on her shoulder and she turned her eyes to the darkening clouds above her as a shiver ran through her body. She wasn't sure if it was from the dropping temperatures or the thick supernatural presence that she felt surrounding her.

"Did I make the wrong choice?" she asked again, letting the necklace drop to her chest.

You made a commitment to love and cherish a man, and you stood by it. The mistake was his when he broke that commitment to you.

"But what if– "

What if's are a dangerous playground for the mind. Don't waste time there. There is no going back, only moving forward. I am with you, I am for you, and I'm going to take care of you. Don't spend another minute wishing you'd done anything differently. Just move forward and let me go with you.

She looked up to the sky, her eyes filling with tears as goosebumps raised on her arms. "I need You, Jesus," she whispered. "I know I'm going to keep screwing up and I probably won't do this right, but I need You."

You don't have to do anything. Let me do it.

The rain started to come down heavier; she felt drop after drop land in her hair and splash in her coffee.

She grabbed the necklace again. "Letting go of them was the hardest thing I think I've ever done," she whispered. "But I did it. The rest shouldn't be that hard, right?"

Why don't you try?

She took a deep breath and brought the pendant to her lips, kissing the beads slowly. "It's Yours. All of it. Over and over again, I give it to You. The divorce, the book, Jason, Elena, this house, the money, everything—it's all Yours," she whispered.

Libby felt as if an enormous weight had lifted from her shoulders as the rain poured down on her. She set her coffee cup down on the bench and stood up with her arms outstretched and her head lifted to the sky. She didn't care that the rain was freezing and that she was getting drenched. There was too much peace in the downpour for her to think about trying to escape it.

Jason, back at the grind in New York, was having a hard time focusing on the resumes that Amanda had presented him with that morning. His self-indulgent weekend with Libby had cost him not only a few hundred dollars (21 Club had been a bit of a splurge), but also some valuable time in the office when he should have been catching up on piles of work. As his eyes took in the list of emails in his inbox plus the printed manuscripts on his desk, he knew that he couldn't go on much longer by himself. He swore at Kevin Crane in his head and had to fight the urge to tip his desk over and walk out.

Where would you go?

You know where I would go, Jason thought.

She isn't ready for you.

I know that. That's why I'm not going. But, God, I need some help here too. I'm drowning under this mess.

Stop procrastinating and hire someone.

I know. I'm trying.

Focus your thoughts, Jason. Daydreaming isn't getting you anywhere.

I can't help it. I want to–

I know what you want, but I also know what you need. Focus your attention.

Jason sighed and hunched over the resumes again, pushing every thought of Libby out of his head.

By the end of the day he'd set up three interviews for the next day and had Amanda shut down the submission page on their website temporarily. There was too much work already and he hated throwing away people's hopes and dreams without even looking at them. He'd also made another important decision. He walked past Amanda's desk and into the conference room where Peter was set up, stacks of manuscripts stacked in heaps on the table.

Peter stood up immediately, knocking over one of the stacks. "Sorry," he muttered and quickly righted the papers.

"Peter, we both know this isn't really working out," Jason started.

Peter's face fell. "But, Mr. Randall, look, I've got these all divided up into rejects, and then genres, and from there killer plot lines and, would you please just take a look?"

Jason grinned. "I meant that the conference room is not exactly the best place for you to office out of."

Peter looked confused. He pushed his glasses up on his nose. "Uh, what are you saying?"

"Tomorrow morning when you come in, why don't you set up in the office next to mine?"

"Are you hiring me?" Peter's face turned pale.

"Only part-time to keep doing what you're doing. If things progress, we'll talk again in a few months. I am going to hire a full-time agent in the next week or two, but I'd like you to get some more experience in the field before I take that step with you."

"In the field?"

"Consider yourself my shadow," Jason said somewhat reluctantly. Peter hurried out from around the conference table to shake Jason's hand.

"Mr. Randall, thank you so much! Thank you! I promise I won't let you down!"

Jason nodded and recoiled his hand after Peter had nearly shaken it right off. "It's Jason now, and you're welcome."

He turned and walked back by Amanda, who was holding her hand to her heart and mouthing the words 'thank you' to him.

Jason rolled his eyes at her. "Hey, would you please get the process started on changing our name?"

Her eyes grew wide. "Really?"

"Yep. It's my company now, right?"

She grinned and nodded. "Why now?"

Jason took a moment to think before answering. "I've been stuck in the mud for too long. It's time to move forward."

"Does this have anything to do with Elizabeth Abbott?" Amanda grinned.

"It has to do with me needing to get my life back into a forward motion."

"And with Elizabeth Abbott, right?"

Jason ignored her jab and picked his satchel off of the floor by his office door. "I'll see you tomorrow, Amanda."

"Good night, Jason," she sang.

He walked to the elevators and tucked his hands in his pockets while he waited.

So what if it does have to do with her? He thought. I don't want to sit around and let life pile up on me anymore like those manuscripts on my desk. I need to be productive. I need to move. forward.

You need to keep your mind off of her is what you're saying.

Yes, but all of these things are things I've been needing to do for a while.

And now she's the motivation to get them done?

Is that bad?

I know your heart, son. You're moving in the right direction.

He sighed with relief.

So how are you going to rule your thoughts when you're at

home?

Jason pursed his lips to the side as he stepped into the elevator. "Crap," he whispered. He hopped back off the elevator before the doors could shut and jogged back into the office.

"I thought you left!" Amanda said, her eyes following him through the door to his desk. She watched as he shoved a stack of manuscripts into his satchel.

"I forgot some things," he said, frustrated, then he left the office again, muttering unintelligible words under his breath.

Chapter 22

Jeremy had never been happier. His days were spent working the ranch and thinking about Sarah while in the evenings he was by her side, fulfilling any number of wishes that he'd had about her during the day. Whether it was helping her with chores after dinner or caressing her skin under the moonlight that shone through the window of her cabin, Jeremy felt complete just being in her presence, knowing that she wanted him there.

He knew he would always pale when compared to his predecessor and that Sarah would probably never love him as much as he loved her, but he felt that he could do right by her, that at least he could love her in a way that no one else who was still alive could.

He had hope that one day they could love each other equally, but right now he needed to love her more than he needed her to love him in return. He told her often how he felt, even though she never said it back. He didn't push her; he was just thankful to be with her.

Libby shook her head. "Oh, Jeremy," she sighed as her fingers hovered over the keyboard. "You have no idea what you're getting yourself into. Can't you see she's still broken? I wish I could make you see. She's not ready for this; even though she wants it, she's not ready. You're moving too quickly. Unfortunately, if I tell you the truth, then the book will end and no one will buy it. I'm sorry, Jeremy."

The similarities between her life and her book continued to unveil themselves, and she prayed that her fate hadn't been sealed when she'd written this book the first time, years ago.

Sarah was terrified at the feelings that were surging inside of her, especially as Red's birthday approached. She had found such comfort in Jeremy's touch, in his presence in her life, but she felt guilty for needing him, for wanting him. She was glad when he left early in the mornings for work. She spent the days trying to find forgiveness and justifications for her feelings and actions, and by lunchtime every day, she was glad that the cookhouse was full of people and that there was no time for stolen glances nor whispers of affection. She would spend the rest of the afternoon battling within herself, but inevitably, every night as she cleaned up the leftovers and felt his gaze on her while he smoked his pipe near the fireplace, her skin would warm at the mere thought of his touch and she would hurry through her work in anticipation of his love.

The closer it got to Red's birthday, however, the more intense her battle became.

As she was washing the last of the dishes one night, she felt his arms slide slowly around her from behind and he kissed her neck. She tensed in his embrace, goosebumps rising on her skin.

"I love that," he whispered, his finger trailing over the bumps.

She tried to shrug him off. "I hate it."

Jeremy took her hand in his and removed the plate she was washing. He spun her around and pressed her against the sink.

"Jeremy, someone is going to see!"

"So let them!" He leaned in, but she dodged his attempt.

Slightly wounded, he pulled back and gave her a searching look. Immediately he released his grip on her wrist.

"What's wrong?" He stepped back.

Sarah shook her head. "Nothing. I just don't want anyone to see us. You know that."

"What does it matter? I love you, Sarah. I'm pretty sure they all know that by now—"

"What do you mean?"

Jeremy gave her a knowing look. "They know, Sarah."

Her breath caught in her throat and she crossed her arms.

"Listen, I want to make this right between us," Jeremy pressed up against her again, putting his hands on her arms. "I want to ask you something," he said with a smile.

Sarah gave him a strange look, and then her face paled.

Jeremy chuckled and kissed her forehead. "Marry me, Sarah. Be my wife."

"Get off of me," she said quietly.

Confused, Jeremy stepped back again, quickly. "Did you hear me? I just asked you to—"

"I heard you," she whispered, her eyes filling with tears. "I think you should go." She turned her back to him again but didn't move otherwise.

"Sarah! I love you!"

"I'm already married, Jeremy. How could you do this to him? How could you?" she cried, displacing her own guilt onto him.

"Me?" he cried. "You were the one who welcomed me into your bed. How could I? He's gone, Sarah. He ain't coming back to beat you for your unfaithfulness. He's dead!"

"Get out." Sarah clenched her fists together, eyes closed.

Jeremy's shoulders slumped forward. "Sarah, please—"

"I told you to leave," she said again.

Jeremy swore and stormed through the door, letting

it slam shut behind him. She leaned over the counter
as tremors shook her body and sobs came tumbling from
her lips. She knelt on the ground and covered her
face with her hands.
  "Happy birthday, Red," she cried.

"SO, HOW DO you feel about tomorrow?" Jason asked. He adjusted
the phone on his ear, stretched his legs out on the couch, and stared
at the chipped ceiling above him.

"I'm nervous. I haven't heard anything from my lawyer about it,
so I have no idea what to expect. And of course, I'm terrified about
meeting alone with Mark. I don't even know what I'm going to say,"
Libby sighed.

"Just be honest."

"Yeah, about what, particularly? That I hate him? That he ruined
my life? That this book deal is the only thing I have to look forward
to? That it's the only hope I have to get my life back on track?"

Jason resisted the urge to point out that there might be a few
other things to look forward to, himself being one of them. "Maybe
just that last part," he chuckled. He heard a splash as she sighed.

"What was that? Are you—tell me you're not in the bath?"

"Yeah, why?"

Jason groaned. "Baseball. My grandmother, My grandmother's
cigarette breath . . ."

Libby laughed. "I don't know what you're doing."

"Never mind. Next time lie to me." Jason opened his eyes wide
and did his best not to picture her in his mind.

"Do you want me to get out?" she giggled.

"No! For the love of all that is holy, don't get out!" He slapped
his hand over his eyes.

She laughed at him. "Sorry. I'm actually in Alaska wearing nothing but a parka and Eskimo boots."

"Not. Helping."

"Okay. Let's talk about something else. How is your new hire working out?"

"She is a life saver. If there were no hope with you, and she weren't forty-five and married to a police officer, I'd totally marry her."

"Forty-five isn't that old, and who said there was any hope with me?"

"Hmmm. Now where did I get that idea?"

"We're supposed to be talking about work. Remember?" Her voice sounded a little nervous.

"Right. Helen is great. She's so much better at this than I am. I'm sure she's wondering why I didn't just hand over the company."

"Another name change in the future?"

Jason grinned. "No, I think The Randall Agency will be around for a while."

"And what about Peter? How's he doing?"

"Oh, he's irritating as heck, but he's learning. I'll be glad when I can finally set him loose." Jason rolled over and snagged a piece of pizza out of the box on the coffee table.

"How long do you think that will be?"

"He's still green. Too concerned with pleasing me and not making mistakes," he said between bites.

"So he's pissing you off and screwing up all the time?"

"How'd you guess?" Jason laughed. "I'm taking the day off tomorrow, though. Like, a real day off. I'm not meeting anyone or reading anything . . . I'm not sure what I'll do with myself."

"You could fly down here and help me pick up the pieces of whatever's left after Mark gets through with me," Libby sighed.

"That's very tempting," Jason said carefully.

"It's just not fair that he can do this. He gets to abandon his marriage, scot-free, and take everything from me in the process?"

"I really don't think that's going to happen. He would be stupid to try that. I honestly can't imagine a judge siding with him in that fight."

"I hope you're right. Darn it, I keep coming back to this. I'm sorry."

Jason cringed at the sound of the water splashing. He balled his hand in a fist, remembering what her skin had felt like under his touch, how her body had melted against him in the hallway of the hotel.

"It's fine. I've got to go, though," he said quickly, sitting up and tossing his pizza back in the box.

Libby sounded surprised. "Okay. I guess I should, too. It was nice to talk to you, though. I like our texts, but it was really nice to hear your voice," she said sweetly.

"Yep. You, too," Jason's tone was clipped. He needed to get off the phone immediately.

"Um, so, bye?" Libby said, confused.

"I'll call you tomorrow. Bye." Jason hung up the phone quickly and tossed it on the couch as far away from him as it would go. He let out a long, low groan.

LIBBY STARED AT the phone in her hand where the call information blinked at her. What had happened to Jason? He suddenly couldn't get off the phone fast enough. She wondered if maybe there was something he wasn't telling her. Maybe he'd realized that waiting for her would be too difficult–but then, he'd been so flirty on the phone with her. Maybe it was a ploy. Maybe he really was a player. As she toweled off, she scolded herself for letting her heart run with the idea of him so quickly.

Be careful with your assumptions, Libby.

"I also need to be careful about just throwing myself into something! I don't want to get hurt again."

Remember that all you have to do is exist. I will water, feed, and prune.

She sighed. "I'm still going to be cautious." When there was no response to that, she continued changing into her pajamas and tucked herself into bed. "That's just being wise, right?" she asked the empty room. "Oh, never mind," she sighed.

ELENA NAVIGATED HER way through the city to David Daniel's office with a very nervous Libby in the passenger seat beside her.

"Thanks for taking the day off for me, El. I couldn't do this alone."

"I wouldn't dream of letting you. I'm glad things are slow right now so that I can be here."

Libby exhaled slowly. She toyed with the pendant around her neck, sliding it around on the chain nervously.

"Any idea what you're going to say?"

Libby shook her head. "I thought about appealing to his emotional side, but then I remembered that he doesn't have one."

"And Jason thinks you should just be honest?" Elena asked with a mischievous grin.

"Yes. Full disclosure."

Elena whistled and shook her head. "He doesn't know Mark."

"Well, it's not like I can deny the book deal. They have our bank statements, even a copy of the check from Emerald."

"That's so shady," Elena sighed.

"Not really. The account was still in both of our names."

The car came to a stop and Elena looked at her friend with an apologetic look. "This is it."

Libby looked up, surprised that they'd already arrived.

"Do you want me to come in or wait out here?"

"I don't have a clue how long this is going to take. I could just text you when we're finished."

Elena glanced around the area. "There's a Starbucks over there," she pointed. "I'll just hang out there. I've got my computer in the back."

"Okay. Thanks, El." Libby gathered her purse and gripped it with both hands. "Here I go." She got out of the car and walked with long strides to the front door of the looming skyscraper.

"Help me, Jesus. Please help me."

I am right here. No matter what happens, I'm here. Keep your hands open, and trust me.

"I promise to try!"

She took a deep breath and pushed through the doors. She gave the receptionist at the front desk her name and was shown to a conference room where Mark and her lawyer were already waiting. There was a small stack of white papers on the table. Libby looked around, confused. Mark's face was about the color of the paper on the table, and Daniels was standing up, closing his briefcase.

Maybe this is good? she thought suddenly feeling hopeful. "Um, I thought we were meeting privately first," she said nervously.

Daniels raised his eyebrows at her. "You are. We just finalized the papers. I think you'll be very pleased," he said.

She gauged his expression carefully. His eyes were wide and bright; he was obviously very happy about the way things turned out.

"I don't understand. Where's your lawyer?" she asked Mark.

He shook his head. "I don't need one anymore."

She glanced between the two men trying to understand.

"I'll give you two some privacy," Daniels said and left the room.

"Sit down, Libs."

She resisted the urge to roll her eyes at him and sat down slowly, her stomach in knots. "What's going on?"

"I don't want to fight," Mark said blankly. He refused to make eye contact.

Libby sat back down and searched his face. "What exactly does that mean?"

Mark pointed to the stack of papers in the middle of the table. "All you have to do is sign and it will be all over today."

"Hold on just a minute—what do you mean that you don't want to fight? What am I signing my name to?"

Mark sighed and stared at the table. "The house is yours in lieu of alimony."

"And you don't care about my book deal?"

He shook his head. "I'm happy for you," he said blandly.

"I don't understand. A few days ago I thought you were going to take everything from me. I thought—"

"Bria's pregnant," he interrupted her.

Chapter 23

THE WORDS HIT Libby like a sack of bricks. She reached for the nest around her neck and squeezed it in her fingers. "What?" she whispered.

Mark still couldn't look at her, his face ashen. "So if you don't object," he motioned to the papers again, "then it can all be finished today."

She was having difficulty computing everything he'd just said. A lump rose in her throat as she flashed back to the sight of her bloody hand in the bathroom; the pain had been unbelievable. Libby shuddered at the memory and tried to find some sense of understanding about what was happening. She felt the chain around her neck snap and the tension went slack. Her hand with the pendant still closed in it fell to the table like dead weight.

She knew that her face was betraying her, exposing every emotion she was feeling. That was the moment that he finally looked at her, and she saw a reflection of her own pain in his eyes. As if he couldn't stand to be in the same room with her any longer, he bolted out of his seat.

"Just sign and leave them there," he said quickly and left her alone in the room.

Her eyes darted from side to side. What am I supposed to do

now? she wondered. She couldn't cry; she couldn't breathe. She swallowed the lump in her throat and looked down at the pages in front of her.

Sign them.

Slowly, without being fully aware of what she was doing, Libby picked up the pen and scrawled her name everywhere that the stickers directed her to. When she was finished, she laid the pen down, pushed herself up slowly from the table, and left the room.

With a knot the size of a melon in her gut, Libby walked out of the building, the broken necklace dangling from her fingers. She located Elena's car and walked up to it. The door was locked no matter how many times she tried to open it, yet she pulled and pulled on the handle. Then she began to beat on the door and pound on the window, grunting and crying, tears pouring from her eyes. All she wanted to do was get into the car and shut out the rest of the world.

By the time Elena covered the distance between Starbucks and the parking lot, Libby was wailing and sliding down the side of the car onto the pavement.

"Libby, what the hell happened?" Elena rushed to Libby's side. She knelt on the ground and pushed the blonde tendrils out of her friend's wet face.

A few people stopped and asked if they needed help, but Elena shooed them away quickly. When Libby's sobs finally slowed, Elena asked again.

"What did he do? Is he trying to take it all?"

Libby shook her head. "He already has everything," she whispered through hiccups.

"What do you mean? What did he do?"

Libby felt utterly defeated. She just wanted the world to stop spinning so that she could get off the cruel ride. She felt cold and alone. She pulled her jacket tighter around her and swallowed a sob. In a shaky voice, she explained to Elena what had happened when she'd walked into the office to meet Mark.

"But that's good! I don't understand! He gave you everything! Why are you so upset?"

"He's not that kind, Elena. There's a reason," Libby sniffed.

"Well, What is it?"

"Bria," Libby whispered. "Bria's pregnant."

Elena seemed as bowled over by the news as Libby had been. She sat back on her heels and covered her gaping mouth with her hand. "No," she whispered as tears filled her eyes. "No."

THEY DROVE IN complete silence back to Libby's house. Elena mourned for her friend and prayed to anyone who might be listening to give her the words to say, to do something to make this right.

She stole glances at Libby whose face was completely blank, staring straight ahead for the duration of their drive.

Elena noticed a strange car on the side of the road in front of the house as they neared it. It wasn't Reggie, or Mark for that matter. She didn't think Libby was coherent enough to tell her if she was expecting someone, so Elena approached the car slowly, trying to see who was sitting in it. Her eyes widened at the sight of the man in the driver's seat, and she pulled into the driveway quickly. She popped the gear into park and then hurried out of the car and toward the strange sedan.

"You're Jason," she said to the attractive man getting out of the black rental car.

He smiled genuinely and held out his hand. "Elena, right?"

She ignored the hand but grabbed his arm. "Man, am I glad you're here." She pulled him up the driveway to the passenger side of her car.

"Um, okay . . ." he said allowing her to drag him with her. When he saw the look on Libby's face, he turned to Elena abruptly. "He took it all, didn't he?"

Elena guarded her expression but didn't answer the question. "I need your help. I don't think she's really with us at the moment," she said cautiously.

Jason sighed and nodded. He opened the door and methodically unlatched Libby's seatbelt and pulled her into his arms.

"Follow me," Elena said and led him into the house, up the stairs, and into Libby's room. He laid her on the bed and covered her with a blanket, sitting beside her for a moment before Elena tapped on his arm and motioned for him to follow her back out.

Jason shut the door quietly behind him and met Elena downstairs in the kitchen.

"Did she know you were coming?"

He shook his head. "She made a comment in passing last night about me coming today, and I just thought it would be a fun surprise–"

"Well, your timing is impeccable," Elena sighed.

He gave her a questioning look. "I'm not sure if that's sarcasm–"

"Sorry, no. I just mean–ugh, I don't know how much I should tell you–"

"Well, I know all about today's meeting, if that helps."

"You know about the miscarriages, right?" Elena asked. She turned and opened the cabinet beside the fridge and pulled out a bottle of vodka. Jason eyed the vodka with surprise as she poured two small glasses and slid one to him.

"Yeah, I know about those."

Elena threw her shot back with ease and put the glass back on the counter. "Mark's girlfriend, you know, the one he cheated on Libby with? She's pregnant."

Jason's expression froze. He grabbed his own glass and drank the liquid in one gulp. "So, he's taking everything, and he gets a baby?"

Elena shook her head, shocked laughter coming from her lips. "No! He gave her everything. The house, the book money, all he wants is what's his."

"So this is her consolation prize," Jason said, shaking his head.

"Something like that," Elena poured herself another drink and offered one to Jason, which he refused politely.

He leaned forward on the counter with his elbows propping him up. "How long has she been like this? What happened?"

"She beat the crap out of my car first," Elena said. "Then she told me everything and cried for a very long time."

"Wow. Does she ever get a break?" Jason sighed and stood up, pushing his fingers through his hair.

"I was hoping that was your role," Elena admitted.

Jason smiled sadly. "I'm not sure that's what she wants right now."

"It is," she assured him. "But she's scared."

"She needs time," Jason said.

Elena nodded. "Yeah, I know. I just hate seeing her like this. She was hoping that after today, everything would be over, and technically it is, but this . . . this is going to hurt for a long time."

Jason crossed his arms, lost in thought.

"How long are you here?" Elena asked.

"Just today. I fly back tomorrow morning."

"Can you stay longer?"

He shook his head. "I've got a new lady in the office, an intern who's like a lost puppy, and a book launch in two days. If I'd known—"

"It's okay. If any of us had known, Mark would be a dead man by now."

"I'll see if I can push my flight back a bit, but I can't stay longer than a night. I booked a hotel by the freeway."

Elena nodded. "Okay. I'm going to call my boyfriend and see if he can bring some food over after work. You like Chinese?"

"Yeah, I'm not picky."

"All right. Do you mind checking on her?" Elena picked up her phone and started towards the back door.

"Elena," Jason called after her. "I'm glad she has you."

Elena gave him a weak smile. "She's supposed to have more than just me."

JASON CLIMBED THE stairs slowly. He had been expecting to surprise Libby when she returned from her meeting, but he wasn't sure that she'd even *seen* him at all. He pushed the door to her room open quietly.

She was lying on her back looking at the ceiling, still tucked under the blanket he'd wrapped around her. Jason knelt on the floor beside the bed and reached under the blanket for her hand. She gripped it tightly.

"I'm not crazy," she whispered.

"I didn't think you were–"

"I just, I just don't know how to process this."

Jason sighed and propped his head on his hand. "I don't think anyone does. I think most women would have responded exactly the same way, or worse even."

"Did I break Elena's window? I can't remember how I got in the car."

"She didn't say anything about a broken window."

Libby nodded and then turned to look at him. Her eyes were heavy with sadness.

Jason's heart lurched at the sight of them.

She pulled her left hand out of the blanket. "It broke," she whispered, holding up the bird's nest that she'd gripped all the way home. There was an indentation in her palm where the wire had been pressed into her skin.

"I can fix it," he said, and took the necklace from her. He pulled her hand to his lips and kissed the indentations in her palm.

"When did you get here?" she asked.

"About thirty minutes ago."

"How?"

"Favor," he smiled.

"You're using all your favors on me," she sighed.

"You're worth every one."

A tear slipped down the side of her cheek. "I'm really not. You should go home, Jason. I'm not who you think I am."

"Scoot over," he said and pulled himself up onto the bed beside her. Gently he pulled her into his arms, and she responded without hesitation, resting her head on his chest. "What do you mean?" he asked as he trailed his fingers lightly across her back.

"I've made everything up. My story, everything you think you know about me, it's all made up. I'm broken and I'm not strong. I'm a failure and I'm so tired."

Jason sighed. "Well, that's too bad. I really thought I'd finally found Superwoman."

"I'm serious, Jason. You should run away from me."

"Why? Because when you're wounded you don't heal instantly? Because it takes time for you to recover?"

"Because I'm unlovable, and no matter how many times I put myself back together again, I still fall apart. Because dreams die inside of me, and then people leave me, and it just happens all over again."

He waited for the reassurance he needed and then spoke, choosing his words carefully. "You're not unlovable, Libby, not at all. Because if you were, then I would be crazy and I know I'm not crazy."

"What are you talking about?" she asked in a tired voice.

Jason tipped her face up and gazed deep into her eyes. "I love you, Libby."

She pulled her face from his fingertip and laid it back down on his chest with a "hmmph."

That went over well, he thought, rolling his eyes.

Be patient.

Jason felt moisture spread on his shirt underneath her. He rested his hand on her head and pulled his fingers through her hair. He was content to let the silence hover like a thick cloud between them and was relieved to finally have her in his arms again, no matter what the circumstances were. He'd missed her more than he'd allowed himself to acknowledge.

Finally, she broke the silence. "How could you?" she asked blankly.

"How could I what?"

"How could you love me? You've only seen the worst parts of me."

Jason smiled and leaned his head against the headboard. "I've seen some of your darkest moments, that's true. But those don't define you; they're not who you are. Who you are is how you respond. Who you are is how real you've been with me in the midst of those moments. Who you are is imperfect, and I love that because I'm imperfect too. I've seen some great moments with you, too, some of your best, if I remember correctly," he tapped gently on her head and continued to stroke her hair. "All of those experiences, though there are few and I'm anxious to get some more in, have shown me that you are beautiful inside and out."

"What if I never get over this?"

"You will."

"But I can't have children."

"It doesn't matter, Libby. If you would give me the chance to prove it, I wouldn't trade you for a thousand women who could give birth. It's you that I want and everything that comes with you. A broken heart or a broken womb doesn't matter to me. It's you."

She looked up at Jason, eyes brimming with tears. "You can't be real. No one is this good."

Jason cupped his hand around her face. "You've just been hanging out with the wrong crowd."

Libby pulled herself up and leaned her face closer to his, eyes pleading. "Kiss me," she whispered.

Jason's face fell. "I want to, more than anything I want to kiss you right now," he sighed. "But– "

"Please, just once," she put her hand on his cheek and leaned even closer.

The fight within him was weakened by her need. He closed his lips over hers softly, carefully, knowing that she was too vulnerable and he was too hungry for her. He kept his lips stationary on hers, despite wanting to roam across them freely and let his hands explore her body. He pulled back and looked into her eyes.

She seemed to understand his struggle and nodded. "Thank you," she whispered and returned to her position on his chest.

Jason sighed heavily and leaned against the bed again, praying silently for strength.

You did good, son.

The problem is that I didn't want to do good.

But you did.

Jason returned his hand to Libby's back and told himself that this was enough for now.

Chapter 24

"WHY DON'T YOU just stay the night here?" Elena asked Jason as she slurped some noodles through her lips.

Jason shook his head vehemently. "That's not a good idea."

Elena shrugged. "There's plenty of room, the couch pulls out, or there's the master bedroom. I think we have a blow up mattress . . ."

"Really, I'm good. I already checked in at the hotel, and, I just–"

"I get it man," Reggie nodded as he chewed his dinner.

Jason was relieved. He didn't want to go into the details with these new acquaintances as to why he couldn't trust himself to sleep anywhere near Libby. She was too vulnerable and he was too weak. They would both regret it, and he wasn't willing to take that chance with her. She was far too important to him.

"Well, if you change your mind–"

"El, he doesn't want to. Leave it alone." Reggie came to Jason's defense.

"Fine! Sorry!" Elena recoiled in surprise and went back to her noodles.

"It's not a good idea, El," Libby's voice came from the staircase. She'd changed into a pair of black yoga pants and a sweatshirt, her hair was pulled into a loose pony, and she'd washed all the streaky black makeup from her cheeks.

"Hey," Elena said softly and got up to meet her. "Are you hungry? I got you some cashew chicken."

"Yeah, thanks." Libby took a seat beside Jason at the bar and reached for the white box with her food in it.

"Girl," Reggie nodded at Libby. "I'll kick his ass for you if you want me to."

Libby smiled. "I know you would. Thank you. I'll let you know."

Jason rubbed Libby's back gently. "You okay?"

She nodded. "Exhausted. But relieved in a way, I guess."

"What do you mean?" Elena asked.

"It's over now. It's all over. All I have to do is sell this house and I'll be set for a while." She looked around the kitchen, her expression difficult to read.

"Is that going to be hard for you?" Jason asked.

Libby shook her head. "This isn't my home. I've known that much for a long time."

"My assistant coach at school, his wife is a realtor, so if you need help I can hook you up," Reggie offered. "And then I can kick Mark's ass."

Libby chuckled. "You just really want to beat him up, huh?"

Reggie gave her an innocent look. "Who, me?"

She sighed and opened her food. "Really. I'm glad it's over. This news today . . . I don't know how to deal with it. But at least he's not my lying, cheating problem anymore."

"That sounds like a toast if I ever heard one!" Elena grinned and went to open a bottle of wine.

Libby turned to Jason. "I don't want you stay the night, but I do want you to stick around after they leave. Is that okay?"

Jason took a minute before answering.

"I'm not going to freak out on you, I promise," she said, lowering her voice.

"That's not what I'm afraid of," Jason admitted.

She nodded. "Just for a little bit? I'll behave." She reached for his hand and squeezed it.

Against his better judgment, he nodded. "Okay."

AFTER REGGIE AND Elena cleaned up dinner and said their goodbyes, Libby took Jason by the hand and led him to the couch. She sat close beside him, still holding his hand, wishing that she could just lose herself in him rather than deal with all that was in front of her. But she wasn't going to make that mistake again.

"So," he said nervously.

"So."

"Libby, I'm–"

"I'm so–"

They both spoke at the same time and then smiled at each other.

"Go ahead," Jason urged her.

She took a deep breath. "I'm sorry about that, up there." She tilted her head towards the stairs.

Jason shook his head. "Don't be. I'm just not that good with self-control when you're around. I don't want to put the cart before the horse here. You're too important to me."

Her cheeks flushed and she nodded. "I appreciate that." She took a deep breath and propped her head against her hand on the couch. "I like you, Jason. I like you a lot."

"But," he said knowingly.

"It's not the 'but' that you think," she said and wove her fingers through his. "I like you a lot. I like you more every time we talk, and the fact that you're here today," she shook her head in amazement, "is so important to me. I know it wasn't a coincidence."

"As soon as you joked about it last night, something told me I had to come."

"God knew what was going to happen," she said with confidence.

"Yeah."

"That alone tells me that you are way too important for me to risk what this might be by doing anything about it right now."

"I'm not sure I follow." Jason narrowed his eyes at her.

"I'm afraid that if this happens now, it won't last. That I'll be using you as a substitute for Mark and that I won't ever really get over it. I have to get over it. Now that the divorce is final, I'm ready to face it. I'm ready to move past it."

"So, where does that leave me?"

She gave him an apologetic look. "Still waiting, I'm afraid. But I don't want you to wait if you decide that it's too much."

"It's not, Libby. It's not too much." Jason leaned forward in urgency. "I'll wait as long as I have to."

"I was hoping you wouldn't say that," she sighed.

"Why?"

"Because I don't know how long it's going to take. How will I know when I'm ready again? What if I jump too soon? I'm terrified of losing myself in another relationship, of being abandoned again."

He rested his hand on her cheek. "I won't let that happen. I won't let you lose yourself in me. I don't want that. And I'm not going to pressure you into anything that you're not ready for. The ball is in your court. You say when."

"Jason Randall, you're a dream come true," Libby smiled and pressed her cheek against his hand.

"I'm just in love with you, Elizabeth. That's all."

"I want you to kiss me again," she sighed.

Jason withdrew his hand slowly. "Not until you say when."

"When?" she whined.

Jason laughed and shook his head. "I'm also a really good listener, and I heard everything you just said," he grinned.

"I still want you to call me, and I want to see you, just not *see* you."

"Deal. What about our working relationship?" Jason asked.

"Should Helen take over my representation?"

"Hell, no," Jason said possessively.

Libby laughed. "Then I guess we'll just have to figure that out as we go."

"All right," he nodded resolutely. "I'm gonna head out then. If I don't, I might not be able to later."

Libby nodded, a sad look on her face. "I'll try to hurry, Jason," she said as they stood together.

"Don't. Don't hurry. Take as much time as you need."

Libby walked him to the door and let him pull her into an embrace. She breathed in the scent of his cologne, trying to commit it to memory, hoping it would last until she could give him what they both wanted.

Jason bent to kiss her forehead at the same time she tilted her face up to say something to him. They stared into each other's eyes for a moment before they both moved forward without a second thought.

Libby slid her arms around his neck and reached with her tiptoes to meet his lips. She felt a sob catch in her throat when they connected, and his arms wrapped around her like they had the first time they'd kissed. She let him lift her off her toes and crush her body against his. His arms were so strong around her; his torso arched against hers as he supported her weight. She forgot about the declarations she'd made moments ago about needing time and distance—she wanted to erase everything that stood between them, and the only way she knew how was to hold tighter and kiss harder.

Slowly, he loosened his grip and let her body slide back down so her feet were on the floor. Reluctantly, she tore her lips away from his.

"That doesn't count," she said in a high-pitched voice.

"This never happened," he said, hoarsely.

Libby brought her arms back down to her sides and stepped away from him.

"Thank you for being here today."

Jason looked a little dazed, his eyes unfocused. "You're welcome," he finally answered after a few seconds pause. Then without saying goodbye, he turned to the door and left, letting it shut quietly behind him.

Libby let out a huge breath. "What am I doing?"

She didn't need God to tell her what a disaster it would be to let her emotions get the better of her again. She did, however, need Him to speak to what had happened earlier that afternoon. She'd managed to distract herself with Jason for long enough to get her to this point, but now, with the taste of him still on her lips, she knew she needed a distraction from Jason himself.

"This is the worst rollercoaster ever," she sighed. She returned to the couch and slumped down on it. The scene from that afternoon replayed itself in her mind until she got to the words that had caused Mark's face to turn so deathly pale.

"Bria's pregnant," she whispered.

The ache that rose in her heart felt like it was strangling her. She ached for her babies, for the chance to hold them in her arms just one time before they'd left her. She ached for the fact that Mark would now finally get to experience that feeling, with the woman he'd betrayed his wife for. Gut-wrenching sobs raked through Libby's body as she lay down across the couch on her stomach.

In spite of the hope-filled conversation she'd just had with Jason less than thirty minutes prior, she felt so desperately alone in that huge house. Part of her wanted to call Jason back, to beg and plead with him to stay with her, to seduce him with her fragile state of being and sleep all night in his arms.

That won't help, and you're not alone. I'm here.

Suddenly the room seemed so thick with His presence that Libby felt as though she were heavier, pressing deeper into the couch.

"How could You send me into the lion's den like that today?" she whispered.

I promised that no matter what happened I would be here, and I am.

"It's not fair," she whimpered.

Sarah had been sick to her stomach for days. None of her attempts to find Jeremy had come up with any new information. He'd done exactly what she'd asked him to-he'd left. She was sick with worry, doubt, and fear. She regretted her words and actions immediately after he'd stormed out of the cookhouse, but she'd been too prideful to stop him and hadn't expected him to actually leave the ranch. The first day, she'd found respite in his absence but still looked for dust on the road with every sound she heard, hoping to see his horse come trotting down the lane. That night she had shivered at the lack of warmth from his side of the bed. And the next day when Jeremy still hadn't returned, she'd locked herself in the pump house to cry where no one could see her. It was like he had died, just like Red. Sarah was alone again, but this time it was her own fault.

It took another week of worrying herself sick before the nausea set in, and she realized she was sick with more than worry. Something else was growing inside of her.

With a purpose she hadn't had in the last few months, the next day when she woke up with the sun, Libby began to pack the things in the house that she wanted to keep. She was ruthless about letting things go. There were no sentiments attached to the possessions in that house anymore. The only things she wanted to keep were things she'd brought into the marriage: photo albums, her grandmother's chest of drawers that she'd refinished, a few paintings, and her desk. Anything that was upstairs that she wanted to keep, she moved into the guest room and pushed against the wall. Downstairs, her belongings went into the dining room. By nine am when Elena knocked on the door, Libby had cleared out most of her personal items from the rest of the house.

"Whoa," Elena said when she walked in. "What happened in here?"

"I'm packing," Libby said breathlessly as she carried a box into the dining room.

"Yeah, you are. Where's Jason?"

"I don't know," Libby called back.

"Are you seriously telling me he didn't stay here last night?" Elena followed Libby's voice into the dining room.

Libby shook her head. "Nope."

"Wow. I'm surprised. You could have cut the tension with a knife last night!"

Libby blushed, remembering how they had almost needed to do exactly that, and then quickly shoved the thought from her head.

"Wait. What was that?" Elena gave her friend a suspicious look.

Libby shrugged and brushed past Elena to go get another box.

Elena's face lit up and her jaw dropped. "I knew it! He stayed, maybe just not all night! You did it, didn't you? You had sex!" Elena continued to follow Libby through the house.

"Oh, geez, El. No, I did not have sex with Jason last night!" Libby rolled her eyes.

"Could have fooled me," Elena said, slightly disappointed.

"We kissed."

Elena perked up a bit. "Well, that's not a total loss then! Was it hot?"

"You know, I'm not so sure you're such a great friend after all . . ." Libby pushed past her again with a box from the living room.

"Okay, so it was definitely hot."

Libby stacked the box in the dining room, wiped her forehead, and then put her hands on her hips. "Listen, this is how it is, I like him, but I'm nowhere near ready to do anything about it. We kissed, it was a mistake, and it's not going to happen again."

"Ever?"

Libby sighed. "Not anytime soon."

"You're so much wiser than I am," Elena sighed and slumped down into a chair.

"Um, present circumstances notwithstanding?"

"Oh, you know that's not what I mean!"

"You never liked Mark," Libby pointed out and then once again walked away. Elena stayed where she was and waited for Libby to return with another box.

"You're right about that, but I never expected him to pull this kind of crap!"

"You warned me, though. You told me you didn't like him and I bit your head off."

"I'm not sure where we're going with this," Elena said cautiously.

"I'm just saying that your argument about me being wise isn't all that strong. I married a man who got someone else pregnant before we were even divorced. And the ink is barely dry and I'm already falling for some other guy!" Libby sighed. Then she looked at Elena pointedly. "You know, you could help me move these boxes!"

Elena jumped up immediately and laughed. "Sorry. I was too excited about you and Jason!"

"Well, there's nothing to be excited about, so help me!"

Elena saluted her friend and followed her to get another box.

"Why are we doing this again?" Elena asked thirty minutes later.

"Because I'm going to have an estate sale."

"A what?"

"An estate sale. To get rid of all of this junk that I don't want."

"I thought Mark was taking the furniture."

Libby shook her head. "Everything in the house is mine now."

"And you're not keeping any of it?"

"Only what you see here and the stuff in the guest room upstairs."

"Seriously? That's most of your house, Libby!" Elena looked at the small pile of boxes and a rocking chair that sat in the corner. "Was that your grandma's?"

"Yes, and I'm keeping her dresser that's upstairs too. The rest of this stuff has Mark all over it. It's not my style."

"You sure you're ready for this?" Elena eyed her friend.

"I've been waiting for the okay to get rid of this stuff for weeks. I put an ad on Craigslist this morning; people will be here starting at 7 a.m. tomorrow."

Elena cringed. "Do I have to be here that early?"

"No, of course not! Not at seven," Libby winked.

"Why are you so chipper and productive this morning?"

"No idea. I just woke up with energy and I've got to stay busy."

"You're going to crash tonight, you know that, right?"

"Maybe, maybe not. But I need to get this done now if that's going to happen." Libby said, and she started up the stairs.

JASON WAS A little relieved to see Elena's car in the driveway when he pulled up to Libby's house. He knocked on the front door with confidence, knowing that his strength would not be as tested as it had been last night. That not-so-innocent kiss had cost him a few hours of sleep.

"Well, hello there, Mr. Perfect," Elena grinned as she swung the door open.

Jason gave her a strange look and stepped inside. "Morning," he said glancing around. "How is she?"

Elena shrugged and pointed upstairs. "See for yourself."

He walked past the dining room and did a double take, sure that it hadn't looked like that the night before. Elena caught his eye and shook her head. Jason took the stairs two at a time and caught a glimpse of Libby passing into her bedroom.

"Hey," he called out.

She turned to him and the purpose-driven look she had in her face melted into a happy smile. "Hi," she grinned.

"Wow, you've been really busy this morning." Jason stared at the boxes in her room in surprise.

"I know. I woke up and was so relieved that it was all over, it was like I couldn't wait to get out of here."

"So, what exactly is the plan?"

"I'm boxing up everything I want to keep and then I'm having an estate sale tomorrow to get rid of everything else."

"Sounds good. What can I do to help?"

"Well, anywhere you see a box that is taped up, I need those moved in here or into the dining room. Then anything that's not boxed up in this room and the office needs to be moved out. I'm going to close those rooms off tomorrow."

"All right. I'll get started. I just have to leave for the airport at twelve-thirty."

"Oh." Libby's face fell. "I guess you have to get back to life in the city, huh?"

Jason smiled apologetically. "Yeah, I do."

"Well, I'm glad you're here now," she sighed.

"I'll go find some boxes."

While Libby continued to pack her belongings, Elena and Jason moved things to the appropriate rooms. When twelve o'clock neared, Elena called for a lunch break, and Jason decided that he should get a move on towards the airport.

"I have an idea," Elena piped up. "Why don't I take your rental back, and Libby can drive you to the airport and then swing by and pick me up on her way back?"

"Are you sure? I have plenty of time," Jason asked.

"I'd like that," Libby said quickly.

Jason's expression brightened immediately. "That sounds good. And we can pick up some fast food on the way?"

Libby nodded.

"Sounds like a plan," he grinned and tossed Elena his keys.

Chapter 25

JASON HELD LIBBY'S hand as she drove in the direction of the airport. He gathered their fast food wrappers into the bag the food had come in and tucked it between his feet.

"I think I'm already in over my head," she sighed.

"It will be easier when I'm gone."

"I doubt that. I seriously doubt that."

Her insistence made him feel good. He didn't want her to be miserable, but he certainly didn't want her to be happy about being apart.

"So when can I see you again?" he asked.

"Can we leave that up in the air for right now? If we set a date then that'll be all I can think about."

"True," Jason said, a little disappointed.

"Besides, I've got to focus on finding a new place to live, selling the house, all of that."

"Don't forget that you owe me a finished manuscript by August."

"There's that, too. Man, that's a lot."

"Do you have to move right away? Can that wait at all?"

Libby shook her head. "I can't pay the mortgage. I mean, I'd have probably sixty days before anything happened if I didn't pay, but I can't lose the house. I have to sell it immediately."

"Where will you go?"

"Probably an apartment."

"Will you have to sign a year lease?"

She shrugged, checking over her shoulder to change lanes. "I'm not sure. I guess it depends on where I end up. Why?"

Jason took a deep breath and looked out his window. "I was just thinking, you mentioned once that there was nothing keeping you in Dallas, so . . . if you have to move, why not make it worth it?"

"To where? New York?" she chuckled.

"I would love it if you came to New York, but I was actually thinking more like one of the coasts like you said you always wanted."

"I'd be all alone, starting from scratch."

Jason smiled. "It's just an idea, and you wouldn't have to be *all* alone."

Libby's cheeks flushed. "I'm aware of that." She took the exit that led to the entrance of the airport.

"I guess this is it," he said as they passed through the tollbooth.

"Thank you for being here, Jason. You have no idea how much it meant to me. All of it." She gave him a look that said she didn't regret anything that had happened between them.

"Oh, before I forget, I fixed it," Jason pulled her necklace out of his pocket and put it in the cup holder.

"Thank you," she said, squeezing his hand.

"Thank you for letting me be honest about some things," he said sheepishly. "I wouldn't have said some of that stuff under normal circumstances, but I felt like the timing –"

"Was perfect," She finished. "I needed to hear it. I was spiraling into a very dark hole, and you pulled me out of it. Which is just more evidence of the fact that I can't let this happen yet. I don't want you to be the one who saves me."

Her words stung him slightly; he didn't understand what she meant, but he let it drop. There wasn't time to get into another heart to heart right now. Libby pulled up to the curb where Jason pointed and put the car in park.

"I'm going to say goodbye out here, if that's okay? I just can't do the whole airport goodbye scene right now. I'll want more than what I should, and . . . this is just a lot harder than I expected it to be."

Jason was confused but he nodded dumbly and pulled his backpack out from the backseat. Libby met him around on the passenger side and hugged him tight. He held her as long as he could. The last five minutes had thrown him into a tailspin of doubt, but the one thing he knew was that he didn't want to leave her, and by the way she kept hanging on, he didn't think she wanted him to go either.

At long last, she loosened her arms around him and stepped back. "So, you'll call me?" she asked, her voice hoarse.

"Yep."

"Okay. Have a safe flight." She breathed out and then went back around to the driver's side and waved as he entered through the sliding glass doors.

LIBBY SAT IN the car for a minute before pulling back into the traffic passing by her. Inside her gut relief and regret seemed to be holding hands and she couldn't figure out which was which. When she arrived at the rental car place to pick up Elena, her expression was sullen. She got out and gave Elena the keys.

"You were right. I'm crashing," she said simply and climbed into the passenger seat.

"Are you okay?" Elena was concerned. "Did something happen?"

"No, I'm fine. It's just like I said. I'm coming down from all the energy I had this morning."

"And you just had to say goodbye to the man of your dreams," Elena pointed out.

Libby gave her a dark glance and Elena clamped her mouth shut and drove back to the house in silence.

"Are you sure you're up for an estate sale tomorrow morning?" Elena asked when they got back to Libby's.

"Yeah. I will be. I'm going to take a nap and then just take it easy the rest of the day. I think I went a little nuts this morning."

"A little? You packed and organized seven years' worth of stuff in three hours. You deserve a nap, a massage, and a happy ending!"

"I'm working towards the happy ending, just not the kind you're thinking about."

"I'll be here at six thirty tomorrow morning with coffee and breakfast." Elena gave Libby her keys back, gave her a hug, and then said goodbye.

Libby did exactly as she'd said she would. She went up to her bedroom and passed out for three hours.

JASON WAS GLAD for a nearly-empty flight and a row to himself on the way home. He needed the quiet to process and let his confusion work itself out.

This is why I urged you to be patient.

But You said—

I did say. She needed to hear that from you, but you didn't ask me about the rest.

Jason sighed. That was definitely the truth. He'd let the moment suck him in and chew him up. I'm sorry, he thought.

You don't need to apologize; you didn't do anything wrong. You just moved a little too quickly.

But what is this all about? I care too much already. If this isn't what You want then it has to stop sometime.

How about you put your trust and faith in me and let me lead you down the path I've designed for you?

Yeah, that sounds easy enough, Jason thought, rolling his eyes.

Let me have the reigns.

So does that mean I need to ask You before I call her?

No. But you need to listen for my voice. I wanted you with

her yesterday. **It was part of my plan, for both of you.**

So I just let it go?

Exactly.

Jason sighed and looked out the window silently for a few minutes without responding. The flight attendant came by with drinks and pretzels and Jason let his sit on his tray for a long time before touching them.

I love her.

I know.

Is that okay?

Give her to me.

Jason closed his eyes and breathed in deeply.

Nothing bad will come out of you surrendering this to me. You know that. I only have the best for you. Plans to prosper you, plans for hope and a future.

But is she in those plans?

Give her to me and then I can show you.

He swallowed some of the soda in the little plastic cup.

"Okay," he said under his breath, eyes closed. "I give her to You, Lord. Libby is Yours and I'll listen for Your voice. Please move quickly."

The pilot announced that the plane was beginning its descent into New York, and Jason gripped the arms of his seat. This was his least favorite part of flying.

THE NEXT DAY, Libby and Elena worked together to clear the house of all that they could during the estate sale. By five p.m., they had banked almost three thousand dollars and had sold all of the large pieces of furniture and decorative items, including paintings and area rugs. The house looked like it hadn't even been lived in.

"I am taking you out for dinner," Libby sighed as she shut the door behind the last buyer who walked out with an iron turkey centerpiece and some Christmas decorations.

"You might have to spoon feed me!" Elena whined from where she lay on the stairs. "I'm so tired!"

Libby yawned as if on cue. "I know. But right now I'm mostly hungry. Come on, we can go to Zini's. We worked so hard today we don't even have to feel guilty."

Elena cringed. "Guilt is not the problem when it comes to Zini's!"

Libby remembered the other problem that the greasiest, most delicious pizza in Dallas had to offer, which was of the gastrointestinal nature. "Oh. Right. What about Campisi's? They're super good and closer, too."

"Yeah, that sounds good. My stomach never revolts on Campisi's."

They drove the short distance to the pizza place and were seated in a small booth in the back of the restaurant.

"This is cozy. I'm not sure I've been to this one before," Elena looked around at the dimly-lit room with deep red walls and mirrors that reached to the ceiling.

"I like the main location better just because of the history behind it."

"The one with the big Egyptian sign?"

"Yeah. Apparently the mob used to hang out there. Someone told me that the owner still has connections," Libby said raising her eyebrows.

"Is there still a mob?"

Libby shook her head. "I'll research it and write them into my next book."

"How is that coming?"

"The book? Not great this week, but I'll get back to it tomorrow, I suppose."

"When are you going to look for an apartment?" Elena asked suddenly.

Libby sighed and sat back while their server set down glasses of water and asked for their drink orders. "Whatever your house red is," Libby said to the server and Elena ordered the same. "I don't know about the apartment," she said to Elena. "Soon. I have to decide what I'm going to do. I can only afford the mortgage for a few months after today, but I don't want to spend the money on that."

"What do you mean 'what you're going to do?'"

"Well, Jason actually had an interesting thought today on the way to the airport."

"Good. Don't think for two seconds that we're not having a conversation about him tonight, too." Elena sat forward and gave Libby a serious look. "Let me guess. He wants you to move to New York?"

"That was a suggestion, but he remembered that I'd told him that I had always wanted to live on a coast somewhere and that you were really the only thing tying me to Dallas anymore."

"I'm not sure I like where this is going."

"Think about it, El, what do I have here? Besides you, nothing! I don't belong here. This place is so not me."

"So, you're just going to move?" Elena cried.

"I haven't made a decision about anything yet. I don't know what I want. I don't want to leave you, but in ten years of living here, I don't have any other friends or networks, not even a job! I can write from anywhere."

"Wow," Elena sighed. "I was not prepared for this."

"It's nothing yet. I promise I'll tell you as soon as I figure out what to do. I'll probably get a six month lease here before I decide."

"I would miss you so much," Elena sniffled.

"I would miss you, too. But I don't think I want to stay in Dallas."

"You should at least go to Paris or somewhere amazing; then I can't be mad at you, I'll just be jealous!"

Libby smiled. "Now you're talking!"

They ordered a pizza to share after the waiter brought their wine, and then Elena dove into the real object of her curiosity.

"So, what was all of that stuff about the other night?"

"What stuff?"

"Why was the idea of Jason sleeping over such a big deal?"

Libby rubbed her hand over her eyes and shook her head, groaning.

"What? It's a valid question!"

Libby took a deep breath. "Besides all of the complications that it would have caused, Jason is a Christian."

Elena made a face. "Oh, well, that explains everything!"

Libby laughed and shook her head again. "I was a Christian once, too. You didn't know me then, but I was. I went to church, I read my Bible, all of that."

"Yeah, so?"

"Ever since I found my grandma's letter–that one that was in my old college yearbook–things have been kind of weird with me."

"What does that mean?"

"She was a really strong Christian. She was the reason I was one, too. So her letter had a lot of that kind of stuff in it, and it just . . . it reminded me of a lot of things that I let go of when I went to college."

Elena pursed her lips to the side. "So, what are you saying?"

"I'm saying that I don't know what the rules are now. As far as dating and sex and all that. I'm divorced now, gosh, that sounds so weird. But it's the truth. I'm not married anymore–" she paused for a moment to let that sink in. "And I'm revisiting some of the beliefs from my past and I don't know what's okay and what's not."

"Wait, revisiting beliefs–does that mean that you're a Christian again?"

"I never really stopped believing in God, El, I just tried to leave Him behind when I went to school and at the same time, felt sort of abandoned by Him. I didn't think I needed Him and I thought that if I didn't keep up with everything then maybe it wouldn't be so bad if I decided to do a few stupid things while I was free."

"And now?"

"Like I said, things have been changing. Certain things have been coming back to me and–"

"You're sure this doesn't have anything to do with Jason?"

Libby shook her head. "No. This started the night that we found that letter, the day before I went to New York. But regardless, God and I have been reconnecting, and even though I did leave Him behind all those years ago to do my own thing for so long, He never gave up on me."

"How do you know that?"

"I feel it. I just know it. I can't help but think that if only I'd kept up the whole Christianity thing, if I'd just kept Him in my life, maybe I would have made different choices, and I would have married someone else and could have had a much different life. But even when I've thought about that, I feel like God says that He is here now and if I let Him, He can still make something beautiful from my life."

"I think your life is beautiful, Libby," Elena said after a moment's thought. "It's full of pain right now, but isn't there a level of beauty in feeling things so deeply and then overcoming them?"

"Exactly. That's totally it. God is showing me that as painful as this time is, there is beauty to come from it. I think the book is part of it. I'm terrified that Jason is part of it, and of course you're part of it. For a long time you've been the only thing of value in my life."

"Oh, good, pizza's here," Elena said, sounding relieved. She grabbed a slice and bit into it, chewing it slowly.

"I know this sounds crazy coming from me . . . we've never talked about anything like this before," Libby continued. "But something is changing inside of me. I don't expect you to jump on the bandwagon, but . . . I'm starting fresh now, and my relationship with God is going to be an important part of that. I've done it on my own and failed for way too long. It's time to give God the chance to show me what He wants for me."

Elena sighed and stared at her pizza quietly for a moment. "Well, I'm surprised, for sure, but then totally not in some ways," she said finally.

"Explain," Libby ordered.

"There have been more than a few times during the last few months that I've prayed for you," Elena admitted. "I wasn't sure who exactly was listening, but I knew someone was. I've always believed there was something out there; I just didn't know who or what. I still don't. But I've prayed for you, begged for something to change. And then the book happened, and this gorgeous Jason guy waltzes into your life right when the biggest idiot ever runs out of it. It all felt . . . cosmic to me. Like there was someone watching out for you."

Libby was touched by her friend's sentiment. "Thank you. Thank you for telling me that. That means so much to me."

"So, that means no hanky-panky, then?" Elena asked.

Libby laughed. "Probably not. I just know that with how fragile things are in my life right now, that would be a huge mistake even without the morality issues that I still have to figure out. If I'm going to be with Jason in any way, shape, or form, it's not going to be until all of this is behind me–like not even visible in my rear view mirror."

Elena nodded in understanding. "So, that's the real reason why he didn't stay. You're not together."

"No, not at all," Libby shook her head. "But I'm really attracted to him. We agreed last night not to let anything happen, but then when he was leaving–"

"You kissed."

Libby sighed, "Yes. Big time." She moaned at the memory.

Elena grinned. "You know what? I haven't seen you act like that in years and years. Before Mark even."

"I was like that with Mark." Libby remembered all too well.

"Maybe I blocked it out because I didn't like him."

"If only I'd listened to you back then."

"Don't do that. Don't waste time on the what-ifs. You'll drive yourself crazy."

"You're right." Libby finally picked up a piece of pizza and bit into it. It wasn't New York deep dish, but it was Campisi's, and it was pretty darn good.

Chapter 26

"SO WHAT ARE you going to do with all that money from the estate sale?" Jason asked over the phone.

"Hopefully find myself a super tiny apartment, rent a storage unit, and maybe treat myself to a mini vacation."

"You know, I hear New York is really pretty in May," Jason offered.

"Ha ha, very funny. I'm actually on my way to look at an apartment right now."

"Oh, yeah? Short-term lease?"

"Yep. That money has been burning a hole in my new bank account for twenty-four hours already."

"Uh oh, are you that kinda woman? The 'have money must spend' kind?"

Libby laughed. "Not at all. I just have things I need to get done with this money!"

"I hear ya. But a vacation sounds nice. Any ideas on where you'll go?"

"Not yet, it was just a thought. If I go, it'd be a working vacation, but it would be nice to have a change of scenery. The house is so empty that it's suffocating sometimes."

"I still can't believe you sold all that furniture!"

"A girl's gotta survive, right?"

"True enough. Well, listen, would you like to hear some really great business-related news?"

"Is it about my book?"

"Yes, ma'am."

"Then yes!" Libby squealed and exited off the highway towards her potential new apartment.

"We got proofs back today for the cover, and there are a few that are really good."

"Oh, my gosh! Can I see them?"

"Yeah, I'm going to forward them over to you; I just wanted to tell you first."

"Oh, I can't wait to see them!"

"Yeah, I think you'll be pretty happy. How is the book coming?"

"Honestly, I've hardly touched it this week, but I'm almost finished with my first rewrite, so I'd say I'm doing pretty well."

"I'm impressed that you're as far as you are with it. With everything that's been going on, it wouldn't have been unreasonable to push the deadline back a little bit."

Libby kept an eye out for her turnoff from the access road. "It's a really good escape, actually. And I can take my anger out on Jeremy if I need to. This whole stupid divorce has proven to be really great for my writing inspiration. I've even changed a few things in the plot that I'm excited about.

"Oh, yeah? What?"

"Can't tell you, silly!" Libby laughed.

"Not even your agent?"

"No way! Oh, I'm here. Man, this place looks like a dump," Libby sighed and looked at the dilapidated two-story apartments in front of her.

"It's short term, right?"

"Yeah, and I definitely don't have to live here."

"Well, I guess I'll let you go. We'll talk again in a few days or so?"

"Absolutely. Talk to you later." Libby tucked her phone into her purse and sighed as she stared at the overweight balding man who approached her with a semi-toothless grin. She plastered on her best fake smile and prepared to endure the next fifteen minutes of her life.

"OH, MY WORD, Jason, I feel like I need a shower after that!" Libby couldn't help calling him when she got back into her car. "A rat ran past us inside the apartment. A rat! And the guy smelled like urine! And did I mention the rat?"

"Well, rats are a way of life here in the city—"

"But have you had them in your home? I mean, really. A rat?"

"Okay, maybe not in my house, but outside, yes. We have roaches though . . ."

Libby shuddered. "Yes, we have those here too. They're horrid little things, aren't they? Do yours fly?"

Jason howled with laughter. "Roaches don't fly!"

Libby didn't bat an eyelash. "Yes. They. Do."

"Please. Show me a roach that flies and I'll buy you dinner."

"You're buying me dinner anyway *and* I'll show you a roach that flies!"

"Was that an invitation?" Jason asked in a sing-song voice.

"No," Libby said in mock-defense. "I'm just saying . . ."

"Why don't you come up here again?"

Libby laughed. "Yeah, that wouldn't be a bad idea at all. The only way I'm coming up there any time soon is if you promise not to be there!"

Jason snorted. "Please. You act like we're not grown adults who are completely in control of themselves."

"If only that were the case," Libby sighed. "Speaking of which, I really just called to tell you about the horrific conditions that man wanted me to live in."

"What, so you don't want to talk to me now?"

Libby sighed. "I always want to talk to you."

"Well, that's a relief!"

"What do you mean?" Libby asked in surprise as she backed her car out of the parking lot and sped away from that awful building as quickly as she could.

"Nothing."

"Jason! Tell me what you meant."

He groaned. "It's not a big deal. I just got some mixed signals from you when you dropped me at the airport. But it's not a big deal and I haven't spent hours dissecting your words the way you would if it were me."

"Um, I'm going to pretend not to be offended by that stereotype and ask, again what do you mean?"

JASON REGRETTED SAYING anything. He got up and shut the door to his office, something he should have done when she'd first called him back. Amanda caught his eye before the door shut and she gave him a very dramatic wink. He rolled his eyes at her.

"You said that you didn't want me to be the one to save you. I didn't really understand what that meant, and then you didn't want to come in to the airport to say goodbye. That's all. Nothing big."

"Oh, Jas," Libby said softly. "I wish you had asked me about that then."

"It wasn't a big deal, just like I said–"

"Can I explain?"

He sighed. "Yes. Please."

"I don't want to look to you to be my savior. I don't want to depend on you to get me out of this crazy place that I'm in. I want to get out of it and then meet you on the other side. If it happens any other way, I'm afraid that it won't work. That it really will be just a rebound relationship. I don't want that. I want to be with you. And the airport thing, gosh, don't you ever watch movies? Airport scenes are the worst. I hate saying goodbye anyway, and doing it in an airport is just so awful. There's always this element of 'will I ever see him again?' Do you know what I mean?"

Jason sat down, shocked. "Completely. That's not at all what I thought you meant."

"Well, that's what I meant. I couldn't deal with an emotional goodbye. Not after everything that's happened, not after our last airport goodbye, and not after our kiss that, um, never happened," she paused. "I can't do all that yet. I'm already in the middle of a bunch of emotional junk tied up in the last guy! Man, that sounds bad."

"No, it doesn't. Not to me. I get it, and like I said, it's a relief. You *want* to be with me?"

"Yes, of course I do. But I can't let that be my focus. And I have to be careful about seeing you too much and talking to you on the phone too much. That's why I want to say goodbye now. Except I don't. At all."

"This seems strange. I mean, I get it, but we both want the same things, don't we?"

"Yes, but Jason, to be honest, I still cry myself to sleep over what happened with Mark sometimes. I don't love him anymore, but that wound of betrayal is still so fresh. Not to mention all the other stuff."

"I'm sorry," he sighed. "I'm not trying to rush you, I swear I'm not."

"I know that."

"Well, I need to let you go, but I'm going to tell you something first." Jason sat forward in his chair and leaned his head in his hand.

"Okay."

"I miss you."

He could hear the smile in her voice when she said, "I miss you too."

Jason sighed long and loud into the phone. "All right. Talk to you later."

"Yep, bye."

Jason sat back in his chair and began to beg and pray for patience for himself, and for healing for Libby. "I know I'm being selfish, Lord, but I need this. Please, move. Please be at work! I'm dying over here!" Jason threw himself into his work and didn't look up again until nine p.m.

WHEN LIBBY GOT home she raced upstairs to check out the cover images that Jason had sent to her. Her favorite was of a woman with a long braid looking over her shoulder underneath the ranch entrance where the words *Red Parks Ranch* were carved into the wood. She gasped when she saw the Sarah that she'd imagined in her mind as she'd first started the book.

"Man, these guys are good at their job," she mused as she opened the file and got straight to work on the rest of Jeremy and Sarah's story.

> Sarah pulled on the waistband of her work pants. They were growing increasingly tighter everyday. If no one had noticed by now, it would only be a matter of days. She was ashamed of her condition and the fact that there was no man around to take responsibility for it. She knew the hands weren't stupid. Jeremy had left for a reason, and it was ridiculous to think that no one had caught on to their affair, what with Jeremy following her home every night and leaving her cabin in the mornings. She was thankful that Abe was doing such a good job in Jeremy's place, but still, she longed for Jeremy to return. At night she prayed that he would forget the words that she'd spoken and hear the true cries of her heart. She wanted to tell him that he'd simply caught her on the worst possible day, that he'd surprised her during a time when she really needed to think about what she was doing. She'd spoken without thought, and now she was carrying the child of a man who had disappeared from everyone who knew him.
>
> One afternoon while she supervised a stove full of food cooking for dinner, she was startled by a jerk

in her belly. At first she thought something was wrong, but then she realized the baby was moving inside of her. She pressed her hand against her stomach and marveled at the feeling, tears filling her eyes as she looked around the cookhouse, desperate for Jeremy to materialize in front of her. The baby kicked again as if to remind her that it was the one who needed her. Sarah squared her shoulders and sliced a generous piece of bread from the loaf she'd made that morning. She couldn't pine for the man anymore. She had to take care of his child. Still, she called to him in her heart and prayed that he would return before it was too late.

Please Jeremy, she pleaded, please come back.

Libby attacked her keyboard, flying through the story, anxious to get to the end. Inevitably there were many interruptions. She continued her search for an apartment and held showings at the house as often as the realtor called. She felt somewhat hopeless about the whole process.

"Every place I go to is either too expensive, too awful, or not willing to take a short term lease!" she complained to Elena one night over drinks at a restaurant near Elena's flower shop.

"I've told you that you can move in with me if you have to. I mean, the couch is kinda comfy . . ."

Libby nodded. "Yes, I know. I'm avoiding that at all costs!"

"I could stay with Reggie for a while," Elena shuddered.

"Oh, lord, I would never ask you to do that," Libby laughed.

"You know he's gotten better. Ever since I found out he wanted to talk marriage and I shut him down because of his nasty apartment, he's really been trying."

"Do you ever think that maybe he just needs a woman around to help him understand how dirty he is?"

Elena shook her head. "I'm not sure. I don't know if I'm prepared to take that on!"

"But you love him," Libby said with a grin.

"So much," Elena sighed dreamily. "If he really asked, I'd say yes. But there would be some serious stipulations."

"Like putting food back in the fridge," Libby cringed.

"And flushing the toilet. I won't even ask him to put the seat down, but flush it! For the love!"

Libby pretended to gag.

"What about you? Any news on the Jason front?"

Libby shook her head. "We actually haven't talked in a few days. I've had my head buried in the book and trying to find a place to live."

"Have you given any more thought to leaving Dallas?"

"Not really. I'm not sure it's the right time to leave and start fresh somewhere else. I don't know. I feel like something is just waiting to happen. I'm not sure."

"Well, you know you have a place if you get desperate." Elena brought her glass to Libby's and clinked them together.

"Thank you. But I'm going to find a place. I have to find somewhere soon. There is a family interested in the house."

"Really? That's awesome!" Elena clinked their glasses again.

"Yeah, they saw the house the other day and really liked it. Know what they loved the most?" Libby said with a telltale tone of voice.

Elena rolled her eyes. "Of course I do. The garden."

Libby grinned. "Wherever I end up, I'll definitely be bringing you along to recreate my sanctuary. That's the only thing I'll miss about that house."

"It was the best part, if I say so myself."

Libby laughed and took a drink, feeling genuinely happy about her life for the first time in a long time.

When she got home that night, the only thing she wanted to do was fall asleep while talking to Jason on the phone. The mere thought of it made her blush, and because of that, she purposely didn't call him. Instead, she pulled out her grandmother's letter and reread it again. She'd read that letter so many times in the past few months that the pages were wearing. For the first time in a long time, Libby had the urge to actually pick up a Bible and read it. Unfortunately, she wasn't sure she still owned one and if she did, it was no doubt packed away. She wrote herself a note to buy one the next day and then climbed into bed.

"I felt happy tonight. Truly happy," she said quietly. Speaking candidly had become their nightly ritual.

I noticed. That makes me happy.

"Thank You for what You're doing in me. Every day it feels easier and easier to look ahead, and I have hope. I can feel Your presence with me."

I love being with you, Libby, and I'm not finished yet. There's still more to come.

Libby breathed in deeply and rolled over. She grabbed her phone off the nightstand to plug it into the charger and see if she had any messages.

She always had one message when she finally laid her head on her pillow at night. "Good night," was all it read and it was always from Jason. She smiled and put the phone back on her nightstand. The fact that it had been months and still any word from him made her heart stutter spoke volumes to her.

"I GOT AN offer," Libby breathed into the phone as soon as Elena picked up.

"On the house?"

"No, on the boat I'm selling. Yes, El, the house," Libby laughed.

"Oh, my gosh. Is it the family you told me about a few weeks ago?"

"Yeah, apparently they had to solidify some details on their end before they could make a legitimate offer."

"Wow. So, this is really happening. Where are you going to go?" Elena cried.

"I don't know yet. But I have just over a month to find out. I have a moving company coming to give me an estimate tomorrow."

"Okay, I'm coming over tonight and we're going to scour apartment listings!"

"Sounds great. I just have a phone date with Jason at four, so don't come until at least five thirty."

"Phone date? You have a phone date?"

"Baby steps," Libby grinned.

"Oh, my gosh, you've got to be kidding me."

"Sadly, I'm not," Libby laughed at herself. "But it's better than where I was a week ago."

"Fine. I'll be there at five-thirty."

Libby wrote all day and then at precisely three fifty-five, she saved her file, grabbed her phone, and went downstairs to brew a fresh cup of coffee.

The phone rang moments later and Libby practically pounced on it to answer it. "Hi," she said excitedly.

"Hi, yourself. What are you so excited about?"

"I sold the house today!"

"What? That's awesome, Libby! Congratulations!"

"Thank you. I'm really happy. I've got a month to be out of here."

"Do you have a place?"

"Not exactly, but I'm going to by then. If not, I'll put everything in storage."

"Wow. You're not worried?"

"No. I mean, if I'm desperate there are plenty of places I can live; I've just been picky because I'm still trying to figure out what I'm supposed to do."

"Have you been praying about it?"

"All the time," Libby said with a smile. Jason had been encouraging her to pray at some point during every conversation they'd had lately. "He's surprisingly silent lately."

"Oh, that usually means He's up to something," Jason laughed.

"Great," she sighed. "Anyway, what's going on in your world?"

She loved listening to him talk about his work, and she loved simply hearing his voice. She asked him about his next book launch and listened while he told her about the worst manuscript he'd ever read, a fantasy novel about a planet of talking dogs.

Suddenly another question popped into her head, one that she had never considered asking before.

"Hey, so um, I have a strange question," she ventured.

"Okay, what is it?"

"You know how you said that I get to say when?"

"Um . . . oh, right. Yes. I remember. The night nothing happened."

"Right." She felt her cheeks warm. "Well, I was just wondering, what happens if I actually do? If I say when?"

"Obviously I can't answer that."

"What? Why not?" Libby exclaimed.

"Because I just can't. But if you say when, then that is essentially you putting the ball back in my court."

"Hmmm."

"Are you saying when?"

"Did you hear me say when?"

"Um, yeah, about four times, I think."

Libby laughed. "No, I'm not saying when. Not yet."

"But you're thinking about it."

"Jason, I think about it every day."

"I like that," he said in an amused tone of voice.

Libby rolled her eyes and returned to her questions about his work.

THAT NIGHT WHEN she climbed into bed, though she was ready to complain to the Lord about the lack of affordable and desirable apartment listings online, she wasn't the one who started the conversation.

You know what the next thing is.

Immediately her heart began to pound. Not yet, she responded. I'm not ready yet.

What makes you ready?

"I don't know!" she whined out loud.

Libby?

"What?" she whispered.

At some point you have to jump.

"But I can't see the bottom."

You still have to jump.

Her heart constricted and she squeezed her eyes shut. "Am I supposed to go to New York?"

You're supposed to say when.

Her eyes flew open and she glanced around in the darkness. "It's too soon!"

Says who?

"Me! Everyone! Society!"

I'm releasing you from all of the expectations that the world may put on you. Don't make decisions based on what other people may think. I know your heart intimately, Libby. I know what it is that you want, and I'm saying that you're ready.

She stared quietly up at the dark ceiling, biting her lip.

What are you waiting for, Libby?

Huh? she thought.

What's holding you back from stepping into the next thing?

"I don't even know what the next thing is! I don't know where I'm supposed to go, to live, any of that! I've been asking You. Have You been getting my messages?"

It was true that things had been progressively better, that her daily conversations with the Lord had brought her more comfort than she'd ever known; she was even inching closer to forgiving her ex-husband. But did that mean that her wounds were healed? They didn't feel healed.

Healing is a lifelong process, Libby. There is no litmus test for when it's over. You have this idea in your head that you have to present yourself as though you are perfect. If that is

true, then you will wait for a lifetime. But you are perfect in my eyes right now, and I want you to live in the abundance that I have for you. It's time.

"But what if I'm making this up, and what if it's too soon, and what if he hurts me?"

What have I told you about what-ifs? They're dangerous, and just like Elena said, you'll drive yourself crazy in those thoughts.

"So, I'm going to New York?"

Just say when.

Libby rolled over onto her side and stared at the outline of her phone on the table. She reached for it, about to text Jason, but then an idea formed in her head and she set the phone back down, pulled her blankets up to her chin, and fell asleep with a smile on her face.

Chapter 27

FOR THE NEXT few weeks, instead of looking for an apartment, Libby focused as many hours as possible working on the revisions for *Red Parks Ranch*. It was the one thing she knew she had to do before she could make any changes to her life. When she finally finished the last sentence, she breathed a huge breath of relief and then immediately texted Elena.

"I'll be over as soon as we close up!" was the response.

Libby printed the manuscript out at home, which took almost thirty minutes and two ink cartridges.

Elena squealed as soon as she walked in the door and Libby handed her the huge stack of papers. "Where can I go?"

"The office or my room, wherever you can find somewhere to sit," Libby said nervously.

"What are you going to do?"

"Finish packing up the rest of the junk that's lying around here, finalize a few details for the movers, just that kind of stuff."

"Okay. I'm too excited about this to even ask if you know where you're going." She eyed the stack of papers and said, "Give me six hours and bring me dinner?"

Libby grinned. "You got it."

Elena took the book upstairs and closed herself in Libby's office while Libby forced herself to focus on other things. She cleaned out a few drawers in the kitchen, double-checked some other rooms and random drawers to see that they were cleared out. That took all of twenty minutes.

She sighed in defeat and picked up her phone and called Jason, promising herself that she would only talk for a few minutes.

"Did you know that I have your number programmed to a special ringtone and every time it goes off, I smile?" Jason asked as soon as he answered.

Libby grinned. "No, I didn't know that."

"The only bad thing is when someone else has that ringtone on their phone, I get jealous and wonder why you're calling them and not me."

Libby laughed out loud. "That's really funny. I promise I'm not calling all those people."

"What's up? I don't usually hear from you in the middle of the day."

"Elena is reading the finished manuscript right now."

"What? Really? Already?"

"Yes. I've been doing nothing but writing."

"What about apartment hunting?" Jason asked curiously. "You're time is running out."

"Overrated. I've decided to become homeless."

"Oh, yeah? Let me know how that goes for you!"

"I've got something in the works; it's not for sure yet, but let's just say I'm not worried."

"Well, all right. You can't give me any more details?"

"I don't want to get into it yet. It's kind of a crazy situation and if it doesn't work out, then I don't want to have explained it a thousand times—you understand?"

"Sure, uh, I guess."

"So, what's going on over there? I need entertainment. It's going to take her, like, six hours to read the book and I might go crazy."

"She's going to read it straight through?" Jason asked in awe.

"Yeah, that's how she works. She devours books."

"Wow. Well, actually we've had some excitement in the office today."

"Oh? What's that?"

"Peter proposed to Amanda last night."

"Aw," Libby gushed. "That's so sweet!"

"Yeah, Amanda's acting like a little school girl," Jason said with a raised voice.

"Can she hear you?"

"Yes. I do that on purpose. Bingo. She just threw an eraser at me," he laughed.

"An eraser? She has an eraser?"

"Yeah, that's weird, isn't it?" Jason chuckled.

The more she listened to him, the more she knew that her plan was right on the money. She knew she was ready.

"I've got to go, Libby. I'm sorry. I have a meeting across town that I need to prepare for."

"Okay. No problem."

"Hey, have you thought any more about coming up here for a weekend? I'd really love to see you, but I just can't get away right now."

"I've thought about it." Libby bit her lip and said nothing more.

"Okay, well let me know what you decide."

"I will. Bye, Jas."

"Bye, Libby."

Fully committed to her plan now, Libby opened her laptop and went to sit on the floor in the living room where the couch used to be. She opened a travel website and began searching for flights to New York City.

ALMOST EXACTLY SIX hours later, Elena emerged from the office upstairs, a blubbering mess of tears. She hugged Libby hard and cried harder.

"Is this all because of the ending?" Libby was astonished.

"It's the whole thing. It's just everything you've been through, and yet writing this amazing book, and it's that you're getting published and . . . Oh, Libby, I'm just so proud of you!" Elena sniffled.

"So, you liked it?"

"I loved it, Libby. It was so beautiful."

Libby took a deep breath. "Thank you. I want to hear all your thoughts about it, but right now we need to talk."

"That doesn't sound good." Elena wiped her eyes and blinked to clear them.

Libby led her to the floor where she'd sat hours earlier and purchased her plane ticket. They sat facing one another, cross-legged.

"What is it?" Elena pressed.

"I made a decision about what I'm going to do."

Elena's eyes grew wide and filled with worry. "Please don't leave me."

Libby cringed and exhaled slowly. "I have to, El."

"No," Elena sighed, tears spilling over her eyelids again. "Where?"

Libby gave her a knowing look and Elena nodded. "New York, right?"

Libby shrugged. "It's time. I'm ready."

"Oh, Libby, I'm going to miss you so much!" Elena cried and flung herself forward into Libby's arms. "But I'm happy for you. I know it's time. I just hate that he lives so far away–"

"I know. I hate that, too. I hate that I have to leave you, but I do, El. I have to go."

Elena released Libby and nodded, wiping her nose on her sleeve. "I know. I think I've known for a while."

"Really?" Libby wiped at her own tears.

Elena nodded. "As soon as I met him, I knew there was no way you'd let him go."

"It's terrifying. I'm so scared, but at the same time, I know that it's right. Like if I've ever known anything at all, it's that this is right.

That he's it."

Elena began to cry again. "I'm crying because I'm happy for you, I swear. I think he's fantastic. He's perfect for you."

"He really is," Libby agreed. Suddenly she couldn't wait for the weekend.

The knowledge of Jeremy's whereabouts continued to weigh on Abe, and as he watched Sarah's belly and exhaustion continue to grow, he came closer and closer to taking matters into his own hands. As far as Abe was concerned, Jeremy had probably run when Sarah had told him the news. Abe cursed the man up and down but knew that within a few weeks, days even, Sarah would be of no use to anyone except the baby she was about to deliver. He continued to struggle over what to do until one afternoon when he saw the telltale signs that he'd seen in his own mother in the five births she'd endured after his own. That day, Abe knew he couldn't wait any longer and quietly saddled a horse and left the ranch.

⋆   ⋆   ⋆

Sarah had never known such pain before. She didn't know what was normal and what wasn't and she was terrified. The pain was a repetitive tightening in her belly and a cramp in her back, over and over. The last thing she wanted to do was birth this child on her own, but she wasn't about to hobble through the fields asking for help. She was embarrassed enough as it was.

Tears streamed down her face as she gathered blankets and sheets beside her bed and labored through another contraction. When she reached her limit with the pain, she lowered herself onto the bed and felt the incredible urge to push. She screamed his name in fury as she bore down with her heels digging into the mattress.

She had cried his name out, calling to him so many times before and he'd never returned, but this time, as if all of her agony had finally reached his ears,

Jeremy shot through the door, his face pale with the sound of her scream.

* * *

The confusion and fear in her eyes as she screamed in pain terrified Jeremy. Abe pushed him into the room and barked out orders. Jeremy followed immediately and then knelt by the bed, offering Sarah his hand.

She stared at him, wild-eyed, as she let out another blood-curdling scream. Then suddenly she fell back against the pillows, breathless and spent. A tiny cry filled the room and Jeremy turned sharply to where Abe sat, wiping at the tiny body.

"What happened? Is she okay?"

"She's fine, let her rest."

"Is the baby . . . is it okay?"

"Your son is mighty fine, boss."

A sob slipped out of his lips and he scooted down the floor to get a look at his son.

"Abe, if I'd missed this—"

"I wasn't gonna let you, even if you did know about it."

"I had no idea. I swear it."

"You wanna hold him, boss?"

Jeremy took the little squirming bundle into his arms as huge tears rolled down his sun-browned cheeks.

Jeremy cradled his son while Sarah slept.

Two days old and already changing so much, and to think, he almost missed it.

He understood now. He knew he had pushed her too far, too fast. He'd loved her too quickly. But had any of that changed now? He turned his gaze to the sleeping woman who had yet to speak to him. He still loved her just as much, even more now that they shared a son.

"God, if You're there," he whispered, "please give me another chance. I won't mess it up this time. I can't. I love them."

On Thursday, the movers arrived just after the storage pod had been delivered. Elena, Reggie, and Libby watched as her entire life was carted out on dollies and packed into the portable pod.

"You're really leaving, huh?" Reggie asked.

"Yep."

"And he doesn't even know?" Elena asked skeptically.

"No. I've purposely avoided his calls and have only been texting. I'm too excited; I know I'll give it away."

"What if he's not there? What if he's—"

"What did you tell me about what-ifs, El?"

Elena sighed. "Yeah, okay. You're right."

"I'll be back on Wednesday to close on the house and tie up the rest of my loose ends here."

"Then we'll fly back with you and meet the pod at your new place," Elena repeated the plan for the twelfth time.

"I'm really excited about that part," Libby grinned. "We're going to have a lot of fun."

"I still can't believe you're moving to New York." Elena pouted.

"Me, neither." Libby smiled.

The element of disbelief was largely overshadowed by the crazy excitement she felt stirring in her belly as she boarded her plane on Friday. Jason still had no idea she was coming. She had only doubted her plan for random split seconds over the past week, but every time, a sense of peace had filled her from head to toe and the doubt would simply disappear. All she had to endure now was a plane flight and a cab ride.

Six hours of torture, she thought. The time passed quickly enough though, and she was surprised when the pilot announced that they'd made record time and were nearing New York. Libby remembered how nervous she'd been the last time she'd flown into New York to see Jason. This time that nervousness was excitement and she didn't feel like she was going to throw up. She gripped the arms of her chair and waited for the butterflies to dance as the plane descended. It was her favorite part of flying.

JASON MADE HIS way home from work slowly. It had been a long week and he was tired. He had tried to call Libby before he got on the subway, but once again she hadn't picked up. He was starting to feel a little insecure about how many times she'd missed his calls that week. She'd texted him every night, though, and always had a legitimate-sounding excuse, but the fact that she never called him back had left him a little uneasy.

He pushed those thoughts from his head and sidestepped a suspicious looking pile of something brown on the sidewalk. All he was looking forward to now was another "CSI" episode and some leftover spaghetti that he had in the fridge. He looked up as he neared his town home, squinting against the sun. It looked like someone was sitting on his stairway. The sun glinted off of something, shining in his eyes.

"That's weird," he muttered. In the two years that he'd lived there, no one had ever just hung out at his front door.

The person seemed to recognize him. As he neared the steps, he saw the woman stand up expectantly. Jason still couldn't make out who it was because of the blinding afternoon sun, but the pendant that had caught the light looked oddly familiar. He was a little irritated that someone was now standing between him and the rest that he needed. Who in the world could it be? He reached the foot of the steps and looked up, his hand shielding his eyes as he waited for his vision to clear of sunspots.

"Libby?" Jason froze.

"Hi," she said sweetly with a huge smile on her face.

He hurried up the steps to where she stood and pulled her into his arms. "What are you doing here?" he exclaimed. "Oh, my gosh!"

She melted into his embrace and Jason felt his eyes stinging with moisture. He sighed deeply and then pulled her back to look into her face.

"What are you doing here?" he asked again.

Her own eyes glistening, she laughed quietly and said very simply, "When."

"What?" Suddenly it was as if a light went off in his head and his eyes widened in understanding. All the air in his lungs seemed to be sucked out and he gripped the fabric of her sleeves in his fist. "Really?" he whispered.

A tear slipped out from the corner of Libby's eye and she slid her hands up so that she was holding his face. "I tried to stop myself because this terrifies me. It's too fast and people will talk, but the fact is, I've fallen in love with you, Jason. I'm starting to think that that was the plan all along."

He breathed her name and pulled her back to him, pressing his lips against her hair, her forehead, and her cheeks before pulling away again and looking intensely into her eyes. "If I kiss you right now, I may never stop," he warned her.

"You don't have to stop," she smiled, pulled his face to hers, and slid her arms around his neck. She felt her feet lift from the ground as his arms tightened around her, leaving absolutely no space between them.

Jason's lips, starved for affection, moved gently over hers, filling their need and savoring the taste of her. There were no more warning bells or words of caution. Now that she was his he didn't worry about crossing boundaries; he knew he wouldn't come close to them because what was happening between them was too precious. He wanted her desperately but loved her more than that, and though he knew he couldn't wait forever, what he had right now, in that moment, was enough.

Chapter 28

"EXPLAIN IT ALL to me again," Jason said as they held hands and strolled through Central Park later that afternoon.

Libby leaned into him and smiled. "Elena and Reggie are coming this weekend."

"And you're moving here. Permanently."

"For now," Libby corrected him.

"Which I'll just pretend means permanently."

"Well, I guess as long as you're here." She smiled up at him.

"I can't believe you're really here." He leaned forward and kissed her forehead.

"It was time. I had to let go of my fears. I mean, they're still there but . . . I'm not letting them get in the way. I know that this is right." She held his hand to her lips, amazed that her plan had actually worked.

Jason was thoughtful for a moment and then he stopped her in the middle of the path. "Call me crazy, but I think I have a solution to your living situation, and you won't even have to look at any apartments."

"I'm listening," Libby turned her head in interest.

"What if . . . what if you moved in with me?" Jason said with a straight face.

Libby chuckled and rolled her head back. "Jason, the only way that would work out for us is if–" She stopped suddenly, her eyes wide as she stared at him in shock.

"If we got married."

A chill ran through her limbs. Her lungs felt constricted and she pulled her hand slowly from his.

"Don't pull a Sarah on me," he grinned. "You can say no, it's just a hair-brained idea that I had–"

"Yes," Libby blurted out before she even realized she'd done it.

"Did you just say–"

"Yes." She nodded and held her hand up to cover a sob. "I can't believe I'm saying this, but yes. If you're really asking, then my answer is yes!"

Jason's face paled and he took her hands in his. "Wait, just wait."

Libby suddenly felt that fear flood back into her heart. For a split second she thought that things were finally falling into place exactly as they should be. Was he going to take it back?

"This is not how I want to do this."

Libby was too insecure to feel relief. "What do you mean?"

He moved forward to kiss her softly. "I want to ask you properly," he whispered against her lips.

Libby let the relief wash over her and she blinked back tears.

"You're not going to change your mind if I leave you for an hour, are you?"

She shook her head vehemently.

"I'm going to drop you at your hotel and then I'll meet you back there in an hour. Okay?"

She couldn't speak so she nodded her head and let him lead her quickly back to the street.

It was agony, pacing her hotel room, waiting for him to return. She'd changed out of her jeans into a knee length black skirt, a short-sleeved red button-up sweater, and a pair of flats. She resisted the urge to call Elena; she wanted the news to be official before she announced it, even if it was crazier than simply moving across the country.

She spent the entire time praying that she was making the right choice, and when Jason finally knocked on the door forty-five minutes later, she had nearly worn a hole in the carpet where she'd been walking, and she knew without a doubt that saying yes wasn't only what she wanted, but that it was what God was confirming in her heart.

She threw open the door, expecting him to be on one knee, but he was standing, with his heart-stopping smile stretching across his cheeks. He'd changed as well, into designer jeans, a black shirt, and a dark grey blazer. Libby's heart thumped at the sight of him.

"Libby, will you have dinner with me?" he asked with a wink. He held out his hand to her.

She slipped her hand into his, amazed at how warm his skin was on hers, and how safe she felt within his grasp.

Jason led her from the hotel–not the same one she'd stayed in before since this time she was paying for it–and to the sidewalk. He walked her to a quaint café just a few blocks from the hotel.

Libby kept anticipating the moment, but even after they'd finished their dessert he still had yet to ask her anything special.

He didn't ask her in the cab on the way to an unknown destination as night fell over the city. He didn't ask her as they walked through the dimly-lit paths at Central Park or as they stared out at Turtle Pond with the beautiful castle beyond them.

Libby didn't recognize where they were headed, having only been there once and this time it was nearly pitch black, but soon she saw a familiar landmark forming in the distance.

Jason's grip on her hand tightened as she caught her breath, realizing what his plan had been all along.

A streetlamp lit up the top of Alice's head and spilled light down her shoulders, casting odd-looking shadows onto the ground around the statue. Libby closed her eyes as they drew near, leaning hard against Jason.

He stopped in front of the statue and turned Libby to face him.

She opened her eyes, which were full of tears ready to spill at any moment.

"You told me once that you loved the idea of Alice escaping from reality, even though the fantasy world wasn't perfect and she had to rise above many things to get back home. You told me that you didn't want me to be your savior, that you wanted me to be waiting for you on the other side of everything you were facing." Jason pushed Libby's hair behind her ear and left his hand on her cheek. "Well, I didn't save you, and I did wait for you. I waited for you to rise above and climb out of that world and into this new reality that we get to create together. I don't want to rush you, if you need more time–"

"I don't!" she whispered quickly.

Jason sighed with nervous relief and dropped one of her hands. "Elizabeth Abbott, will you marry me?" Jason opened a small grey velvet box that he'd pulled from his pocket and held it into the light for her to see. A simple gold band with three diamonds in the middle sparkled at her.

"Yes," she spoke with confidence.

Jason slipped the ring onto her finger and as she leaned forward to kiss him, he stopped her gently. "One more thing," he whispered.

She gave him a curious look and waited for him to continue.

"We will have our Alice," he said softly. "I don't care how it happens. But we will have our Alice." He held out his palm, which held a bead the same size as the ones in her necklace. "And when we do, we will add this egg to the nest."

Libby drew in a stuttered breath as her tears unleashed themselves and Jason's lips finally met hers in the sweetest kiss she'd ever been given. He pulled away slowly and held her face near to his, gazing at her, and whispered fiercely, "I will never leave you, nor forsake you, Libby. Ever."

She had never known so much peace, so much joy. She smiled and began to laugh, feeling giddy like a child. She knew that this had been the plan all along.

"YOU FOUND A place already? I thought you weren't going to look until tomorrow!" Elena sounded extremely surprised.

Libby leaned against the wall and pulled a pillow into her chest. This hotel certainly wasn't as nice as the one Jason had put her up in, but she could stand it for a few more days. "It kind of snuck up on me," she said cryptically.

"So where is it?"

"About twenty minutes from downtown. It's a townhouse."

"A townhouse? In New York City? Are you crazy? How can you afford that?"

"Um, it's kind of already paid for, sort of . . ." Libby trailed off.

"I feel like you're not telling me something."

"Um, okay. First of all, I'm going to need to give you power of attorney so that you can go to the closing for me. Second, I'm moving in with Jason."

"What? Wow. There goes the Christian values, I guess," Elena laughed.

"Not exactly." She hated doing this to Elena, but it was oh so much fun.

"Spill it, sister."

Libby took a deep breath, knowing that Elena was about to freak out. "We're getting married." She cringed and immediately held the phone out as Elena screamed loudly into her end.

"What? You're joking me!" Elena continued to squeal and yell into the phone. "Isn't that fast? I mean, super fast?"

"All things considered, yes and no. I know this is right, El," Libby sighed. "I'm so sure of it I can almost touch it. This is right."

"Oh, Libby. I'm thrilled. I really am. I'm so happy for you!"

"Thank you. So that means that when you guys come up this weekend, we'll have just a really small ceremony and–"

"Wait–this weekend? Are you kidding me?"

"The movers are coming and I have to have a place to put my stuff. I can't stay in this hotel forever and . . . it's *right*."

"Wow. I can't believe this. You're getting married! This weekend. I have to get a dress!"

Libby laughed. "Of course you'll use anything for an excuse to shop. It's just going to be the four of us, El. You don't have to buy a dress for this—"

"I'm going to pretend that you didn't just say that. Please tell me that you are going to buy a new dress? Please?"

"Well, of course I'm going to," Libby giggled.

"Oh, you better not shop without me! I'll come a day early even!"

"Can you do that?"

"Of course I can! Samantha can run the shop. I'll go to the closing on Wednesday and then fly out after that. Then we'll spend all day Thursday shopping in New York! Oh, my gosh, I'm so excited!"

LIBBY'S HEART BRIMMED with excitement over the next few days as she anticipated Elena's arrival. She and Jason had their work cut out for them, trying to make room in his house for her and her things. She wasn't bringing a ton of furniture into the mix, but she did have boxes and boxes of things that she couldn't part with.

As she took in his bachelor pad for the first time, she realized that it was going to be a challenge to bring their styles together. She made a passing comment about it and Jason stopped short.

"You call this a style?" He laughed. "You can get rid of whatever you want in this place, Libby. I didn't do anything with the place when I moved in; I just let things end up in places that made sense. If you don't like my grungy leather couch, get rid of it. If you want to move it to a corner instead of five feet from the TV, then we'll move it. Whatever you want."

"Are you serious?" Libby asked, incredulous.

"Absolutely. I'm not attached to any of this." He waved his hand around the room. "I got that coffee table from someone's trash pile. Seriously, those were dark days. I didn't care what the place looked like. But I want you to have a home that you want to be in. I want you to make this your home."

"Do you think we could decide on some of this stuff together?" she asked.

Jason sighed and pulled her into his arms. "I think you're perfect."

She closed her eyes and melted into his kiss, almost afraid to open them again for fear of finding out he really was too good to be true.

WHILE JASON CLEANED out his closets and cleared out an entire room for Libby's office, she made a list of the big things that were coming from Dallas. The bedroom suite from the guest room, her grandmother's chest of drawers, the office furniture, and the rocker were among the most important.

On Tuesday, while Jason was consumed with a box full of old baseball cards that he'd found, Libby ventured up to the third floor to the bedroom they would soon share. It was the first time she'd even dared set foot up there in the two days they'd been working together in the house.

The room was very plain. His bed sat on a simple frame with no headboard and his dresser was vintage, but still the original brown color. There were no pictures on the walls, and plain blue curtains hung on the window. She tried to imagine her own things in that room and then turned to the dresser again. Inspiration hit her suddenly and she raced down the stairs to where Jason was working.

"Where is the nearest paint store?" she asked breathlessly.

Jason gave her a questioning look. "What are you going to paint?"

"Your dresser," she grinned.

"Uh, okay, well let me get my shoes on–"

"No, I can go. I need to figure this city out. Just tell me where it is."

Jason gave her directions and Libby set out excitedly on her adventure. She returned thirty minutes later, the wheels in her head spinning as she took the stairs two at a time back up to the bedroom, paint in hand.

AFTER A FEW hours, Jason made his way up the stairs to check on her, unsure of what he would find. His dresser–boxers, socks, and all–had been emptied out onto his bed, and Libby was on her knees with a paintbrush, carefully painting black strokes across a drawer.

"Wow," he breathed. "I didn't know you could do that!" His old, ugly brown dresser frame was now painted black and looked slightly weathered even though the paint was fresh. "How did you do it?" He stepped towards it with an outstretched hand.

"Don't touch!" Libby squealed and Jason froze. She breathed out when he dropped his hand back to his side. "It's called antiquing. I'm going to paint my bed frame to match it."

"I'm impressed. You keep surprising me!"

Libby grinned up at him and he noticed a black streak of paint across her face.

"That's cute, too," he pointed.

"Job hazard," Libby shrugged and went back to painting the drawer.

"So, you're in my room," he said awkwardly. "And that's my underwear."

Libby didn't look up at him but bit her lips together as a smile played about them.

"Did you just, uh, dump them out, or–"

"Oh, I picked them up with my hands. Even put a pair on," she teased.

Jason made a whining sound and Libby burst into laughter.

"I'm leaving now" Jason said and turned on his heel, practically running down the stairs.

As promised, Elena arrived on Wednesday night and joined Libby in her hotel room.

"What's going on with the book while you're busy planning a wedding?" Elena asked from the bathroom while she washed her face.

"It's being edited and proofread right now; then I'll get it back and make whatever changes they feel necessary and go through the process one more time before it goes to print," Libby explained as she changed into her pajamas.

"You have to change stuff? Will that be hard?" Elena asked as she crawled into bed.

"I don't know. I guess it depends on what they want to tweak. We'll see."

"Wow. This is crazy. Look at where you are right now versus a year ago!"

Libby lay down beside Elena and stared at the ceiling. "I can't even comprehend it." She held up her hand to admire her ring and Elena pulled it over to get another look.

"He picked it out on his own? And it fit and everything?"

Libby nodded. "Yep. It's perfect."

"Dang. Someone should write your story."

Libby grinned and turned on to her side. "I think someone already is," she sighed and closed her eyes, knowing she was going to need hours of good sleep to prepare for a day on the town with Elena.

After hours of being dragged into extravagant store after extravagant store, Libby finally had to sit Elena down and remind her that she had a minimal budget for her dress and that she only wanted something very simple.

"Fine," Elena pouted and looked up some more affordable stores in the area on her phone. "Okay, here's one. It looks like a knock-off store. Maybe we can both find something here." Elena pointed in the direction of the store and once again, Libby followed.

The shop looked more promising than any others that they had been in, simply because of the peeling paint and aged window display. Libby was hopeful while Elena cringed and commented at the smell of the place.

An Asian woman greeted them from behind a sewing machine.

"Look! She's making a dress right now!" Libby pointed and watched for a minute before Elena reminded her why they were there. Libby turned her attention to the small inventory of white dresses while Elena went for the racks with color.

It took Libby all of five minutes before she found what she was looking for. She checked the tag and saw that the dress was in her price range but was two sizes too small. She pulled it off anyway and showed it to the woman at the sewing machine.

"Do you have this in a six?" she asked the woman.

She was met with a blank stare.

"Um, six?" She pointed to the dress and then drew a six in the air with her finger.

"Ah, yes. One minute." The woman excused herself into the back of the store and then came out with a dress identical to the one Libby was holding. "Six," she said and handed it over.

Libby thanked her and then looked around for a changing room. The woman pointed to a curtain behind the rack of prom dresses that Elena was looking through. Libby didn't let the woman see her expression of surprise but took the dress behind the curtain and thanked her lucky stars that they'd found a reasonably affordable place to buy dresses in New York City.

She stripped off her clothes and pulled the dress over her head and then turned to look in the mirror. "Elena!" she called as she stared dreamily at her reflection.

The curtain snapped to the side and Elena gasped. "Oh, Libby. It's beautiful!"

The strapless dress was incredibly simple but elegant. The white sheer overlay gathered in the front under a small string of delicate cream-colored fabric roses and then fell to the floor like drapes around her feet, swishing softly when she moved.

"You can pull your hair up loosely and tuck some roses in there. It will be so beautiful!"

"That sounds perfect," Libby sighed. The sight of herself in a wedding dress made her stomach knot in fear. "Am I really doing this again, El?" She turned to her friend and grabbed her arm. "Tell me I'm not making a mistake!"

Elena stepped into the makeshift changing room and pulled the curtain shut, grabbing her best friend's hands. "You're not making a mistake. I would tell you this time. I wouldn't let you go through all of that again. I've never seen you so happy before. You're ready, Libby. You're ready to live the life you were always meant to have."

Libby nodded and breathed through the small anxiety attack. "I know you're right. I know it. I just get scared sometimes."

"I think that's totally normal. You just need him to remind you of who he is. They way he looks at you, Libby . . . let's just say, I've never seen anyone look at you that way before. He loves you the way you deserve to be loved. And you said it yourself: this is right."

"Yeah. I did, didn't I?"

"Are you going to buy that dress?"

Libby nodded. "Yes. And I'm going to marry Jason."

"And I'm going to try this one on now that I've seen that." Elena held up a grey, one shouldered, knee-length chiffon dress.

"That's really pretty, Elena."

"Yeah? You like it?"

Libby nodded. "Try it on."

Elena did so as Libby changed back into her clothes. "This is really cute." Elena turned and her skirt followed the movement. The fabric gathered in the front a little more dramatically than Libby's did and a satin grey sash around the middle held it all in place.

"I love it, El."

"If you love it, then I love it," Elena grinned. "I think we're set!"

"Finally! I'm exhausted and I can't wait to get back and see what Jason has done with the furniture we bought for the living room!"

"Listen to you guys, buying furniture together. I still remember when you came home to that awful bedroom suite—"

"Don't remind me," Libby rolled her eyes. "Come on, let's get out of here!"

SATURDAY DAWNED MORE quickly than Libby had anticipated it would. Thursday evening and Friday had been spent moving boxes and furniture in and out of the townhouse and finalizing what few details there were for their ceremony the next afternoon.

Libby took her time waking up, thankful that Elena had stayed with Reggie the night before so that she could get the best sleep possible. Slowly she raised her arms over her head and smiled as the plans for the day played themselves out in her mind.

"I'm getting married today," she sighed and sank deeper into her pillows.

Enjoy today, Libby. Keep your eyes on me and nothing will get in your way. Just enjoy what I've planned for you.

"Thank You for not giving up on me when You should have. Thank You for being patient with me and loving me even when I didn't care about You at all," she prayed quietly.

My promises are true, always. I will never leave you.

"Nor forsake me, I know. I believe it now. I know it."

I love you, Elizabeth.

"I love You, too."

ELENA AND LIBBY met Reggie at an entrance to Central Park and he led them down a path in the opposite direction of Alice and the castle, through some trees, deep into what felt like a forest rather than a park. A few passersby commented on Libby's dress, oohing and aahing over the idea of a wedding in the park. One little girl begged her mom and dad to follow them, and when she almost started crying, Libby turned to them and invited them to come along and watch.

"It won't be very long, and it's just a few of us. Please, you're welcome to come along."

The mother was mortified, but the dad shrugged and said, "Let's do it! Come on Amber!" He swung his daughter onto his shoulders and followed the small procession along the path.

Libby grabbed Elena's hand and squeezed hard as they neared the steps that led to the Bethesda fountain where Jason and the minister were waiting for them.

"You okay?" Elena whispered.

Libby nodded. "I'm just overwhelmed. This is too good to be true."

Elena stopped walking and turned Libby to face her. "For once, Libby, it's not. It's exactly as good as it's supposed to be."

Smiling through her tears, Libby hugged Elena tightly.

"You're going to crush that pretty white rose. Go on," Elena whispered, pushing her away gently.

Libby smiled, checked that her solitary rose was still in one piece, hiked up the skirt of her dress a little, and started moving down the steps. The view of the fountain and the lake behind it was breathtaking. Libby couldn't help smiling as she finally saw the Loeb Boathouse in the distance. Their lunch at Tavern on the Green later would complete her Central Park bucket list. Small things when compared to the man who was waiting for her by the railing, but important things nonetheless.

After what felt like an eternity, she finally reached Jason's side.

"You're beautiful," he said, eyeing the mass of curls that cascaded down one shoulder. "As beautiful as you've ever been."

"I love you," she whispered.

The minister directed them to stand facing one another and began to lead them in their vows.

"Elizabeth, with the Lord as our foundation and our strength, I vow never to betray your trust and never to treat this gift that you've given me as carelessly as it's been treated in the past. I promise to love you and cherish you and to call out the best in you, every day. I promise to support you and provide for you and do my best to give you everything you will ever need. I will never leave you nor forsake you," Jason said quietly as he slipped a gold band onto her finger.

Libby's cheeks hurt from smiling so wide, but she couldn't help it. She took his hand and the ring from Elena and spoke her promises over him. "With the Lord as our foundation and strength, I vow to be loyal to you until the end of our days and to never forget what a gift you are to me. I promise to support you and fight for you, to love you and honor you as my husband. I promise to submit to you and to God within you, and to do whatever is in my power to give you everything you could ever need. I will never leave you nor forsake you."

Jason grinned as she struggled to get the ring over his knuckle, and then when it was safely in place, he took both of her hands in his again.

"Jason and Elizabeth, it is my honor to proclaim that what God has brought together, no man may come between. In the name of the Father, Son, and Holy Spirit, and by the state of New York, I pronounce you husband and wife."

A sob left Libby's lips just before they met Jason's and she fell into him with such force that he had to take a step back to steady himself. She threw her arms around his neck, crying as his lips took to hers.

Everyone laughed, and as Libby and Jason released each other, Amber danced right up to Libby, despite her mother's cries of, "Amber! Come back here!"

"You're a beautiful princess," Amber gushed and hugged Libby around the legs.

"You are going to be a beautiful princess one day, too," Libby bent down and handed the little girl the white rose.

Amber's eyes and mouth opened wide.

The little girl took the flower delicately and held it as if it might crumble and die. Amber trotted back to her parents and showed them the flower. Her mom mouthed her thanks to Libby and touched her hand to her heart.

"Are you ready to go see Alice?" Amber's dad asked the little girl.

"Yes!" Amber cried and ran off ahead of them.

Jason squeezed Libby's hand and she stood and returned his gaze. He pulled her into his arms and put his lips close to her ear. Libby gripped on to his suit jacket as she heard the Lord speak to her.

I make all things new. Where you have asked me to put broken pieces back together, I have wiped the slate clean and I am painting you with broad, fresh strokes of bold, beautiful colors. The old is gone and the new has come. You have never experienced what is ahead of you so don't be fooled into thinking that you know where you're going. Put your trust in me and believe that I am always with you, and together we will create a portrait so beautiful, not even the flowers of the field could compare.

They both exhaled at the same time. Libby had never heard Him so clearly. There was no more fear or doubt left in her heart; she was the happiest she'd ever been.

"Let's go, wife," Jason grinned.

"EVERYTHING OKAY IN there?" Jason asked rather urgently through the bathroom door.

Libby was on the other side of the door putting the finishing touches on her surprise for him. She grinned at herself, her stomach balled up in knots of anticipation. She smoothed the silky red fabric over her waist one more time and then took a deep breath.

"Okay. I'm ready," she said just loud enough for him to hear.

She heard a shuffling as he moved away from the door, and the creak of the mattress. She bit her lip and opened the door, gazing seductively at her husband.

Jason's eyes bulged out of his head and a low chuckle came from his throat.

"I thought you might want to see this dress again," Libby grinned sheepishly.

He stood up and approached her slowly, his fingers sliding gently up her bare arms. "You're brilliant, you know that?"

"Well, I try," she grinned and met his incoming kiss.

THE MOONLIGHT STREAMED from the window above the bed, casting shadows of the trees outside on the wall across from them. Libby watched as dark leaves danced across the doorway to the bathroom, Jason's chest rising and falling underneath her cheek. His chest was smooth to the touch as she drew circles on it with her finger. The faint sound of traffic wafted in through the window, but it was comforting to her because she knew she was where she belonged.

"It's going to be good, isn't it?" she whispered.

"It already was," he said sleepily.

She laughed and poked him in the chest. "You know that's not what I meant."

Jason draped his arm across her back, trailing his fingers on her skin. "It'll be amazing."

She felt his lips on her head.

"I will do whatever it takes to make sure you are happy and taken care of," he promised. "Even if it means whisking you away to the East Coast first thing tomorrow morning."

Libby gasped and pushed herself up, staring into her husband's face. "What?"

He grinned from ear to ear. "You said you've always wanted to go, and my parents felt bad about missing the wedding, so this is their gift to us. We'll have a week to ourselves and then they'll be pounding down the door because they're dying to meet you."

She pulled herself up and kissed him hard on the mouth. "I can't believe this."

"I love you," he whispered.

She laid her head back down on his chest. She doubted she would be able to sleep tonight, but she didn't care. She loved the sound of Jason's heart beating in her ear. She loved how he smelled, even hours after his cologne had faded. She loved the way he loved her, and she knew she would love him for a lifetime.

"I love you, too."

Sarah caressed the sweet little face, in awe as he suckled at her breast. She'd never been so in love in her entire life. She knew Jeremy was watching her from a safe distance across the room. She still hadn't brought herself to speak more than a few words to him. She'd been working on building her courage up and finding the right thing to say.

Watching him with their son over the past few days had nearly ruined her decision to keep him at a distance. But there were things that needed to be said. Things she needed to tell him.

"If you'd just waited," she finally blurted out. "I wasn't ready."

Jeremy stood up immediately from his seat at the table and cleared his throat. "I didn't understand, Sarah."

"It was his birthday that day, Jeremy. It was Red's birthday."

Jeremy sighed and sank back into his chair. "Hell, Sarah, I never know what day it is. All I knew was that I loved you."

"And then you just disappeared. You didn't even give me the chance—"

"You didn't give me the chance!" He snapped back.

"You surprised me at the worst moment," Sarah sniffed. "I didn't know what to do. I didn't want you to leave the ranch. I just needed time."

"I told you that if I couldn't be with you, then I couldn't be here."

"So you just left?"

"Believe me, if I'd known about the baby, I would never have left you here alone."

"So that's the only reason you came back?"

Pain shadowed his eyes. "You know that's not true."

She stifled a sob and took a deep breath. "By the time I figured out what was happening, no one knew where you'd gone."

Jeremy picked his hat up off the table and spun it

in his hands.

"I wasn't far."

Sarah swallowed. "You were gone a long time. You meet somebody?"

Jeremy stood again and this time rushed to her bedside.

"No, Sarah. Never. There's only you. There will only ever be you."

"Red will always be the man I loved first, Jeremy. I can't do anything about that." She sat up, careful not to disturb the baby. "But that doesn't change the fact that . . . that I do love you. I do. I tried to hate you, but every time this child moved inside of me, I knew it was part you and part me, and I would fall more in love with you."

"I can't give you everything he wanted to give you."

Her eyes glistened with tears. "You've already given me more than he ever did."

Jeremy knelt down in front of Sarah, kissing their baby, kissing her mouth. "Sarah, I promise you, I'll never leave you again, and I'll give you as many more sons as we can manage." He cried like a child. "I'll marry you as soon as we can get the minister here, if you'll have me."

She couldn't mistake the hope in his gaze. With one hand cradling the child, and the other wrapped around Jeremy's neck, she pulled him closer to her, opening her mouth against him and welcoming him back into her heart.

"Of course I'll have you," she whispered. "You're the only man I want."

As Jeremy peppered kisses across her face, the truth of her words settled in her heart. She'd recovered from her loss and had managed to find true love and happiness again. For the first time in years she lifted her thoughts to the heavens and breathed a quiet prayer of thanks.

Epilogue

LIBBY GRIPPED THE bathroom counter so hard her knuckles were white. "Please, God, don't do this to me again. Please. I'm begging You," she prayed. Her chest was tight with panic and she was having a difficult time breathing. The small plastic tube sitting on the back of the toilet seemed to be screaming obscenities at her.

Jason knocked on the door. "Babe? Are you okay?" His voice was as strained as her heart felt.

"Thirty more seconds," she said just above a whisper.

"Can I please come in?"

Libby closed her eyes and focused on breathing in and out slowly, trying to calm the nerves inside of her.

"Libby?"

Finally, when she knew more than thirty seconds had passed, she opened the door and Jason came in slowly. He rubbed his hands along her arms from behind.

"Did you look?"

She shook her head. "I can't."

He kissed the back of her neck, stepped over to the toilet, and picked up the pregnancy test.

Jason swallowed and then picked up the box to see what the results were. "Two lines. That means—"

"I know what it means," she whispered.

"Libby, we don't know what—"

"Can you just give me a minute, please? Just leave me alone."

"No, honey. I'm not going to let you face this alone." He put the test and the box down and pulled her rigid body into his arms.

"Whatever happens, I will not leave your side."

Libby didn't respond. She was numb. For six months their lives had been absolute bliss. When they weren't in the throes of passion and newlywed bliss, they worked alongside each other, Jason planning her book tour schedule for the fall while Libby's time was spent weeding through edits and changes that came down the pipeline from Emerald.

For the past few weeks though, she'd been feeling under the weather. The cause hadn't occurred to her until one morning when she was searching for a bottle of nail polish remover and had noticed her feminine products still sat new in the package though it had been well over a month since she'd restocked. She popped up so fast she'd almost hit her head on the countertop. All day that day she had prayed and prayed that it was a fluke, but even as she prayed she had spiraled into that dark place from her past.

That darkness seemed to call to her. It wanted to swallow her whole. Last time she had fallen in headfirst and had worked to pull herself out on her own, and when she finally emerged, she'd discovered that her marriage had disintegrated.

This time her new husband was holding so tightly to her that she wanted to beg him to just let her go. Instead, she stayed, like a carcass in his arms, detaching herself mentally and saying goodbye to the happiness that she'd naively become accustomed to.

"We're going to the doctor first thing in the morning," Jason whispered.

Libby finally pulled away from him and pushed the test and the box into the trash. She left the bathroom and crawled into their bed, pulling the blankets around her chin.

〜

JASON STOOD IN the bathroom and stared at himself. What am I supposed to do?

Remind her of my promises.

I don't really think she's listening to me right now.

Remind her of the promise I gave you on your wedding day.

Jason sighed and left the room. He went into Libby's office and pulled the framed picture of the two of them on their wedding day off the wall. He tucked it under his arm and returned to the bedroom where she was curled up in the fetal position. He sat down gently on the bed beside her and stared at the picture of their faces, turned toward one another and smiling widely at each other, laughter in their eyes.

Jason turned it over and traced his fingers over Libby's handwriting, which flowed across the back of the frame in gold ink. As he read it again for the hundredth time, he begged the Lord to give him strength. Then he read aloud:

"I make all things new. Where you have asked me to put broken pieces back together, I have wiped the slate clean and I am painting you with broad, fresh strokes of bold, beautiful colors. The old is gone and the new is come. You have never experienced what is ahead of you, so don't be fooled into thinking that you know where you're going. Put your trust in me and believe that I am always with you, and together we will create a portrait so beautiful, not even the flowers of the field could compare."

He heard a sniffle come from Libby's side of the bed.

"'For I know the plans I have for you,' declares the Lord," Jason recited from memory. "'Plans to prosper you and not to harm you. Plans to give you a hope and a future.'"

Libby turned over and faced him but didn't look him in the eye. "I can't lose another baby, Jason. I can't do this again," she cried.

Jason scooted down and lay on his side at eye level with her. He placed his hand on her cheek, rubbing his thumb across it. "Maybe you won't! And no matter what happens, I'm going to be here. You won't be alone and I'm never going to leave you."

"You don't know what it feels like, Jason. Part of you is growing inside of me right now and in a few weeks, it might be gone; you don't know what that loss feels like."

"Right now I know that it would hurt worse to lose you. I won't let you push me away. We're going to get through this together."

Libby closed her eyes and didn't open them again that night. When he knew she was asleep, Jason sighed and pushed himself off the bed. He began calling OB/GYN offices to see who had an appointment available the next morning.

LIBBY WAS SILENT all the way to the doctor's office and while she changed for the ultrasound. She knew the drill. She inserted the long phallic-looking probe herself and squirmed uncomfortably while the technician took pictures of her insides. She didn't say a word while they waited in the examination room for the doctor to see them.

She shifted uncomfortably in the paper gown while Jason stood at her side, holding her hand.

"I spoke with the doctor last night and told her about the previous miscarriages and that you were concerned this time."

Concerned doesn't even begin to describe it, Libby thought, but she kept her mouth clamped tightly shut.

The door opened with a creak following a brisk knock, and an older woman with grey hair and bright blue eyes walked in. She wore a lab coat with a flowery scarf at her neck.

"Hi, there, you must be Jason and Elizabeth," the woman gave a genuine smile and held out her hand. "I'm Dr. Brown."

Jason shook the woman's hand. "Thanks for fitting us in so quickly. I really appreciate it."

Dr. Brown nodded. "Well, let's take a look then, shall we? Go ahead and lie back, Elizabeth."

Libby obeyed but didn't let go of Jason's hand. The fact that he was there meant more than she could say. She'd always done this kind of thing alone before.

The doctor pressed on her stomach gently. "Any nausea?"

"Yes," Libby said, clearing her throat.

"Good. How about spotting or cramping?"

"No, none of that."

"Good. Do you drink or smoke?" Dr. Brown positioned herself at Libby's feet and began the internal exam.

"We drink wine, but I haven't had any lately because I've been so nauseated."

Libby tensed as the doctor pressed on her stomach.

"Let me just check the pictures of our little nugget," Dr. Brown said, sitting up and snapping the gloves off of her hands. She held the sonogram pictures up and studied each one carefully. Then she opened the file folder with Libby's name on it.

"Oh, good. We've got your file from your doctor in Dallas already. So it says here that you miscarried at five and then eight weeks?"

"That's right," Libby said, her voice cracking.

"And you never did any kind of fertility testing?"

"No."

"Go ahead and sit up, honey." The doctor said.

Jason helped Libby sit up, and he put his hand on her back as she leaned into him.

"Tell me about before," Dr. Brown said. "Tell me how you miscarried."

"Uh, is that really necessary?" Jason asked.

Dr. Brown smiled and rolled forward. "Jason, Elizabeth, I know the past is painful, but it will help me determine how we're doing if I know how things went before. If you'd rather he told me?" She looked between the two of them.

"He doesn't know. I mean, we weren't together then."

"Oh, so there was a different father?"

Libby nodded.

"One or two?"

"I'm sorry?"

"One different father or two different fathers."

Libby swallowed and shakily pushed her hair out of her face. "One. Just one. My ex-husband."

"Okay. So tell me what happened."

Libby took a deep breath and looked to Jason for strength. He pulled himself up on the table behind her and put his arm around her waist.

"The first time it happened at home," Libby said quietly. "I had really bad cramps and went into the bathroom. The blood, it wouldn't–it wouldn't stop coming."

"Okay, and the next time?" Dr. Brown prodded gently.

"I went in for my first ultrasound and there was no heartbeat. The baby had already died."

The doctor consulted the file again. "And that was the one that was at eight weeks, correct?"

"Yes."

Dr. Brown sighed and looked Libby in the eyes. "Well, dear. Today you are ten weeks pregnant, which is further than you've ever been, and I can't see anything wrong with that baby you're cooking in there."

Libby's hand flew to her face and she broke into hysterical sobs right there on the exam table.

"Oh, sweetheart. What an awful thing to carry around for so long," Dr. Brown joined Jason in comforting the sobbing woman. "We're going to make sure you stay pregnant this time, all right, mama?"

Libby nodded in between sobs.

"You take as much time as you need," the doctor said to Jason, and then left them alone.

Jason cradled Libby in his arms and let her cry until she was spent.

"Twelve weeks," Libby hiccuped. "Twelve weeks is when the chances drop." She looked up at Jason, her cheeks splotchy and red.

"Do you hear me? It could still happen."

Jason's face fell. "Baby, don't think about it like that. The doctor said everything looks fine!"

"I don't care. I'm putting myself on bed rest until twelve weeks." Libby sniffed. "You won't change my mind."

"Can we celebrate though?"

"No. Not until twelve weeks."

Jason sighed and pulled his fingers through his hair.

"Please, Jason. I can't celebrate yet."

He nodded. "Okay. We'll wait. We'll come back here in two weeks."

LIBBY DID JUST like she said; she stayed in bed for two weeks, only getting up to go to the bathroom (and puke if necessary) and eat. She didn't even call Elena.

"Last time I didn't spot at all. They had to do a D and C," she said as they drove toward the hospital for their appointment.

Jason cringed. He had had two anxiety-ridden weeks and he was going stir-crazy. He wanted to go out with his wife again instead of sit on the couch and watch TV until she needed him. He wanted to make love to her again and to simply enjoy life with her again. He missed her, and on top of that, he was as anxious about the pregnancy as she was.

"If she tells us that everything is fine, can we celebrate tonight?" he asked as they pulled into a parking spot.

"Let's just see what she says," Libby said, fidgeting with the straps on her purse.

"LOOK AT THAT!" Dr. Brown exclaimed as the ultrasound technician moved the wand over Libby's belly. "Look at that heartbeat just a-thumping away! Would you like to hear it?" She grinned at Libby and Jason.

Jason grabbed Libby's hand and beamed down at her. "What do you think? You want to hear our baby's heartbeat?"

"Yes," she whispered anxiously.

Dr. Brown pulled out her fetal doppler and pressed the probe against Libby's stomach. Soon the 'chug-a-chug-a' train-like sound of a heartbeat filled the room.

The doctor looked from Libby to Jason in surprise. "Are you two gonna blubber like this through every appointment? I might need a Xanax!"

Jason laughed through his tears and kissed Libby's head. She gripped on to his arm and shook with relief. She pressed her other hand to her belly and wept with joy.

"Everything looks fantastic here. You two can relax and come back to see me in a month." Dr. Brown grinned at them, and she and the technician left the crying pair in the room alone with their sonogram printouts.

"OH, MY GOSH, Libby, I'm so glad you called. We need to talk."

"Can I go first?" Libby asked nervously.

"Sure, but mine is big."

"Well, I'm twelve weeks pregnant," Libby blurted out.

It was the first time she'd spoken the words, and it felt amazing to say them out loud. "I'm pregnant, the baby is fine, we heard the heartbeat today, and I'm going to be a mom," she sniffed and felt the familiar shiver of goosebumps run through her body.

There was a gasp and then silence.

"El?" All she heard were sniffles. She smiled at Jason through tear-filled eyes.

"Oh, Libby," Elena finally croaked out. "I can't believe it!"

"I would have told you sooner, but I was terrified. I mean *terrified*. But we've made it this far. I've been sick as a dog," she laughed, "and . . . I think it's really going to happen this time."

"I know it is. I just know it is!" Elena sniffled again. "I'm going to be a godmother!"

Libby laughed and leaned her head against the headrest, staring at her husband. "You get to be a godmother, I get to be a mother."

"Crap, I've got to go. I've got a customer and Sam's on lunch. But you better be free tonight because I have to tell you about a certain little box I found in Reggie's sock drawer."

"Elena!" Libby cried.

"*I know.* I gotta go. Call you tonight. Love you!"

"Love you too, El."

"Everything good?" Jason asked curiously.

She nodded. "Everything is amazing. Take me home. I want to celebrate." She flashed him a coy smile.

Jason caught the look in her eyes and stepped on the gas. "You got it, baby. Whatever you want."

Four years later

"THAT IS A beautiful necklace!"

Libby looked up and smiled in the direction of the voice. "Thank you." She rubbed her thumb over the beads in the nest around her neck as she had become accustomed to doing subconsciously.

"You're Elizabeth Randall, aren't you?" The woman who had been eyeing Libby said suddenly.

Libby blushed and nodded. "Yes, I am." She still wasn't used to being recognized in public even though her first two books had both hit bestseller lists within months of each other and her Facebook page was always blowing up with comments and likes.

"My name is Stefanie. I'm a big fan, and . . . this is going to sound bizarre, but . . . I think I was at your wedding."

Libby sat a little straighter and studied the woman harder. "Are you Amber's mom?" she asked, pleasantly surprised.

The woman nodded. "Yes, I am. I can't believe you remembered! That day meant so much to her."

"Is she here?" Libby looked around at the playing children, trying to recognize Amber.

"No, no. She's in school now, but my son is over there, in the blue T-shirt."

"Oh, yes. I can see the resemblance." Libby smiled.

"Well, I thought that was you. When I read your book and saw the picture on the back, and then went to your Facebook page, I showed my husband but he was sure I was wrong, but . . . it is you!"

Libby smiled. "That was a very special day for me. I've always remembered Amber. I wished that we had gotten a picture of her back then."

"Oh, well, I could give you one, if that's not weird," Stefanie chuckled nervously.

"Not at all. Maybe we could meet for coffee after school sometime and I could say hello to her? That would mean a lot to me."

"And to her! She's told every one she's ever met about the princess wedding she went to in Central Park."

Libby laughed and then adjusted herself on the bench she was sitting on. She waved towards a group of children climbing over the giant Alice's shoulders. "Let me give you my number so we can get together. I'm afraid I'm going to have to start back now. I'm planning a surprise for my husband tonight. We just stopped here for a few minutes because my daughter was begging me to see Alice."

"Oh, of course! Which one is yours?"

Libby pointed to the little brown-headed girl that was running toward her.

"Are we leaving, Mommy?" the little girl asked.

"Yes, but first I'd like you to meet Miss Stefanie. Stefanie, this is my daughter, Alice."

"Hi Miss. Tefanie. Nice-a-mee-you," Alice said, her pigtails bouncing.

"It's very nice to meet you too, Alice. You have a lovely name."

"I know. It's hers!" Alice pointed to the statue she'd just been climbing on and grinned. "Mommy? Can I see the new egg again?"

Libby smiled at Stefanie and nodded. "This is part of our surprise." She held her palm out for Stefanie and Alice to see the new bead.

"It's going in the next!" Alice said excitedly.

"Nest, honey," Libby laughed.

"Right. Next."

Stefanie gave her a strange look and then looked at the necklace hanging from Libby's neck.

"Oh," she smiled. "Congratulations! I bet he'll be really excited!"

"Yeah, if this one can keep quiet just a little bit longer, we might pull off the surprise."

Libby gave Stefanie her number, took Alice by the hand, and began her slow journey back into the real world of New York City, ready to celebrate adding another egg to her nest.

She marveled again and again at where the past five years had brought her, and as her daughter skipped along beside her, she breathed in deeply and thanked the Lord, yet again, for being true to His promises.

"Thank You," she whispered, lifting her eyes to the treetops. "Thank You for saving me."

The End

Acknowledgments

As of May, 2016, Nor Forsake is six years old. I can not believe that it took six years to get this book out. Those six years were extremely full and had my emotions twisted in every direction. This book sat on my computer, taunting and sometimes mocking me for the last three of those years. I wasn't sure it would ever see the light of day so the fact that I am writing these words now is truly a miracle and a gift, and I had some amazing people helping and cheering me on along the way.

To my editors, proof-readers, and last-minute-tweakers, Rosemond, Megan, Mary, Jennifer (JBB), and Jana, JJ, Bethany, and of course, Mama Dotti, how am I doing, on, my, commas? JUST KIDDING. You guys are amazing and I'm so thankful for the many hours you put in helping me perfect this story!

Sojung, my cover designer, you put up with a lot and still managed to create an absolutely beautiful cover. Thank you for being a patient artist!

My new friend and fellow author, Amy Matayo, thank you for all of your advice and wisdom. I so appreciate your time, your patience, and your friendship.

Campaign contributors, your investment in this project blessed me beyond words. Thank you so much for believing in Libby's story!

Launch team, comment, like, share—oh sorry, I've said it so many times . . . You guys did such a fantastic job getting the word out about this book! Thank you for exploiting your social media outlets for me!

The Splendid Society, #Realtalk, #the4500 . . . you've changed my life this year. Thank you for being a safe haven. Thank you for receiving me in my brokenness and for helping me to be brave enough to talk about it. You are some of my dearest friends in the world.

Becky, my very own Elena, I would not be where I am today without you. My heart is whole because you helped pick up the pieces. Sarge and Jubes forever.

Salem and Josiah, you are my joy, and you are my favorites. Thank you for being proud of me even when you don't really understand what it is that I'm doing and why you can't read my books yet. I love you *this* much.

Rocky, your insistent encouragement of my dreams is everything to me. This book would never have happened without your support, your grace, and your tolerance for my crazy. Thank you, I love you more today than ever before.

Father, human words can not express what we have. Thank you for not leaving me, for not forsaking me. Thank you for saving me.

And finally, to you, my dear readers. Thank you for your words of encouragement and for continuing to read and resonate with the words of these pages. It is for you and your hearts that I write.

Julie Presley lives somewhere in Texas and has hopefully moved for the last (13th) time. Between a day job, two active ministries, a husband, two kids, and a very love-deprived (yeah, right) Corgi, she manages to find time to pursue her true passion: writing realistic Christian romance novels. Her first book, *Stones of Remembrance,* received rave reviews from her mom as well as a few other people.

She loves Jesus, worship, dark chocolate, red red wine, and courteous reviews on Amazon and Goodreads.

You can read more from Julie on her blog at www.juliepresley.com, as well as connect with her through social media:

Facebook: facebook.com/authorjuliepresley

Twitter: @jpresley48

Instagram: @juliepresley

Made in the USA
San Bernardino, CA
17 June 2016